ELLE GRAY | JAMES HOLT

THE FLORIDA GIRL

FBI MYSTERY THRILLER

RESORT TO KILL

PROLOGUE

NOW, ST. MARTIN'S ISLAND, FLORIDA COAST
I. 9:00 AM

"Kage, you got eyes on your 3?"

ALEXA'S VOICE WAS A TIGHT WHISPER AS SHE PRESSED HER hand to her ear, activating the radio mic that connected her to her partner, who was little more than a stick man in her vision at the end of the long driveway.

FBI Special Agent Alexa Landers frowned. She knew that there was statistically about zero chance that anything should happen, but she still didn't like it. Alexa didn't really like statistics. She preferred facts.

The island had been cleared by herself and her partner, FBI Special Agent Kage Murphy, and then it had been scoured by the Secret Service this morning.

And those guys were SERIOUS, she reflected on the hour-long interview and background check that she and Kage both had gone through last week – and that was even with her father being a well-known Navy man!

But still, there was a reason for such things. And that reason was waiting in the small black car that stood beside her, its engine on.

'Skip' Jackson. Senior Presidential Advisor along with a couple of Hill staffers, straight from Washington. The President's right-hand man, or at least that was what Coast to Coast News said. Other news outlets might say such feverish things as 'the power behind the throne' or 'the hand in the glove,' but Alexa wouldn't have gone that far. Truth was, 'Skip' Joseph Jackson, a man well north of his sixties, six-foot-one and still built like a tank, had seemed pretty guileless and straightforward as far as Alexa could see.

"Alexa? Where the hell is my 3 again?" Kage's voice returned a fraction of a moment later, and Alexa could even hear the grin in his voice.

"Goddamnit, Kage! It's your right. Due right!" Alexa hissed back. She knew he was teasing her, but, like statistics, she was very selective about when humor applied and when it didn't.

And right now, standing with the warm Gulf winds teasing at her hair, on a small scrub of a private island as they waited for the representative from Cuba for a secret diplomatic meeting, it really didn't.

"My right is fine, Alexa. We already cleared the marina there and there's nothing. No one in or out, and no boats approaching," Kage said with a touch of firmness to his voice. Alexa winced. She hadn't intended to tell him how to do his job. He was her senior in this relationship, after all. Alexa had only been deployed to the

Miami field office for about fourteen months now, straight out of the Academy, whereas Kage had been there for years.

Maybe Kage was right to be more relaxed about it all, Alexa thought to herself as she pursed her lips and scanned back behind them. The road was wide and went straight back to the double iron gates and white walls of the private St. Martin's Conference & Spa Resort.

The island of St. Martin was tiny and overlooked; a bare, remote thumbprint directly west of Sarasota, some twenty miles from the main coast. There was nothing around it but water on all sides, and the island itself was a reedy, swampy, tidal spit favored by no one but bird watchers and deep-sea fishermen.

The fact that there was a private resort here at all was a wonder, Alexa thought. Maybe bird watchers had more money than she realized.

Heaven alone knows what the other guests are thinking, Alexa mused, trying to control her free-floating anxiety. Apparently, the powers that be in their collective wisdom had decided to only hire out the 'premium' lodges at one end of the resort, which meant that there were actual guests still in residence in the main resort building on the near side of the island.

Anyway. That didn't matter. The two regions, the premium lodges and the rest of the resort were locked down. No one but Secret Service and FBI had been anywhere near here for the past twenty-four hours, hadn't they?

Pull it together, Alexa! She cleared her throat, turning back as she cast a long, slow look at all the green around them. There were brackish ditches on either side of the road, which led to the solitary helipad, and one of the island's small marinas on the far side. Kage was up there along with a handful of Service guys (you could always tell them because of their perfect suits and very, very serious attitudes, Alexa reflected) waiting for…

There!

A low droning hum broke over the constant whistle of the winds. Alexa turned to shield her eyes against the sun to see a small dark blip appear in the sky, quite high and moving at a steady pace.

"Agent Landers?" There was a whirr from Skip's window as the old man stuck his head out. He had a long, brick-like face, deeply lined from stomping on decks most of his life, but his eyes were a crystal-clear blue.

"Is that a bird or a plane or our man? Representative Martinez?" Skip cracked a smile, and Alexa was suddenly reminded of her father. They both had that same ex-military way about them. Good with the people below them. Friendly, but only up to a point.

"Sir, I think it is, yes, sir – but please, protocol was that you stay inside your vehicle until Representative Martinez has exited his transport," Alexa said quickly.

Skip pulled a face. "Ah, of course. No open windows, I take it? Even when it's doing a Florida one-thirty out here?" he quipped.

Alexa took a risk as the drone of Representative Ramon Martinez's chopper grew louder and closer.

"That's what A/C is for, sir, if you please," she said, as Jackson laughed and threw a salute, raising the window once again.

"*Target approaching landing site,*" Kage reported as Alexa saw him and the Secret Service guys start to walk backward, away from the helipad in a wide circle.

"Give them a lot of space. You see anything?" Alexa whispered, feeling a little bit useless stuck out here at the far end of the driveway. She would much rather she was up there with Kage, following the mission parameters to a T…

1. Positive ID on target.

2. Sweep perimeter of the landing site one more time as they come into land.

3. Hold positions until Representative Martinez has exited the vehicle.

There was no answer but a howl of wind in her ears for a long, long moment. The Cuban helicopter was far larger now, and the whirr of its propellers was almost deafening as it started to lower itself toward the ground.

"*Absolutely nothing. Same old weed and ditchwater as it was last night and this morning-*" Kage said as the helicopter came into land, lowering to twenty feet…

Ten…

Five, three…

It was right about then when all hell broke loose, as the helipad erupted into a ball of fire.

CHAPTER
ONE

10 DAYS EARLIER, SOMEWHERE
IN MIAMI DOWNTOWN

II. FBI FIELD OFFICE, MIAMI
[UNDISCLOSED LOCATION]

"Agent Landers, whatever you're working on is canceled. I need you in my office right now…"

S O BEGAN, AND ENDED, THE MESSAGE FROM FIELD CHIEF Williams that would lead Alexa Landers from the sweltering heat of Miami to the roasting fireball of St. Martin's Island.

Whatever it was, the young, twenty-four-year-old Alexa Landers knew it was important as she looked up from her desk to see that Kage was pushing back his chair opposite her, too.

"You got the chief's message?" her partner, the large and athletic, black-haired, Irish-Japanese Kage Murphy asked. His brow was furrowed, and Alexa could well understand why. Williams was a hard ball, but he wasn't usually so demanding. The field chief was the kind of guy who wore suits all the time on the job and had a contained, professional air in everything he did. In her past year and a half on the job, it seemed to Alexa as though she had never seen Williams become unsettled, not even once, even when they had cornered a professional assassin in a busy waiting room of the University of Miami Hospital.

The chief wasn't the kind of man to break a sweat, in other words. Knowing this, Alexa and Kage were quick to grab their things as they made their way out of the small data analysis room in the discreet, underground FBI Field HQ and down brightly lit corridors to the chief's office.

"Landers, Murphy, take a seat," Williams said as they came in, his back still turned to them as he hurriedly moved between two keyboards, cradling a phone on his shoulder.

Kage shot her a look with those large, dark eyes of his. *Oh crap,* it said. Whatever it was, Chief Williams wasn't just uptight, he looked *unsettled,* which was a bit like waking up one day to find that the White House had disappeared overnight.

"Sir?" Alexa asked.

Williams held up one finger as he finished typing, then spoke into his cradled phone. "Yes, I see. All calendars cleared. I'll send over their background files to you right away."

There was a murmur from the other end of the line, and Williams sighed as he leaned back in his chair, setting the phone down in its cradle and turning to skewer them both with a sharp look.

"I see that someone has made some friends..." Williams said in his gravel and oak baritone. Even seated, Chief Williams was a big man. Alexa thought he would have made a stunning NBA player in his earlier years.

"Friends, sir?" Kage asked.

"That was the Departmental Liaison for the White House. Secret Service," Williams intoned, his brow knotting momentarily, and then clearing.

"Secret Service." Alexa blinked. That was a new one. She'd only had a brief encounter with them before, back at the Academy, when a trio of servicemen had been invited to give a talk to the young Bureau hopefuls about the interconnected nature of their departments, and the sort of work that an FBI agent could eventually migrate to, should they be successful with their current career.

A six-to-nine-month background check. Fitness test. Entrance exam, and then you also have to be personally selected to even get in... Alexa remembered that fleeting sense of wonder and glamor at the notion of being selected by the highest law enforcement role in the country. They were the best of the best, of course, tasked each day with either protecting the leaders of the nation or investigating some of the most critical attacks against the nation's infrastructure.

The actual agents who had given the lecture, Alexa remembered, had been just what she had always expected them to be: tight, contained, with a deadpan delivery that made them seem more robotic than human.

What was so important that the Secret Service was interested in our little Miami field office?

"That's what I said, Agent Landers. We have a new case. A very important case, and I have just been ordered to assign yourself and Agent Murphy to it," Williams said with a slight glower. Alexa got the impression that the man didn't like taking orders.

"You were both *personally* requested," Williams clarified, looking at both of them as if they had done something wrong.

"Us?" Kage scoffed a slightly nervous laugh. "I mean, why us?"

Williams turned back to his computer, his hands skittering over the keys for a moment before the printer started barking out paper.

"What do either of you know about Cuba?" he asked as he retrieved the paper files and laid them out before Alexa and Kage.

Alexa picked hers up to see that it contained a picture of a rather young, handsome Cuban man in his early forties perhaps, with dark hair and bronzed skin in a light blue suit.

"This is Minister Ramon Martinez, a young firebrand in the Communist Party of Cuba. He's been making waves these last few years, apparently, railing against the US-Cuba Trade Embargo, and rising pretty quickly from the CDR to the Politburo," Williams stated.

"CDR?" Alexa winced a little, wishing that she knew more about Cuban politics other than the revolution.

"Committees for the Defense of the Revolution," Williams supplied. "A dispersed, widespread arrangement of local-action neighborhood committees that do most of the work of disseminating education, medical aid, public health programs – as well as reporting on anti-Communist activities. Minister Martinez garnered support from his local CDR, becoming a small-time soap-box agitator, before he went for the big leagues three years ago, and was elected all the way up to the Politburo; an eight-man department that pretty much governs how the party operates in Cuba."

Kage whistled in surprise. "Sounds like a firebrand."

"You'd be right there, Agent Murphy. Look here, from his speech last year at the 34th International Conference of National Communist Parties in St. Petersburg, Russia..." Williams turned on the large screen at the back, and, a few moments later had called up a video of the same young Cuban politician standing on a podium and addressing a huge room of delegates from all over the world. The hall they were in was bedecked with bright crimson red banners everywhere, and each party of delegates had their own table along with small name tags and speaker systems.

"*My friends and comrades, it is intolerable that el bloqueo – the blockade – still exists in the modern world. Where else in all of our globe has a nation been so deprived of access to opportunities, to healthcare, to business, to industry, than that of Cuba!?*"

Alexa could see why people were drawn to Ramon; he was a passionate speaker whose words burst from his chest one moment, for his voice to turn soft and mournful, full of pathos, the next.

"My people curse el bloqueo. We grew up knowing that the United States had a hand at our throats and that they would not let go until we choked! How many times have I, in my own neighborhood in Havana, listened to the despair and frustration of young owners, or of builders, tradespeople, entrepreneurs, starting families – all of whom are unable to live with basic dignity, or afford their own skills – because of el bloqueo? How many generations of Cubans have been crippled!? That is why I am calling on all delegates here to join me in calling for a renewed resolution from the United Nations that will demand the end to the Blockade … !"

He was met by clapping and calls of approval before Williams froze the video.

"And that is our Representative Ramon Martinez, one of America's fiercest critics on the international stage, who is set to come to American soil for the first time ever in a little over two weeks," the field chief stated. "And you two, Special Agents Landers and Murphy, have been personally asked to be the protection detail for our diplomatic envoy."

"What!?" Kage burst out, before hurriedly correcting himself. "What, *sir,* I mean?"

"Joseph Jackson, I guess you've heard of him?" Williams raised an eyebrow, but both agents only looked back at him in confusion.

He harrumphed. "Presidential Advisor Joe Jackson, who has been a member of the President's staff for the past two years. He keeps himself out of the limelight because he mostly advises on defense issues. He's the one who will be meeting Representative Ramon Martinez, and he is the one who personally requested your team."

But something pulled at Alexa's memory. She'd heard that name before, hadn't she? It sounded awfully familiar.

No, it couldn't be …

"Do you mean Skip?" Alexa burst out.

"Bingo."

The truth was that Alexa did know 'Skip' Joe Jackson, but she had no idea that he was now a presidential advisor. Or rather, her father had known him back from his Navy days, when her father had been a lowly commander, then captain before he retired in case they dispatched him to a desk job.

'Skip' – short for Skipper to his friends – had even been a regular at Thanksgiving for a short time in Alexa's childhood years. That had been before the illness that had taken her mother, of course, and the long quiet that came after which stopped her dad from ever hosting again.

Alexa remembered a middle-aged, white-haired man with clear blue eyes, friendly, not exactly warm, but could make them all roar with laughter when they needed to. She also remembered her father and Skip walking out to the porch after dinner to toast brandy and cigars, and have hushed, ominous-sounding conversations that her mother had said 'wasn't our clearance, honey.'

Phew. Well. Skip – who had almost been a distant, estranged godparent to Alexa and her brother Brad – had certainly done well for himself, hadn't he?

Alexa looked up to see Williams and Kage looking at her as if she had just sprouted an extra head.

"You all know I'm a military brat, right? It was my father. I think they served together, or my father served under him, I think," Alexa explained hurriedly.

Williams made an agreeing 'that explains that' sort of noise. "Well, you must have made an impression because Skip Jackson asked for you two specifically. In fact, he said that 'in light of your recent outstanding success with the Senator Gunderson case, I could think of no one finer' or so he stated in his email." Williams cleared his throat, then hastily tapped on his computer for a new image to appear on the screen behind him.

It was an island. Little more than a pulled rhomboid shape covered with lots of green, with the washes of a sandbank running across from one side. A little way away was a coastline, and a main road.

"This, ladies and gentlemen, is St. Martin's Island, way remote even for the Keys. This is where Advisor Jackson will be engaging in secret talks with Representative Martinez," Williams said.

"Next stop Havana, right?" Kage said.

"Precisely. You will be going in with Jackson's Secret Service detail to clear the island, check the resort, and generally oversee the personal security of the meeting for as long as it continues," Williams stated.

"How long will that be?" Alexa asked. She felt a little breathless. Being involved in international diplomacy, no matter how far removed, was not exactly something that she had been prepared for when she woke up this morning.

Williams gave a small shrug. "I've been told to schedule you for a couple of days, but the details haven't been released. The advisor and Martinez are booked in at a private residence at the St. Martin's Spa and Resort complex, so I presume you will be doing general door-guarding duties."

"A private residence?" Alexa asked. That didn't quite sound right. Why didn't the meeting happen at Camp David, or some other entirely private location rather than at a resort?

"I don't know a lot about this either, Landers, but I have been told that the location was selected by Martinez's team rather than ours. St. Martin's Spa and Resort is a members-only resort, but it is divided into two areas: a main resort hotel where, yes, there will be paying guests and smaller, private lodges. It is at one of these lodges where the meeting will be happening," Williams stated.

"There's going to be civilians on-site at the same time? That is going to be a security nightmare," Alexa groaned as Williams nodded heavily. Alexa was starting to see what was putting her chief on edge.

"Huh, it makes kinda sense, from the Cuban point of view, right?" Kage offered. "They want to chat in private, of course, say the things they have to say without the world press listening in. But I'm thinking this guy Martinez might want the cover of somewhere semi-public, too. If anything goes wrong..."

"Or maybe he just wants a free hot tub and sauna on the American dollar," Williams quipped. It took Alexa a moment to realize that it was a joke. She wondered about laughing, but the chief had already moved on.

"But the possibility here is that Martinez and Jackson will be negotiating the US Embargo of Cuba. There might be concessions, who knows. But it does mean that for us, whatever happens on that island will be big news."

You mean do it right. Don't mess up, Alexa thought. "Understood, sir."

"St. Martin's itself is about nine miles at its widest point. Seasonal flooding; the Army Corps put in service roads and irrigation in the sixties, but since then it's mostly been left to itself. Nothing there but beaches, palm trees, and mangroves."

And gators, I bet... Alexa groaned. One thing she had yet to get used to since coming down here was the sheer number of things that were trying to kill you, from sharks to alligators to pythons, spiders, and a host of other horrible things, it seemed.

"And birds. Plenty of bird life apparently, which is why St. Martin's attracts bird watchers from across the globe." Williams scanned down a sheet he had at his side. "Other than that, the resort has a marina, and there's a pier and a helipad on the near side of the island. The only thing going for us is that the only way to get there is by boat, which rather limits any unwanted attention."

Only by boat, Alexa nodded. Her recent experience with assassins and stolen yachts didn't exactly fill her with confidence. She was already wondering whether she could call the Coast Guard and encourage them to double up their patrols when Williams collated all of the papers he had outlined and handed them over.

"I advise the pair of you to spend the next few days clearing up whatever investigations you're working on and make yourselves ready. The Secret Service will likely want to interview you, and when you're called, it will probably be at very short notice."

"Yes, sir," they both said, standing up.

When they got outside, Kage turned to Alexa with an excited elbow to her ribs like an excited teenager.

"This is going to be *easy*, right? Why didn't you tell me you had family connections on cushy jobs? Cuba wants the deal to go through. We get to stay in a resort for a weekend watching nothing more interesting than birds. What could go wrong?"

What indeed, Alexa thought.

CHAPTER TWO

ST. MARTIN'S ISLAND, FLORIDA COAST

III. APPROXIMATELY 9:20 AM

"GET THE ADVISOR BACK!" ALEXA SHOUTED AS THE after image of the fireball was burned over her eyes. Even from this far away, she had felt the shockwave hit her like a fierce, hot wind in the already sweaty Florida morning.

Skip. Kage. The Cuban. Kage.

Alexa's thoughts were a delirious blur and there was a ringing in her ears. *What was it?*

It was the explosion, its echo still reverberating through her eardrums as large, blackened, and smoking pieces of helicopter were raining down on the helipad.

Kage was still out there!

Beside her, the Secret Service detail that had been in the car had already put it in motion, throwing it fast into reverse and screeching back down the tarmac and asphalt road at an almost breakneck speed.

"Open the gates! Code Red, Code Red!" someone was shouting in her ear, and for a moment Alexa didn't recognize the voice as one of the Secret Service agents.

"What's happening? Do we have shots fired? Team Two, come in!"

Another voice was answering the first, as the Secret Service detail was scrambling to try and locate the enemy. Alexa hit the floor and rolled, her heavy Glock already in her hand.

But this wasn't the protocol. Not the one that they had been briefed in. She was to follow the car and advisor, stay close until they were behind closed doors – no matter what.

Unless there was an active shooter. Then you neutralize the threat…

And that was just the thing. This wasn't an active shooter. But what the hell was it?

Ahead of her, the helipad was a smoking pile of blackened and twisted wreckage, with burning fuel giving the air a sick, greasy scent.

(Where was Kage? How far back was he?)

"Team Two, secure the perimeter. Team One, protect Wolfhound!"

Wolfhound. That was the Secret Service's official communications nickname for the man she knew as Skip. It fit him well.

Alexa felt her body treacherously stay for a moment longer as she looked at the terrible vision of hell before her. Several of the nearby palm trees were burning, too. There was no sign of movement from the helipad. Whatever had taken it had been powerful enough to completely eviscerate the craft. Nothing but a propeller and a tail was recognizable.

"Murphy!? Murphy – come in!" Alexa hissed over her comms, but then her training kicked in. She had to protect her partner, but her orders were to protect Skip at all costs.

But Kage was still out there.

Another terrible moment of indecision as Alexa's eyes scanned the burning green. She still couldn't see any movement, but there were a lot of trees out there. Maybe Kage and the Team One agents were right now trying to locate the shooter.

(Because it had to be a shooter, right? What else would have happened?)

"Team Two at the gate. The bird is through-"

Crap! Alexa stood up, sweeping the area around the road with her Glock, but could see no movement. No glint of metal against the green. No secondary attack. She jogged back to the gate as Skip's car spun a handbrake turn on the far side and accelerated along the winding road that started to curve toward the row of private peaked-roof lodges that they had already locked down for the diplomatic meeting. By the time Alexa was through the gate, the Secret Service was already swinging it shut behind her, and she could see that the black SUV that housed her almost-godparent was already surrounded by more Secret Service agents, practically body-checking the seventy-ish Skip as he was bundled out of the car and into the chosen lodge.

Someone was suddenly in her face, walking up to gesture at her. For a moment all she could hear was the roar of the explosion still pregnant in her ears, but then the words resolved themselves.

"Agent Landers! Wait here. You're with me, we're securing the gate."

It was one of the agents, big and clad in a dark blue suit, light blue shirt, and shades. She had her gun in her hands, and waving Landers to the opposite side of the long, double wrought-iron gates that looked straight out to the burning pyre outside.

For another moment Alexa hesitated. "My partner... Agent Murphy is still out there," she offered to the Secret Service woman.

"So is my team. If he's alive, he'll be with Team Two. They were scouting the perimeter."

There. She said it in such a perfunctory way that Alexa found herself nodding.

If he's alive. Her partner might already be dead.

Blood hammered in her chest, and suddenly Alexa was thrown back into her training again as time appeared to go fast and slow, fast and slow. She ran to the other end of the gate and took up a crouching position as the Secret Service woman was doing across from her.

"I'm not seeing anything. No active shooters," Alexa whispered as her ears crackled with updates on Skip. He was fine, a little shaken up, but hadn't taken any damage, and he was secure in the living room of the private lodge as they were making arrangements to get him off the island and onto a private jet straight back to Washington.

"Hold tight," the Secret Service woman said to Alex before touching her earpiece.

"We got nothing at the gate, either. I didn't see any shots fired..."

"Neither did I," Alexa said, as now, instead of feeling useless, she started to feel angry.

What the hell am I doing sitting here when my partner is back out there!?

Wait.

Alexa forced herself to take a long, slow breath, and then double the time it took to breathe it out. This anger was natural. To be expected in the chaos of the moment. She knew that she had to trust the team she worked with; otherwise, there would be no point at all.

And with each breath, as Alexa scanned the burning helipad and the mangroves around it, her thoughts started gaining just a little clarity.

Kage had been quite a ways back from the helipad at the time of the explosion, hadn't he? He and the rest of Team One had been expanding the perimeter around the helicopter, moving out in an ever-widening circle as they swept. Maybe that had put him back further behind the line of trees already.

(*Burning trees, behind the line of the burning trees…*)

"Check your LOS," the Secret Service woman said.

LOS – Line of Sight, Alexa registered. A part of her was aware that the woman was giving her orders probably to stop her from going into shock.

After all, I just saw a guy get blown up. How many people did Martinez have with him? A full complement of guards, like Skip did? How many people did I just see die!?

Line of Sight, she repeated to herself. Alexa turned slowly, surveying what was around her, her eyes scanning for movement from potential attackers.

There was the long curve of the white, Mediterranean-style wall that surrounded the resort. On this side, there were decorative palms, sculpted lawns, and lily-pad pools with rockeries. There were the three private lodges, black-peaked roofs, each one built to look like a tiny house. Outside of one was the SUV and a grimace of Secret Service agents.

The road curved around in front of each lodge, meandering past some more sculpted lawn areas with trees until it came to the main resort hotel itself; an impressive, three-story white building with two wings. Alexa could see an awful lot of windows looking down at her, but they all appeared to be dark. If the guests were inside, then they had probably been locked down and told to stay away from the windows.

And then, through the glimmer of the trees and past the hotel was the line of shining blue. The warm seas of the Gulf of Mexico, and the distant gleam of dark green that was the Florida Coast.

No shooters. No one running toward them. No muzzle flare.

"Okay. We're clear!" the woman called. There was a squeal of tires from behind them as Skip Jackson was whisked back into the black SUV and hurtled to the marina connected to the main resort building. Alexa's ears were still ringing with voices on the radio as someone was calling for an air ambulance on site, and an alert to be sent out to all the local agencies. Emergency codes were being given, and split-second decisions were being made.

"What do we do now?" Alexa asked as she saw the Secret Service woman eyeing Skip's SUV for a long count until it vanished, and then she was up on her feet, reaching for the gate controls and pulling the automated lever.

"Now we sweep and neutralize. Hopefully, work out what the hell happened," the woman replied as Alexa sprang up, and, alongside the jogging woman, started to run back up the roadway they had just come.

"Kage! Damnit, report back!" she hissed as they started toward the helipad, but her second called her back.

"Don't get too close! Forensics will want that-"

There was a snarl of static in her ears, and suddenly there was a figure, several figures, emerging from the thick mangrove brush, and one was big and athletic and waving a hand at her.

It was Kage. He was fine apart from mud all over his ripped, rumbled suit.

"My comms got knocked out by the blast, but I've been sweeping with Team One. There's no one out here!" Kage called out as they jogged toward each other.

"Team One? No one injured!?" The Secret Service woman with Alexa realized that, under all her tight control she, too, had been desperately worried about her friends.

"None of ours. We were all too far away from the blast when it happened," Kage responded, turning to look at her with wide eyes. He had a graze over his eye where the blast must have severely stunned him.

"You were right here. Did you see what happened to Martinez's copter!?" Alexa asked, still twitching her head to one side and the next as she scanned the burning greenery around them. Still no attackers – and there was clearly nothing they could do about the burning wreckage on the helipad.

"I don't know, but I'll tell you this for sure," Kage said as he turned back to the pyre of burning smoke. "Something with that much force and power? That was a bomb. I'd bet money on it."

CHAPTER THREE

THE INVESTIGATION DAY 1
IV. 10:45 AM

"THE ENTIRE ISLAND IS ON LOCKDOWN, NO ONE ON OR off apart from Skip Jackson and his people," the words of the field chief came a few seconds after his image spoke to them on the small screen that Alexa and Kage huddled around.

"Skip managed to get the governor of Florida to announce a localized active emergency, which buys a bit of time. You have a few enhanced powers, such as restricting the movement of people, but tread carefully – the federal emergency decision has to go through the President, and that opens up an entirely different can of worms. It's not an option they're pursuing as of yet, for reasons I can't get into right now. You understand," the field chief stated.

Alexa didn't quite understand, but she wasn't in a position to quibble about it. "Yes, sir."

At any other time, in any other situation, Alexa might have thought that this was perhaps the most extravagant place that she'd been asked to work yet. The pair sat in the living area of the same private resort lodge where Skip and Representative Martinez had been scheduled to hold their meeting. Unlike the faux-Greek or Spanish Mediterranean style of the buildings outside, these elite buildings had been decorated to look more like hunting lodges straight out of old Europe, with plush Chesterfield sofas and antique writing desks, and long, red mahogany tables. Deep purple curtains sectioned off this area from a door leading to a small wing of rooms. There was art on the walls of ancient sea battles and galleons amidst raging seas. Somewhere out back there was a private sauna room, a plunge pool, and a games room complete with a billiards table.

Of course, now was not the time to admire the décor, Alexa thought as one of the Secret Service doctors finished flashing a light in Kage's eyes before turning to the camera.

"Your man is medically fine and fit to serve, Chief Williams. A light abrasion to the forehead, but no concussion as far as I can see. I would normally advise a few days off work all the same, but, given the situation…"

"It's critical, thank you, Doctor," Field Chief Williams said, and the doctor nodded at them all before hurrying out of the room to attend to the other agents who had similarly been thrown to the ground by the helicopter blast.

"Sir? You were saying. Lockdown. But the meeting is canceled. What do you want us to do?" Alexa asked.

Williams gave her one of his 'I'm not happy about this, but' frowns—which generally looked like every other frown he wore, except that there was an extra wrinkle on his forehead.

"Change of mission, Agents. I just got off the phone with Skip himself, who said he already has the Cubans demanding an explanation of what happened..."

"They're denying responsibility," Kage said flatly.

"Yes. They're blaming *us* for whatever went wrong with Representative Martinez's flight, or at least that is the threat Skip passed on to me. Right now, this situation still hasn't made it to the mainstream press because no one on the island is allowed any phones, but that won't last," Williams explained as Alexa nodded.

Everything leaks, given time, she thought. Especially given social media.

"So... Skip impressed upon me the importance of having a Bureau presence right there, at the heart of the scene, taking a lead on the investigation from hour one."

Alexa blinked. There was a low ringing in her ears which she was sure came from the explosion, like tinnitus. Had it really only been almost two hours?

"You want us to lead the investigation?" she said, feeling slightly light-headed. "Isn't this a little... beyond our clearance?"

"Not really. We don't know if this is even a criminal act, and we have the skills. I've gotten permission for Dee to be flown out to join you, and of course, the Service agents there will be isolating the... remains to be sent to our pathology lab," Williams said.

"But, sir..." Kage echoed, his voice sounding a little higher than normal.

This is an international incident? Alexa silently echoed Kage's unspoken concerns. Relations between the US and Cuba were tetchy at best, and at worst...

No one wants to be the first to say 'Missile Crisis' or 'Bay of Pigs' around here, do they? she thought. In fact, everyone so far had very carefully NOT said anything like that.

"This is an investigation into a crime, agents, just like any other," Williams said heavily, his words finally syncing with his image briefly. "Skip passed on this message. That he could think of no better agents to take on this task," the field chief explained as Alexa felt a certain doom settle on her shoulders. "He wants you both on this and, despite my quarrels with the politicians, on this I have to agree with him. I believe in you both. You have all the training and skills necessary for this, and the Secret Service will be helping you in the initial scene investigation."

"The Secret Service will be assisting *us*?" Kage said a little faintly.

"Indeed. This is a Bureau matter, not Service. You'll be collating evidence and conducting interviews with all residents on the island. In short, *find out what happened to Representative Martinez!*"

"Yes, sir," both Alexa and Kage said solemnly.

There was a small amount of talk after that – general authorizations and plans for the boat that would bring over Dr. Dee Hopkins, the FBI's forensic specialist along with her mobile lab, as well as where they would set up the war room, the initial priorities this morning, and whatever else they might need.

By the end, when Alexa cut the connection and closed the laptop, she turned to look at Kage and wondered if he had the same ringing in his ears as she did, or whether she looked as he did; determined, worried.

"Here we go again, I guess?"

CHAPTER FOUR

V. 12:15 PM

T HE ISLAND WAS AWASH WITH PREGNANT TENSION AS THE Florida sun grew hotter and hotter. Their lodge had air-conditioning, but it was still too stuffy for Alexa as she did her best to convert the space into a makeshift war room.

Her laptop was on the table, connected via a secure adapter to the FBI hotspot, allowing them some private communications back to their field office. They had very little in the way of paper, whiteboards, cameras, printers, or any other general equipment that they might need, but she'd managed to find a set of notecards at least in the guest area. Each one was embossed with a tiny bird and 'St. Martin's Resort and Spa' on the bottom, so Alexa presumed they were there for the guests or staff to write compliments or notes.

Alexa stood in the center of the room, with a spray of notecards on the large, polished mahogany table arrayed around her, with a series of cryptic one-line sentences that she hoped would make sense to anyone else as well as her.

DIPLOMAT – RAMON MARTINEZ
DIPLOMAT – SKIP JACKSON

ST. MARTIN'S RESORT
- Air and Sea Access ONLY
- Recent Arrivals?

HELICOPTER – HAVANA To St. MARTINS
- Access to Helicopter?
- Access to Helipad?

EXPLOSION
- Fuel?
- Engine Malfunction?
- Shooter?

Her eyes scanned over the fragmentary information they had, finding that they had not very much at all.

Ugh, she groaned and tried to forget about the distant roaring sound that she still had in her ears. It wasn't going away, like she was constantly listening to the sea. She wondered if she should have told the doctor about it, and then hurriedly shook her head.

I'm fine. Been through worse; and it wasn't as bad as what Kage went through, was it?

But still, her eyes circled back around to the word 'explosion' and for a moment she saw that flash in her eyes all over again, felt the world stop and her heart hammer.

"Alexa?" It was Kage's voice as he re-emerged from the front door, with one of the Secret Service agents following close behind him; a large, bald man in a steel blue suit who could have been anywhere from thirty to forty, as his face had that toned, peak-fitness quality that defied attempts to age him.

"Agent Marinsburg, Team Leader," Kage said with a jerked thumb back to the man. "We've just come back from the crash site and he has some news."

Alexa nodded, trying to read their lips as that ringing in her ears was only getting louder.

"No survivors at the site. The helicopter, which was an Airbus H155, standard civilian long-distance helicopter. We have recovered and accounted for three dead, which, although we need a pathologist to positively ID, we believe them to be Cuban Representative Ramon Martinez, a pilot, and probably a bodyguard or aide. We have a makeshift crime scene room in the small marina garage nearest the helipad," Marinsburg wasted no time in debriefing.

Alexa nodded, trying to keep up with the information, and adding notes to her incident cards as it went along. Of course, as was the case with any criminal investigation, this raised more questions than it answered.

Like, how far does a helicopter fly anyway? What if one of the people on board was a bad actor? Could Cuba have decided to assassinate one of their own?

Alexa felt out of her depth, despite the assurances that Chief Williams had given them. The white noise in her ears sounded like a storm, and in that storm was just herself and Kage, surrounded by far too many variables and options.

Breathe, Alexa demanded of herself. This was what she had been trained to do, after all.

"You will want to see this, ma'am, may I?" Agent Marinsburg held up a small data-stick as he walked over to their laptop, and Alexa nodded distractedly.

"The marina has a set of security cameras connected to the resort, which the resort manager agreed to pass on the recordings to me-"

I bet they did, Alexa couldn't help but think. You don't really get to say no to a Secret Service request, do you?

"One of them was pointed north to the coast and so didn't have eyes on the helipad, but there were another two. One was knocked out by the blast but, luckily for us, one set of footage remains. This needs to go through a thorough digital analysis, of course, but I believe the footage is fairly clear," Marinsburg stated, as Alexa made a note to get a copy to Dee. She'd *love* working on stuff like this…

The screen flickered, went dark, and then Alexa was looking once again at the large octagon of tarmac in the early morning light, and Alexa could even see the small black SUV and the tiny stick figure of herself in the distance. A haze of green surrounded them, and a moment later she saw movement to the edge of the camera vision, as the black dot of the helicopter was growing nearer and larger.

"No sound on this?" she asked.

"No, ma'am, unfortunately just visuals only, but wait and see…" Marinsburg leaned forward so that he could put the video into slow motion, the frame rate dropping to half-speed, then one-quarter of normal speed.

Even though there was no sound, Alexa felt the humming in her ears start to rise once again, a gentle roar as the helicopter grew closer and larger, then larger still as it slowly circled the helipad and then started to lower.

"Right here," Marinsburg mentioned and slowed the video down even more, as Alexa's palms began to sweat. The video resolution was terrible, but she was kind of glad about that. She wasn't sure that she really wanted to see the actual face of the diplomat peering excitedly out of the window…

As it was, the windows were blurred and darkened anyway.

"What am I looking for?" she hissed as the H155 Airbus started to descend; twenty meters, fifteen, ten.

Watch out! Panic spiked in Alexa's chest. Which was ridiculous, wasn't it? Why was her heart hammering so hard and so fast?

Five feet, and then-

There was a sudden burst of white, a star blowing out of the ground where the helicopter started to land, and Marinsburg tapped the pause button quickly.

"I – I don't understand…" Alexa shook her head in confusion. She was looking at an explosion that she had already lived through and to which she'd nearly lost her partner. What was the benefit of this?

"The glitch, you see the way that the light is too much for the camera's optics? That is the epicenter of the explosion, the detonation itself," Marinsburg explained, quickly pressing play so that the explosion once again engulfed the helicopter, the entire scene growing a lurid white and then-

No.

Alexa had to get out. Suddenly the roar in her ears was deafening and she couldn't breathe. Without thinking, her body reacted, turning as she pushed past Kage and stumbling through the door of the lodge.

I need air. Air!

Alexa's feet skittered down the gravel path as she felt her chest heave; she could still taste the acrid and burning, greasy smoke in her lungs, as if the particles of that terrible event were still lodged inside of her. Particles of smoke and engine oil and even worse than that, too…

The sun was mercilessly hot, but there was a breeze, and – *thank god!* – it was a fresh, clean breeze laden with the salt of sea air. Not smoke. Not death.

"Alexa!?" Kage's worried voice followed her outside as he appeared at the doorway, then hurried to catch up with her as Alexa realized she was still walking, stalking back and forth on the roadway outside the lodge, heaving great lungfuls of that clean, pure air.

"Damnit. You should have said something-" Kage started to say.

"Say what?" Alexa snapped at him, instantly annoyed at him for suggesting to her that she was weak, but a part of her also more annoyed at herself.

What is wrong with me? I've been shot at, I've had guns pointed right at my head.

"Hey, hey, I get it-" Kage opined, and Alexa shot him another hard look.

Do you, Kage? Do you?

Kage very wisely didn't say anything but stood there as Alexa took long, slow lungfuls of air that didn't smell anything like explosions.

Of course, Alexa knew all the reasons for it. Her training at Quantico had included courses on 'operational mindfulness' as well as combat stress, emotional first aid, and yes, PTSD. But she had never even been in a war, or a combat zone, that was what was confusing her. This was just something, another event that happens in the life of an FBI agent, wasn't it? Why was her heart racing and her ears ringing and her lungs feeling like they were choking on that acrid smoke every time she thought about the explosion?

It's natural. Delayed shock reaction. My body didn't know how to deal with the threat, didn't even see the threat coming, Alexa told herself.

"I'm just... still processing it, I guess," she managed in the end. Once again Kage wisely didn't say anything, which Alexa was very thankful for.

"I'm good. I just needed the air," she said, feeling stupid as Kage nodded silently, and they turned and walked back into the private lodge once more. To his credit, Agent Marinsburg didn't say anything, but Alexa noticed Kage giving him a pointed look, the sort of look that said, *Don't,* and that seemed to be enough for Marinsburg, who had cut the video but held up the data-stick instead.

"What you saw just now, agents, was proof that the detonation occurred on the helipad, not on the H155. There wasn't a shot, as far as we can discern, and our initial scene inspections concur. The explosion originated under the surface of the helipad, right where the helicopter was about to land."

Agent Marinsburg paused, then looked at them both steadily.

"It was a bomb. And it was very well hidden, as my team didn't spot any sign of tampering with the helipad when we swept three consecutive times. Someone had time, opportunity, and skill to bury a device under the helipad."

Alexa blinked at the serious implications of what the agent was saying.

"But they must have re-patched the helipad tarmac afterwards, or repainted. They would need to have access to the helipad not just today, or this morning, but perhaps for much longer than that. And the service tools required to do it."

"Yes, ma'am, they would," Marinsburg said heavily. "It is my recommendation that the killer was already on the island, and is *still* on the island, as no one has been allowed to leave yet."

Alexa spun, all thoughts of burning air forgotten.

"The resort manager. We need to get a full list of all the guests and staff right here on the island, right now."

CHAPTER FIVE

VI. 1:35 PM

"**M**'LADY, I CAN ASSURE YOU THAT EVERY LAST *ONE* OF my staff here comes with the best credentials and prior employment references!" said the large, portly gentleman who looked to Alexa as though he had walked straight out of a *Gone with the Wind* amateur dramatic production, with his white suit and his blonde handlebar mustache.

Bartholomew Price was the owner of St. Martin's Resort (*"-sadly no, I am not the beneficiary of this entire slice of oceanic idyll, but merely just the land these four walls sit upon, as well as yonder* helipad marina where such an unfortunate and obscene tragedy has occurred-" as he had explained a moment earlier).

The man in question stood inside his rather lavish office on the ground floor of the main resort building, accessed through a wing that gave Mr. Price his own estate room, private sauna, and even a private kitchen where "I have a chef, he comes in four times a week, whenever I am here, and is truly remarkable with sea bass, let me tell you!"

The man was a fool, Alexa had decided, and worse than that, he was an over-paid and scared fool. He had clearly not been expecting what had happened this morning at the helipad, and Alexa noted the nervousness in the way he kept on fiddling with his cufflinks (gold, of course) or smoothing the tips of his mustache.

You got anything to hide, Mr. Price? Alexa wondered for a moment, casting an eye around the wood-paneled room with wide windows looking out over the sculpted lawns and fountains of the resort, a spray of trees, and then the wide, vivid blue waters of the Gulf.

Of course, Alexa knew that everyone always had something to hide. It was the nature of being human, but the skillful trick for the investigator was working out whether their secrets were merely tawdry, or whether they were criminal...

He's a powerful man, but he thinks he's more important than he is, and he wants more power, Alexa surmised. He was powerful enough to have a presidential advisor and a Cuban diplomat here, after all...

"I am sure all your staff are impeccable, Mr. Price," Alexa said acidly. "But I am still going to need a complete schedule of all the staff you've had working here over the last year, as well as all the registered guests, and in particular everyone who was working or present here over the last week," Alexa smiled, looking down at her phone as she looked at the notes she had cribbed from Agent Marinsburg on their way over here.

"I believe that St. Martin's Resort was shortlisted for this meeting out of a potential top three. Do you know why that was,

Mr. Price? They wouldn't have chosen any old place in Key West, now would they?"

Beside her, Kage gave a small cough, and Alexa knew that he was trying to restrain his amusement.

Bartholomew managed to turn a deeper shade of pink. "Why, why St. Martin's is one of the premier resorts in all the Gulf, m'lady-"

"*Sir* or ma'am, if you must," Alexa said, fixing him with a sharp glance. For some reason, it appeared that people seemed to forget that she was FBI just because she was a woman.

"Yes, of course. We cater to an elite clientele, who desire peace and quiet and the glory of nature. Of course, I do not wonder for a moment why my humble establishment was chosen-"

"Your establishment where a terror attack was planned and executed? A perfect venue for it, one might say..." Alexa stated. She paused and allowed those words to truly sink in. This place was *chosen* and it was *easy* for the attack to take place. Did Bartholomew want to start asking why that was, too?

She saw Bartholomew reach the same conclusion she had, and then suddenly he blurted out.

"You don't think I... Are you suggesting that I..."

Alexa cleared her throat, overriding him. No, she didn't seriously think that Bartholomew was directly linked to the attack. But she couldn't rule him out. He was a man hungry for power, and it felt like he had more to gain from providing a playground for the rich and famous than he did from hosting their death site.

"I have been made aware that you made several large donations to both the Republican and the Democratic parties over the last seven years," Alexa went over Agent Marinsburg's notes.

"Why yes, yes I did," Bartholomew spluttered. "I believe it is my civic duty to give back, you see..."

I'm sure, Alexa thought as Kage gave another small cough. There it was, in her book; she was looking at a very rich man who was trying to buy his way into political influence, and finally, his number had come up with his resort being selected for a possible world-changing political meeting...

And we can see how that turned out, she thought.

"Very commendable, Mr. Price. Those staff lists?" Alexa prodded, and Price stood dumbfounded for a moment, then blinked as he turned to the filing cabinet and started to leaf through the available sheaths of paper, drawing out several.

"We haven't changed the staff much in the past few years. Once we get a good man or uh, a woman as well, of course, we tend to keep them. But this top sheet is everyone we have on our schedule at the moment…"

"How many of these are currently on the island right now?" Alexa asked.

No way off the island. The killer is probably still right here, and they had access to the helipad…

"I, uh, let me see…" Price turned to pull another time sheet detailing the last week, with names printed next to boxes labeled Kitchens, Rooms, Grounds, or Spa.

"Thank you." Alexa took a photo of the sheet of paper before turning to hand it to Kage.

"Can you get that to Marinsburg?" she said in a slightly lower voice. "I think the Service will have much better background checks than we do…"

"Uh-huh," Kage agreed, pausing to give Alexa a look before he left the room.

It was a worried look.

What!? I said I was fine! Alexa shot back at him before dismissing the thought. The last thing she needed right now was to have her partner being overprotective of her and take his mind off the task at hand.

Of finding the killer. Clearly someone good with explosives.

"Ma' – Agent?" Bartholomew cleared his throat. "This lockdown. Can I ask how long it'll be for? You see the guests are starting to wonder what is going on, as we have their phones and all…"

Oh yeah, the guests. Alexa almost groaned. That was a whole new ball game, as well.

"Excellent question. I'm going to need all the information about the current guests as well. Who they are, when they booked in, receipts of payment, how they got here…" she listed off. "And of course, we'll be interviewing each one, as well."

"Interviewing them? Personally?" Bartholomew's face fell.

Why does that bother you? Alexa wondered. Was it merely because they would probably leave a very crappy review online?

"Ma'am – Agent, I mean, I feel that I have been helping you out a *lot*, and I have already offered full refunds to my guests, but some of them are threatening to sue me for a breach of human rights! I can't have St. Martin's associated with-"

"Would you rather have it associated with the attempted assassination of a presidential advisor, or a kerfuffle of disgruntled guests?" Alexa asked as the large man once again flustered and flushed a deep red.

"*Dear suffering saints!*" Price muttered under his breath, reaching into a drawer in his desk and taking out a decorative crystal bottle and a glass, to which he poured himself a very stiff drink.

"This will ruin me, Agent Landers," Price said in a much sharper tone. He didn't forget her rank *this* time, Alexa noted.

"We have only five guests at the resort at the moment. Like I say, it is a very prestigious place, we pride ourselves on our privacy, and I was told to whittle the numbers down as much as I could," Price grumbled. "As it is, I'll be taking a monumental loss this month…"

"I'm sure the United States government will help you with the cost of the helipad," Alexa said acidly. Her ears were ringing again, and she was trying not to reveal how much she detested the pure and unadulterated greed she saw oozing out of a man like Price.

"Where are they right now, these guests? Let me speak to them," Alexa groaned.

Price made a surprisingly perky come back. "You – you will? Right now, I have them in the main reception area. It's been hours now, and I've had to offer them free food from the kitchens, of course-"

Price kept on burbling as he led the way out of his office and his private wing, the corridor connecting the main hallway to the larger service kitchens and laundry rooms.

Any of the staff could make it to his office pretty easily, Alexa noted.

From the service area of the ground floor, they went up some steps that led into the lobby itself, and into a wall of murmuring noise. Alexa was met with the sight of a very large room with a rounded, wooden reception desk opposite a set of double glass doors, with a larger lobby area to the right of that with low sofas and decorative plants. Two sets of stairs went up to a balcony around the lobby area, which Alexa guessed had to lead to the penthouse-like resort rooms.

There in the lobby were the five guests, mostly seated on the leather sofas, and standing at the doors to the resort and blocking the stairs leading upward were the steel-blue-suited Secret Service agents in shades.

"Now look here, I know my rights. This is a breach of human rights, you can't just take people's phones and refuse them access to the outside world! We're not prisoners! I have people who care about me out there, and they need to know I am okay-"

One of the men, a thirty-something guy with a close-cropped beard and shaved sides to his head was berating a terrified-looking resort staffer at the reception desk. Alexa saw the nearest Service agent flicking them a mildly disinterested look.

And then the man saw Price and Landers, arriving up the stairs to the service area.

"Ah. Price. There you scuttled off to. It's about time you showed your face in here and told us just what the hell is going on!" The man started to march straight up to them, with a gait that said he wasn't going to back down until he had his way.

Alexa stepped quickly in the way between them, one hand held up as the other smoothly flipped open her FBI badge.

"Stop right there and take a breath, sir," she said quickly as she looked him in the eye, and tried to judge if he was the sort of man to listen to a woman.

He was, or at least he was the sort of man to listen to an armed FBI woman, anyway. Alexa thought she would take that. He wasn't much taller than she was, with a vaguely rounded, gym-rat weight-lifting sort of figure dressed in khaki shorts and a loose T on top.

"FBI? Who are you? You should know what I'm talking about then! The hotel took all our phones and devices! I *work* online. You can't just steal people's stuff!" the man said.

"Been doing much work this morning, sir? Y'know, given everything?" Alexa raised an eyebrow.

That stopped him in his tracks as he blinked, looking confused.

"No, of course not – but the principle-"

"The principle is that I am Special Agent Alexa Landers of the FBI, and this morning we have had a very serious incident," she raised her voice as she cast a look at the others. There was a middle-aged couple, a young woman in a flowery and flowing dress, and finally another middle-aged man in a large sun-hat nursing a bottle of water.

Everyone looked at her silently for a moment. They looked tired, worried, and scared.

"I am sure that you know what's happened by now, but I can share with you that there was a very serious breach of national security this morning, at this resort. There were fatalities." She looked around the crowd, as the younger, angry hipster took a step back as if this was all terrible news to him.

Alexa frowned a little, then took a gamble. "Perhaps some of you have already surmised this much already, but these good men and women here are representatives from the United States Secret Service, and *that* should show you how serious the incident this morning was."

There was a small gasp from the woman of the middle-aged couple, and the younger woman looked at the Service men with wide but interested eyes. "Are we, like, in trouble?" she asked. Her voice carried the unmistakable valley-girl twang of Southern California.

Before Alexa could even answer her one way or the other, Angry Hipster but in. "Secret Service? What do you mean? What happened?" he snarled. "We have a right to-"

"You have a right to safe, secure, and respectful treatment," Alexa overrode him, before continuing. "I am afraid that, given the nature of the events this morning no one will be able to leave the island. Not until I say so. If anyone wishes to question this further, then you are very free to talk to me about emergency powers.

"Also due to the nature of events this morning, I have had to confiscate all of your devices, as they may pose a risk, whether knowingly or not, to national security… At the moment, we are asking for your full cooperation," she stated clearly, taking a breath before she moved onto the next part of that sentence.

"As this is an active investigation and possible national security threat, I have to remind you all that first, we must look after each other. If you spot anything suspicious then you must, you *must* report it either to myself or the nearest Service member that you see… Also, I have to remind all of you that if you fail to cooperate with my recommendations, then you may be in danger of interfering with federal procedure, which is a very serious offense…"

She stated the last bit as she looked at Mr. Angry Hipster full in the face.

I could also go on to say that you are all suspects in an active case, but let's save that for later, shall we? Alexa thought as Mr. Angry Hipster first looked scared, and then puzzled, and then finally angry.

"I am not sure that you can do that…" he began, as Alexa stared at him.

Don't ask it, bucko, she silently begged as her ears started to ring.

But Angry Hipster was clearly intelligent. He asked it.

"Has a state of emergency been declared?" he said, his eyes glowering.

Damnit.

Alexa had really not wanted to go into this with them, as it would be very easy to cause a panic, and if word somehow leaked out of here that it had been declared, then it would be mainstream news before the hour was out.

Maybe it already is, Alexa thought. She hadn't even seen the news yet.

"Yes. A localized emergency response was declared for St. Martin's Island at approximately eleven-thirty this morning by the governor," Alexa repeated what Field Chief Williams had told her this morning.

And that emergency declaration only lasts so long, if they're not doing it federally. I might have a few hours; I might have 24 before these people can legally leave the island…

And the killer along with them.

"*Sir?*" It was one of the St. Martin's Resort staff, dressed in white and blue, and appearing on the stairs which they had just come down. She was young, in her twenties, with scraped-back dark hair and a very worried look on her face, and she was hissing something in Bartholomew Price's ear.

"What is it?" Alexa said immediately. From the look on the young woman's face, it wasn't good – and the look on Price's was even worse.

"I'm sure it's nothing, it's just-" Bartholomew tried to bluster, motioning Alexa to one side, out of earshot of Mr. Angry Hipster and the others.

"One of my staff, Miguel Figuera, didn't come in this morning, that's all. Abigail here just informed me, but I'm sure-" Price started to explain.

"One of your staff? I thought your staff lived on-site?" Alexa hissed back pointedly, aware of the gathered silence from the lobby behind them, and all the ears that were straining to hear what was said.

"They do, in the staff wing," Bartholomew said, as Alexa reached for her phone, and quick-keyed Kage's number.

"*Murphy,*" he answered right away.

"Kage, we might have something. Meet me in the staff hall…"

CHAPTER SIX

VII. 1:55 PM

THE STAFF WING WAS NOT ESSENTIALLY A WING OF THE main resort building at all, but rather a discrete long, single-story building pitched next to it, surrounded by palm trees and rhododendrons so presumably, the high-paying visitors didn't have to be bothered by the sight of the inner workings of this place.

Alexa huffed, pushing down her feelings of resentment. So far in her time in Miami, she had spent an awful lot of time around very rich people, whose lives were right next to the poorer communities of Florida.

The wing itself sat outside the back of the resort and to one side, connected by way of a small gravel courtyard that led directly to the kitchens and storage rooms. By the time she arrived, Kage was already making his way up the gravel path by the side of the building, edged with gravel and pruned, decorative rhododendrons. Alexa was suddenly struck by the incongruence of the scene, the beautiful, slightly scented flowers with their large blooms…

And Kage Murphy, stalking forward in his dark athletic gear and anti-glare shades, with his Glock already drawn.

"Kage?" Alexa breathed, holding up a hand for Bartholomew to stay back at the door to the main resort.

"Marinsburg put a call into their data people, we were already going through the service staff, just as you requested…" Kage said in a low growl, nodding to the main door as he slid along to one side of it, while Alexa took up a covering position on the other as she slowly took out her gun. She didn't know why Kage came in armed and hot, but she trusted him enough that there was a reason.

"On the staff sheet, Miguel was a groundskeeper and general maintenance worker for the resort. He maintained the marina – and the helipad," Kage explained.

He had opportunity, Alexa thought. But did this Miguel have motive?

"Room 5," Price called out nervously from the doorway, where he had already taken several steps back into the relative sheltering darkness of the hallway beyond. Alexa could hear the fear in his voice as she nodded and waved him back further still.

"Make sure no one comes out here. *No one!*" she insisted to Price, turning to nod at Kage that she was ready.

Kage moved silently and with a grace that didn't seem in keeping with his cheeky, twitchy humor. He gripped the door and handle and opened it quickly and smoothly as Alexa stepped forward, her pistol up and scanning the corridor.

"Clear."

There was but one corridor on one side of the building, with sunlight streaming in through the windows to illuminate a series of doors set at intervals down the long opposite wall. From one of them, Alexa could hear muted, tinny salsa music playing and she hoped that whoever was inside wouldn't choose this moment to come out.

"Kage!" Alexa whispered, gesturing at the door where the music was coming from. It wasn't number one, but two.

He stopped, looking at her.

"We should evacuate," she whispered. "If Miguel is responsible for what happened this morning, then…"

Then he could have a bomb inside there, couldn't he? she thought. Kage pulled a face, as that would make this much harder than they had first thought, but he nodded all the same.

Alexa moved down the hallway, half-crouching as she counted off the doors as she did so, *1, 2, 3, 4…*

"Five," Alexa whispered and paused, one hand hovering over the handle, looking back to see that Kage was tapping on the door to the room where the tinny music was playing.

Don't hear us. Don't do anything rash, Alexa silently willed any possible occupant to room 5, as the door to 2 opened and she heard a soft gasp behind, and then Kage's low muttered voice urgently whispering back. A moment later, with the music still playing behind her, the woman left, walking quickly down the hallway and then running across the gravel and back to the resort as Kage joined Alexa at door 5.

"She says she's the only one in here, apart from Miguel," he said, his voice in a low murmur before he blinked and looked up at Alexa, his eyes saying the words that his mouth didn't: *Is this wise?*

She guessed what he meant. What if this Miguel was in fact the bomber, and that he was some crazed fanatic who would rather kill himself than be taken into custody? Or that he had booby-trapped the building?

Or he might just have been sick for work this morning, Alexa also figured.

If we wait and pull a whole locked-down operation here then Miguel inside would know for sure that we're coming for him.

Which might make it worse.

No, they would have to do this quickly and quietly – and face the consequences if it went badly, too.

"On three," Alexa whispered, putting her gun away as she lightly touched the door handle and held up one finger.

1.

Her ears started ringing again, that distracting tinnitus that matched the beat of her blood...

2.

Alexa swore that she could taste the burn of acrid, greasy smoke in her lungs...

3!

Alexa grabbed and twisted the door handle, pushing it open suddenly as Kage stepped forward, his gun up and scanning.

Nothing happened. No explosion. No sudden fireball. No oily, black smoke. Past the door was a simple, single bedroom, a desk and a wardrobe, and an open window.

And on the bed, there was a mess of papers, charts, and maps.

"Huh?" Kage said, sweeping the room as he carefully moved into it. They filed in quickly to find nobody there, but it did little to slow Alexa's racing heart.

"Everything's clear," Kage reported. He put his gun back in the holster and stopped over the bed where the disheveled papers were scattered.

One, clearly, was a map of the island with the nautical depth markers ringing St. Martin's. Another two items were newspapers in Spanish, and on the front cover of one was an image of the now-deceased Cuban Representative, Ramon Martinez, shouting and railing at something off-camera.

"He knew he was coming," Alexa whispered. "Miguel knew Ramon was coming to the island..."

Kage made a gruff, agreeing noise. "And it looks a lot like he was preparing something for him, too..."

CHAPTER
SEVEN

VIII. 3:15 PM

"**M**IGUEL FIGUERA." THE WORDS OF MARINSBURG were an announcement, not a question, as he stood looming over them in Figuera's small room, as Alexa and Kage did their best to document the scene.

"Born in Miami, parents Cuban immigrants; he's twenty-nine. Has lived in just about every city in Miami-Dade. Seems to move every couple of years or so into increasingly ratty apartments. Currently resides in Doral."

"Ouch," Alexa murmured. She remembered her statistics lessons from Quantico. There were multiple indicators of extremist activity, and one of the largest indicators was gender and age. Males in particular had a higher opportunity for extremist thinking in their twenties, and then later on, in their late forties.

I guess when they're young they're full of the passions of life, and later...? Alexa blinked. At only just approaching her thirties herself, she felt like she had her whole life ahead of her, but she could still guess at the yawning gap that perhaps lay, twenty or fewer years out, when it might become obvious that the world really *didn't* match up to your expectations.

But that was where the danger vectors ended; Alexa knew that she couldn't jump to conclusions. It was far more likely to be homegrown, ethnically Caucasian men who were prone to extremism, and after that, the likelihood fell on the children of immigrants, as they often struggled to come to terms with a society that did not value them for their ancestry.

"Got a job here at the resort last summer, after a string of good contracts at hotels and resorts along the Florida coast. No misdemeanors, no connection with the law up until now..." Marinsburg was reading from a sheet, sent over by whatever shadowy database that the Secret Service had access to.

"However, Mr. Figuera was also apparently leading a double life," he said.

"I can see that," Alexa's eyes flickered to the maps and the various newspapers, all of which featured Representative Martinez, and the maps appeared to have lines marked across them. *Routes? Attack lines?* It was hard to decipher the scribblings of someone else, but to Alexa, they looked an awful lot like a plan about to be set in motion...

"Figuera was masquerading online as 'CubanTruther94', which set him out as a member of the 'Truther' movement of ex-Cuban nationals..." Marinsburg said.

"Truthers? Aren't they religious in some way?" Kage asked.

Marinsburg rolled his eyes. "The name is used by a number of anti-establishment groups, almost all grassroots, citizen-led, and tend to fall into the conspiracy theory sector. In this case, the Cuban Truthers work to expose evidence of corruption and inhumane behavior by the Cuban regime, with some claims being far out – boat loads of slaves being shipped over from Mexico, and similar…"

"Ah, I got it," Kage sighed, and Alexa had to agree. A lot of 'Truther' movements had sprung up over the last few years, and almost all of them were concerned with trying to expose the powers that be in belonging to some strange, shadowy cult. It appeared that this movement had even come to Cuba itself.

"He was online, apparently railing at the terrible sins of the Cuban regime, as well as the ineffectiveness of the United States in exposing it, and he has said some pretty volatile stuff…" Marinsburg muttered before repeating something about 'taking back the Cuban lands' and 'invade to liberate' slogans.

"He wasn't flagged before this?" Alexa asked, thinking that surely this would be a cause of concern for any intelligence sweep of the diplomatic meeting site.

"He was using multiple VPNs and an alias, and in general even the Secret Service has to comply with digital privacy laws." Marinsburg's face said just how much he respected that.

But the law is the law, Alexa countered silently. *It's there for a reason.*

"Given the state of emergency here, and that Miguel is an active person of interest, we have… a few extra tools in our toolbox," Marinsburg said. "We have a team at his apartment in Doral as we speak, and they are updating me on what they find." He tapped his ear where the wireless mic was permanently in place.

"Right. So we have a potential extremist on the island, who had a serious beef with the Cuban authorities…" Alexa began.

"And the American ones as well," Kage pointed out.

"Yes. This is clearly motive, but…" Alexa shook her head.

There were still missing parts here. Time frame. Expertise. Tools. Did a grassroots citizen activist know how to build a device capable of what she had seen with her own eyes?

"He had access to the helipad, and days to plant the device," Kage pointed out. All of the items were now in plastic bags, with Alexa having filled in the tags that were no more than office sticky labels to be placed on top, as well as recording descriptions of each item into her phone.

But what was it that I remembered from the academy? Alexa struggled to recall her classes, most of which she had aced. "Don't explosives usually require some sort of, I don't know... dedicated area?" she asked. It was Marinsburg who nodded.

"Yes. Well, only for the potential of damage, that is. In the past, culprits have usually been isolated loners, and so have access to rooms or outbuildings or warehouses where they can work where, if anything goes wrong..."

"They won't kill everyone they might not want to kill," Kage finished.

"Precisely."

"Right, well..." Alexa looked around the room. "That is clearly not here. In fact, I don't see anything much more chemical or technical than a wall clock and a bottle of aftershave."

They had checked these items nonetheless into the plastic bags, sealed with adhesive tape. It was a terrible way to manage a crime scene, but the Secret Service's resources were currently still concentrated on the helipad.

"So, we need to find a site where Miguel might have worked, if he had been the one to commit the crime," Kage affirmed. "I guess we're looking at everything from spare rooms to abandoned sheds..."

"There's a whole island," Alexa said, somewhat irritably. "But we need to *find* Miguel ASAP. He didn't show up for his shift this morning, and he's not here now..." Her eyes moved to the window, which was still open.

No one had brought their fingerprint powder or brushes, or their formula latex which would set hard on surfaces before allowing any prints to be lifted when they peeled it off. Alexa winced, then an idea struck her.

"Got it." She moved to the desk where they had piled the office supplies they had used for the evidence collection, and instead of any high-tech solutions, she picked up the roll of adhesive tape and started layering it over the window sill, as firmly and as evenly as she could.

"Old school!" Kage grinned, instantly getting what she was doing.

"Just a little trick I learned at the academy," Alexa stated. "It's best if you dust the area with talcum powder, even fine flour will do, but I guess we'll have to make ends meet..."

She waited for a moment, and then slowly, very, very carefully pulled up one of the strips nearest the window seal and held it up in the hot Florida sun.

"Bingo," she said, as there was a line of wedge-shapes on the tape.

"Photograph this and the next," Alexa requested, as she laid the tape to one side and carefully teased up the next line of tape, and then the next, too. Together, they clearly looked like the toe print of a boot.

And the only reason a toe print would be here, would be someone leaving the building via the window, right? she thought to herself as Kage took the photos.

"But we don't know how long that has been there. It might be Figuera's, but it might not. How many staff have stayed in this room before him?" he asked, when there was a bluster at the door. It was Bartholomew Price, coughing and spluttering as he peered inside.

"It was Miguel, was it?" he announced loudly and with clear outrage in his voice. "I never trusted him, you know. Never trusted him! But my staff manager said that I couldn't be biased, so I had to hire him."

"Thank you, Mr. Price," Alexa cut him off with a sharp tone. The last thing she wanted to hear right now was Bartholomew Price. But perhaps he had information that could help.

"Mr. Price, it seems that we have a man missing on the island, and the island isn't that big. Is there any other way off this island apart from the two marinas?"

"No, not easily, anyway," Price coughed, shaking his head. "I mean, if you had a boat you could always pull up anywhere along the beaches I suppose, and sometimes we get fishermen who try to do just that – but right now the island is off limits, isn't it?"

Price said the last line a little heavily, and it was clear that he was still smarting at the fact that they were all stuck here, on lockdown.

"Thank you," Alexa said, before turning back to Marinsburg and Kage.

"The Coast Guard is on high alert. They would have warned us if they had picked up a boat leaving these shores. So that points to Miguel still being out there on the island somewhere…" Alexa's eyes went to the window and the green lawns beyond, the trees, and the shaded glimmers of the wall, on the other side of which sat about two square miles of nothing but greenery, sand, and swamp.

"Any buildings out there, Price?" Alexa asked. *If he was the culprit, he would need a space to work, right?*

"Uh-huh, a few. Nature-watching blinds, for the most part, a couple of tool sheds and the like for when we have to repair some of the board paths. I can get you a map if that would be helpful?" Price said, who must have realized that this whole nightmare could be over if he tried to help more.

"I can start a search," Kage said immediately. "But we need people here, too, keeping an eye on the others."

Alexa sighed. "All the guests need interviewing anyway. I can start on that if you want to check out the buildings first?"

A shadow crossed over Alexa's face, as she suddenly remembered that flash of brilliant light, the smell of burning meat in her nostrils.

"Be careful out there, Murphy. Be *real* careful."

CHAPTER EIGHT

IX. 4:45 PM

"REALLY, IS THIS SOMETHING WE SHOULD BE DOING before dinner?" griped Eddie Kendricks, or Mr. Angry Hipster, as Alexa preferred to think of him right now.

Alexa once again stood in the main lobby room of the resort, with the crowd of guests still gathered.

Maybe he has a point. Maybe this would be easier after they've eaten. Alexa might have considered this further, were it not for the silver platters already laden with goods from the kitchen laid on every available surface from the low-slung tables to the receptionist's desk. Bartholomew Price seemed intent on at least supplying food for the duration of this incarceration, presumably in an attempt to stop any lawsuits being fired at him.

But crowd management had never been one of Alexa's strong suits at the Academy. She had scraped through the course with a 65, despite ending the training with a distinction anyway thanks to her exceptional scores in procedure and physical assessments.

It's not that I don't like people, she considered once again. It was more like she had never been that good at people. There was something in them that she found messy, confusing – like why Eddie Kendricks here was angry and aggressive right now over this when just this morning three men had been killed. Murdered, in a horrific shock of violence. All she was asking of them was to wait it out. In a resort. Which they had all chosen to do anyway.

Yes, people were confusing and unpredictable. They didn't seem to obey the laws of principle and reason to which she adhered so strictly. Even her partner Kage Murphy was another fine example in Alexa's eyes. He was an experienced FBI Special Agent; he was highly skilled, very good at what he did, and quick to act when needed...

But then why does he goof off all the time, throwing reckless, crooked smiles or pulling faces behind the backs of the Secret Service agents? she wondered. It was something that Alexa couldn't understand – that disconnect between what Kage should be proud of, celebratory of, and why he acted as if nothing mattered in the world.

Anyway. Her attention snapped back to Eddie Kendricks as he took a step too close, railing as he gestured wildly to the doors that the Service agent was still guarding.

"And they're no use at all. All they do is stand there like statues. You might be lucky if they follow you to the toilet. They don't tell you anything that's going on!" he burst out.

It was the near movement. The sudden shape right next to her focused all her attention, bringing Alexa slamming back into the moment.

"I think you need to calm down, Mr. Kendricks, and take a seat. There looks to be plenty of food, very kindly provided by Mr. Price already," Alexa attempted.

"It's not what I paid for, though!" Kendricks barked back, but at least he did turn back to one of the unoccupied sofas, grabbing one of the smaller china trays of sushi already laid out as he did so.

Alexa resisted the urge to call him a name. That wouldn't get anyone anywhere, and it certainly wasn't professional.

Right. Where to start. She looked over the guests, who had already been told that she was going to start taking statements from all of them. It was only five o'clock; she might be done by midnight, she thought...

But I wish I had more time.

There was Mr. Angry Hipster, or Eddie Kendricks according to the guest sheet. She thought she'd probably let him cool off for a while longer yet.

Then there was the middle-aged guy in the sun hat, who had looked vaguely annoyed but appeared to be keeping it together. He had the air of someone in retirement. A widower, maybe.

Then there was the younger, Californian-looking woman. Despite her social-media-worthy fashion and the oversized sunglasses pushed up to her forehead, she looked scared, currently lying down on the sofa with her eyes closed.

Finally, there was the middle-aged couple, both in shorts and looking like they had been about to go on a hike before everyone's plans were completely turned over.

Well, none of them looks as good a suspect as Figuera does right now, Alexa thought. But they might be able to fill in some details. There might be some small thing they noticed that no one else did...

That was the thing with investigations, Alexa knew. You could never say what was going to be the clue that would break the case wide open. All it took was one cast-iron, irrefutable fact to convince a jury. Just one.

Her intuition guided her to pick the middle-aged couple first, or *Antonio and Maria Luca* on her printed-out guest list. Of all the guests here, they looked like they were probably the most likely to be up and about around the time of the incident, and perhaps they had even seen something when they were preparing for their hike.

"Mr. and Mrs. Luca, would you come with me please?" she asked, remembering to give them at least the smallest of smiles as well, as she gestured toward one of the not-as-big side rooms off the lobby.

Actually, the room was larger than most of the data-analysis offices in the entirety of the Miami field office, and looked to be a place where private bookings could plan entire banquets, with its long table and chandeliers hanging from the ceiling. Alexa pulled a trio of chairs out from one end of the table, as it probably would have been ridiculous for her to be sitting at the far end.

"Agent…? Can I ask, I'm sorry to bother you – but my wife has pain meds for her arthritis, you know," Antonio Luca began, with his graying short hair and a worried look on his face as his brow creased and he wrung his hands. "Early onset, it's a burden – can I ask when we'll be able to go to our rooms?" he asked a little apologetically.

Alexa had already decided on this. So far, everyone had been kept in the lobby by the Service agents, with only trips to the bathrooms allowed. But that couldn't last forever, even under the state of emergency powers. She would have to decide to charge people, formally placing them as suspects and holding them for questioning if she wanted this situation to go further.

These people have to sleep somewhere tonight, too, she sighed to herself. This situation was starting to go beyond a criminal investigation and more disaster management...

"The agents are doing a sweep of all the rooms as we speak," she said, knowing that it had been on Marinsburg's list of things to do. But nothing had suddenly come through on her phone or her in-ear short-wave radio comms, meaning that the agents hadn't discovered a stash of weapons and explosives anywhere, obviously.

But Marinsburg was also pressed for people, Alexa knew. His prime focus was protection, and so most of his team had gone with Skip back to Washington, leaving a skeleton force here to mainly help with cataloging the helipad scene until her CSI backup could arrive.

But nothing has been found so far, Alexa considered.

"After this interview," she confirmed, "I'll take you to your rooms, and, if everything is in order, we should have you back there by tonight." That seemed to placate them, so she nodded.

"So, shall we begin? Let's start by your visit to St. Martin's, what brings you here, and then I would like you to walk me through all the events since your arrival," she initiated, turning back to confer with the sheet that Marinsburg had provided for her.

Antonio & Maria Luca, 64 and 67, Groveland, Florida. Retired Investors. No Priors.

Well, that was an awful lot to go on, Alexa thought as her eyes flickered up to the pair. Antonio was walking her through their general reasons for being here, this being the first time they had come to St. Martin's as they have become keen 'watchers' – amateur bird watchers to be exact – in their middling and latter years.

The pair were in love even after all their years of marriage, and, despite the day that everyone had had, Alexa was touched to see them make small asides to each other, mention other trips they had been on – one to Greenland, another to the Pacific Northwest last year. Antonio reached out and took Maria's hand, massaging her aching knuckles gently as she spoke.

They confirmed they were retired, having made their money in New York and Belgium as high-stakes investment advisors for a variety of firms, making enough to retire early and spend the rest of their lives on their passion... until coming here, that is.

"Well, we were already up, as the best time to see birds is right around dawn or sunset," Maria explained, leaning forward as she did so. "The resort provides a packed lunch to those going out, and trail maps, and so we took the east circular trail."

"About what time was that, Mrs. Luca?" Alexa asked.

"Oh, I guess it must have been coming on five-thirty, six in the morning maybe," the woman said with a cautious smile. She still had red hair that probably was blazing crimson in her younger days, though was now a little faded to a wiry carrot.

"I remember thinking how quiet it was, there were more boats out yesterday–" Maria went on.

That would be the shutdown for the meeting, Alexa nodded to herself. The Coast Guard had been warned to keep everyone away from the island for the duration of today.

"–but as this was only our second day here, we didn't really know if it was anything different at all! There was one boat we saw on our trail, up by the northeastern side. Someone catching those early morning fish I guess!" Maria said with a little delight.

"A fishing boat?" Alexa suddenly realized what she was saying. "What do you mean, nearby to the island? What time would that have been?"

"Oh, it must have been a little after six, I suppose. It was just skirting the shallows, coming up to one of those little boat garage things they have right out over the water. Rusted tin shack, didn't look of much use at keeping the rain off, let me tell you!" Maria said before describing a point halfway around the island, heading eastwards and then north from the resort where the shack was.

There shouldn't have been any boats out this morning. No one at all! Alexa thought as she tried to remain calm, picking up her phone and tapping a quick message to Kage.

Boat Shed. About a mile out east from resort. DON'T GO W-OUT BACKUP! Tomoz morning!!

She fired the message off and then looked up. Suddenly, that sound was back again; a distant, muted ringing that wouldn't go away. She felt her palms sweat just a little. Kage was out there, alone.

"Right, so, shall we move on to the events of the day? Can you describe exactly what you saw?"

"Oh well, a bunting, for one..." Maria said lightly before the woman clearly realized that Alexa wasn't interested in birds. Not as much as these people clearly did, anyway.

"Ah, I see, well... nothing that I saw was out of the ordinary..." Maria looked at Antonio, who shook his head briefly.

Alexa probed a little deeper, but there was little that they could confirm. They had seen a few staff members that morning but couldn't quite remember their faces. The woman behind the counter, a man who had brought them their packed lunch, nothing much else at all. No one out on the trails, nothing but birds.

"Right, well, thank you, I'll ask one of the agents if your room is clear," Alexa said, vetoing her earlier plan to check herself, as her heart was hammering to the beat of one thought.

Find Kage. Get to the Boat Shed.

"Agent?" Alexa called as they emerged from the room, and the nearest bald man in shades stepped forward quickly.

"Can you see that the Lucas' room is cleared please?" she asked, for the man to glance at his fellow Service agents briefly, receive the okay from them, and invited the Lucas to follow him.

Right. Kage. Alexa was already turning when there was a familiar, annoyed voice calling her back.

"I bet it was that little Cuban fella, right!? I saw him this morning, you know, when I got up."

It was Eddie Kendricks, Mr. Angry Hipster.

"Little Cuban fella?" Alexa repeated in a very serious tone as she turned and pierced the man with a glance. "Do you want to clarify that, Mr. Kendricks?" If there was one thing that Alexa tolerated less than fools, it was casual racism.

"The guy who works here. The little guy. Clearly Cuban, y'know?" She watched in disgusted curiosity as Kendricks made some vague gesture to his face, which she presumed meant he was talking about skin complexion.

"Are you suggesting that you saw someone of Hispanic descent this morning, Mr. Kendricks?" Alexa asked, seeing the Lucas look worriedly over their shoulder back at the almost-argument unfolding behind them. Eva Montgomery, Miss Floaty California, was making a face at Kendricks and turning over on her sofa with a huff. The final guest, the middle-aged and white-haired Saul Staniforth, looked positively riveted as he enjoyed the spectacle of Kendricks making a complete ass out of himself.

"That is exactly what I said. I came out of my room must have been, seven? Seven-thirty? To see if there was anyone alive behind the bar, right? Anyway, there he was, the little *Hispanic* guy who works here, heading off to the back. He looked, I don't know, *furtive,*" Kendricks said, adding the last word in a loud whisper that everyone in the room could clearly hear.

"I had my suspicions about him because of the way he looked at my watch when I signed in. He was cleaning this room, and he saw this…" Kendricks brandished the gaudy and goldy slab of metal on his wrist.

"I get looks all the time, of course, but I can tell a thief when I see one."

"Oh dear god, please stop!" Eva, Miss Floaty California with the long, dark hair snorted, sitting up suddenly. "Do we have to put up with your racist bullcrap as well as being stuck in here!?"

"Racist!? I'm not a racist! I saw him looking at me! When you get to *my* position in life, you get a good sense of-"

"What position is that? White frat guy who had his friends give him jobs straight out of college, right?" Eva shot back.

"People-!" Alexa raised her hands. She didn't have time for this. She really wasn't good at people management… That ringing was in her ears again, rising.

And somewhere out in the swamps is my partner, probably walking into a trap without me…

"Look who's talking, snowflake!" Kendricks laughed sarcastically.

"*SHUT UP!*" Alexa yelled at the entire room, and Eva and Kendricks suddenly fell silent and looked at her warily. Even the Secret Service agents had leaned forward a little, looking ready for whatever needed to happen next.

There was a moment of complete silence, apart from the tinnitus in Alexa's ears.

Breathe. Smile. Show them who's boss, but smile as you do it, she thought, musing over what her dad would have said. Her dad with his years of dealing with cramped, frustrated men on boats for months at a time.

'Don't let 'em give you any crap, kiddo…'

"Everyone will be allowed back to their rooms once the agents have performed a sweep of the rooms, okay? That should be tonight." She checked with the waiting agents (there were only two of them left down here now) who glanced at her, unsmiling.

Yeah, sorry, but it looks like you guys are trained to not get any sleep either. Alexa threw them a sympathetic look before moving back to the crowd.

"Now, if you please, try to remember that this will go more smoothly if we keep our cool. We are going to conduct our investigation, and you will all cooperate with that, and then you should be free to go," she said, and a part of her hoped that she wasn't lying.

Why can't I be as good with people as Kage is? Alexa groaned to herself as she turned and started walking quickly to the door, grabbing one of the resort trail maps on the way as she did so. It was nearly five-thirty, but there would still be another couple hours of daylight, she figured.

Maybe Kage's reckless, easy-going agreeableness was actually an asset, she considered.

But would it be much good out there in the wilds with an extremist?

Alexa started to run as soon as she got out the door.

CHAPTER NINE

X. 6:18 PM

ALEXA HAD MISJUDGED THE EVENING. SHE SWORE UNDER her breath as she jogged along the fairly wide, maintained path that led from outside the resort around St. Martin's Island in a wide loop. To her right there mixed either pristine white beaches, dotted with palm trees, or the denser cover of mangrove swamps and brushes, as the path sometimes detoured more inland than seaward.

Inland was a bit of a joke, however, at least as far as Alexa had seen of the island so far. This entire place might barely be just a few feet over sea level at its highest, she thought. She imagined what it must be like in hurricane season, which she had been warned to be prepared for when it came every year.

But that time wasn't yet, thankfully. There was a light breeze in the air, laden with clean salt and slight ozone – and Alexa was glad for that. No smoke. No fires. Nothing greasy in the wind...

Other paths met this one, with small wooden signs and color-coded markers picking out different trails across the island. Checking the map, Alexa saw that several such loops existed, and all of that was bad news for the job of finding the missing Figuera.

The sky over the distant resort was starting to purple, and Alexa was feeling annoyed at herself. She should have called Kage back; they should have gone over in the morning...

But Maria saw a boat out here. What if Figuera had a boat? What if he had a way off the island?

She also wondered if she should have tried to requisition any of Marinsburg's agents, but the man was starting to look more and more worried as more expectations of investigation were laid on him. It was hard enough trying to conduct and hold a crime scene investigation without any specialized officers or a clean zone, she thought.

No. We can do this. One guy. That's all it is. One guy.

One guy who planted bombs for a living?

There was a thin needle of light from up ahead of her on the path, a sharp spike of blue radiance, and Alexa knew that it was Kage with his pencil light. A moment later there was movement from the side of the path, and the dark figure of Kage appeared.

"I thought I told you to wait until morning..." Alexa repeated the angry text conversation she'd had not long before.

"I thought you agreed we should take a look right away, given everything..." Kage shot back at her, but there was no hint of rancor in his voice. If anything, he looked amused, his head turning to one side as he talked.

Does nothing faze you? she could have asked, but didn't. She knew that there was one thing that had. And that had been long ago, and she wasn't supposed to know about it.

"The shed's just up ahead, I spotted it but held position," Kage murmured as Alexa fell into line with him to turn the corner of the path, seeing that the edges were deeply crowded with mangroves and spiky, elongated, and thin trees. The vegetation must have gone right up to the sea from there, as Alexa could hear the gentle wash and lap of the waters, and see a glimmer of darker blue between the green.

Up ahead there was the edge of a rusted, corrugated iron building; a garage, with doors that looked locked.

"Do we have to worry about alligators out here?" Alexa whispered as they slowed, moving to the sides of the path so that there was less chance of being seen by any potential suspect inside.

"Always," Kage replied, throwing a mock-shocked look back at her before grinning. "Nah, not so much. Alligators are more freshwater animals; they don't like salt water so much… it's the crocodiles you have to look out for."

Alexa couldn't be sure if he was joking or not. This was Florida. He probably wasn't.

"Right," she said testily, pulling out her gun as Kage did the same.

They sidled up to the barn, seeing that it was actually on a wooden platform with thick posts driven into the dirt.

"Hey, look. The door isn't locked," Kage whispered, nodding to where one of the double doors was slightly ajar.

Alexa took aim and nodded for Kage as they reversed their roles from earlier.

Kage lightly touched the old handle with his free hand, then looked up at Alexa.

One moment, nothing. The next: Light and fire and smoke and burning bodies, raining down on the wet ground…

No. Alexa blinked, shaking the memory out of her mind quickly as she focused. Her heart was thumping, but this was okay. This was natural. She nodded.

Kage pulled open the door, stepping back as Alexa stepped forward, one step, two-

"Watch out!" Kage shouted suddenly as Alexa stumbled and caught herself before she walked off the very short wooden landing and straight into the dark canal of water that occupied the center of the boat shed.

"*Whoa!*" She stumbled back to the edge of the building, seeing that there was a wooden planked walkway that went up each side of the boat shed, allowing the vessel to dock securely in the middle. The opposite side was open to the elements and looked out onto the water.

There was no one here. But there was a boat; a fairly simple speedboat with wooden sides painted white and red, and an outboard motor.

But no Miguel Figuera. No anyone.

"What's that?" she murmured, seeing that, tucked under the pilot's chair, appeared to be a strong box.

"It could be regular emergency supplies, flare guns, first aid kit, the sort of thing every responsible pilot is supposed to have, but…" Kage murmured.

Yeah, but… Alexa steadied the side and stepped gingerly into the boat. "Hand me that light, will ya?" she said as she crouched by the side of the box, hunkering down as she shone the blue light all along the edge. Once again, the box wasn't locked, and it was so old and rusted that parts of the metal had warped – which was good.

There were no wires that Alexa could see. No flash of silver foil, which was a good thing. She had only performed the most rudimentary of classes at Quantico on what to do in this situation, but 'look for electronics' was a good start.

"I think we're good…" Alexa whispered, as her ears started to fill with the sound of ringing.

"You think?" Kage asked, sounding not very impressed at all. "Maybe we should-"

Alexa teased open the lid of the box, before letting out a relieved sigh as nothing went bang.

But what she *was* looking at, however, was still alarming.

There were no flare guns, but there was very clearly a heavy service pistol, as well as a stock, barrel, and central body of a modular rifle.

"That's a pack-down sniper's rifle," Alexa said, shining the flashlight inside gingerly to see that no, there were thankfully still no signs of wires anywhere. What there was, however, were sets of magazines for both the sniper's rifle and the smaller service pistol.

"A pack what?" Kage asked, as Alexa carefully brought out the body, being careful to only hold it on two tips in case of fingerprint contamination. It had been painted a matte brown and green, but she was fairly sure that if she scraped at it, the underneath would be a light cream-gray.

"You can 3D print these things and buy the rest of the parts online that you can't print," Alexa looked up at him and shrugged. Her specialization had been ballistics. She knew her way around guns.

And the only reason you 3D print a gun is if you can't legitimately get a license or buy the item from the local store, Alexa knew, looking at the modular rifle.

And the only reason you'd get a modular sniper rifle is if you had some very exact, very particular shooting to do.

Like murdering the Cuban representative.

CHAPTER
TEN

XI. 11:45 PM

IT WAS LATE BY THE TIME THEY GOT BACK TO THE PRIVATE lodge they were using as their war room and temporary accommodations. Alexa had to cancel the rest of the interviews with the guests for the night, and instead asked (nicely, with a smile!) that Marinsburg find the people to complete the searches of the guests' rooms, and alert her if they found anything.

It was a few hours later and there had been no alert, so Alexa had to presume that either Marinsburg hadn't done it and the guests were still being held in the lobby, becoming angrier and angrier, or that he had, and they had found nothing more than mosquito lotion and swim shorts.

"You let the guests back to their rooms?" Kage yawned as he slumped against the plush Chesterfield and rubbed his eyes. For a second Alexa thought that he was criticizing her, but then he looked up with a grin.

"Bet they're happy about that. Nothing lifts the mood as much as a good night's sleep," he said before taking a long, lingering look in the direction of their own rooms (which had very comfortable beds with real feather cushions and coverlets, Alexa had noticed).

"Yeah, well, I had to weigh either keeping them in there against their will, possibly getting the FBI sued down the line, and of some of them apparently eager to kill each other," Alexa shook her head.

"You don't pin them for the explosion this morning then?" Kage said with a yawn as he struggled to his feet.

Alexa frowned at that. It was always like this, she was just about coming around to see the need for Kage's looser attitude, when he went and said something stupid.

"It's not a matter of that, it's a matter of evidence," Alexa said.

"Aw, c'mon. You must have your gut feelings, right?" Kage said in an off-handed laugh.

How can you laugh! You were almost blown up! Alexa blinked.

"Like, my money is on Figuera as it makes the most sense, right? But that Eddie Kendricks has been eager to get off this island from the moment this began…"

Alexa wrinkled her nose. She didn't suspect anyone for it, but Kendricks felt a little showy. Like if he had a problem with Representative Ramon Martinez he would boldly storm straight up into him, get into his face, and *make* everyone see him having a problem…

"Okay, okay. The older couple then. They shot the helicopter out of the sky because they think it was a threat to their beloved birds or something," Kage opined, as Alexa stood stock still.

"Still nothing? No laugh? *Sheesh*, tough crowd…" Kage murmured before turning to wave her goodnight.

"I'm hitting the sack. We've got the evidence, we just need our man," he said, his tone dropping back to serious. "You did really good today, Agent Landers. I'm proud to serve with you."

"*Pfft.* Get going, looks like that blast rattled your head," Alexa whispered.

"Ha! I see! You can joke. I knew it!" Kage said as he turned, still grinning on his way to bed… leaving Alexa in the room, as her smile faded from her face. The thing was, Alexa knew *how* to make jokes and be social, technically, it was just that she didn't understand it much of the time.

Kage has to make fun of the investigation, the blast, the fact that he almost died, Alexa considered. It was probably his way of dealing with the fact that he had almost died, and then had seen three people die right in front of him and had been unable to do anything about it at all.

Once again, Alexa smelled that memory of burning flesh, and her palms went clammy. But she didn't rush out to get fresh air this time. She waited. Breathed through it.

'You've always been a tough cookie, kiddo.' That was what her dad would be saying to her right now, wouldn't he?

In a few moments the smell and the wave of threat response had faded, her heart rate had returned to just jogging, not sprinting, and she was able to look at the evidence and the notes arrayed before her.

It had taken them a good while to bring the metal box back from the boat shed, partly because it was a good half-an-hour's walk, maybe forty minutes from the resort – and partly because they had to do what they could to secure the evidence. That meant photos, lots and lots of photos, and lots and lots more plastic bags.

We just don't have the manpower for this, Alexa thought. They didn't have the spare people to secure the boat shed and maintain a guard to make sure no one else tampered with it, just as they didn't have enough people to keep an eye on all the guests.

The metal box was sitting by the side of the wooden table, wrapped in plastic, as were the various guns and gun parts they had found, each bagged and wrapped with sticky labels on them. Alexa sighed, moving to her notes to update:

Miguel Figuera. Cuban Truther.
- Maps
- evidence of plan-making
- last seen MORNING

Not that it helped to learn where he was right now, apart from that he was out there somewhere.

A thought struck Alexa suddenly. He hadn't gone for the boat. Why?

It was the one thing that didn't really make any sense. If Figuera had indeed set the bomb (*he had access, he had time, he had opportunity*) and that he got his target (*he had motive, a court would convict him*) then why didn't he flee on the boat, as surely that had been his intention?

Alexa winced. Clearly, Figuera had already stashed his murderous tools of the trade there, and that was perhaps why he had never shown up to work that morning, but why not make a run for it? It didn't really make any sense, especially as he had decided not to stick around and try to sweat it out.

"Maybe he got scared of all the agents and the activity," Alexa said to herself, scowling at the evidence. Maybe he had never realized the monumental error of his undertaking until it had happened, and now he was hiding somewhere out there in the swamps, trying to work out how to stay alive.

"Stay low, wait for it to blow over, take the boat and flee, to..." Alexa tried to think it through, and couldn't really see an easy way out for Figuera at all. He clearly couldn't go all the way back to Miami, and he would never get to liberate Cuba personally, would he?

Whatever, Alexa shook her head. The fact was, this man had the tools, the time, the opportunity, and the motive. Any court in the land would convict, she was sure of it. She also knew the terrible truth was that the vast, vast majority of criminals were usually in some form of emotional duress at the time of their crime. Figuera, with his conspiracy theories of elite slaving clubs, was borderline paranoid, perhaps even mentally ill.

People didn't make easy, sane, or logical choices at the best of times. Which was why Alexa found them hard to understand. People rarely always acted in their best interests, she knew, and that likelihood only accelerated when you were dealing with the sorts of people who decide to try to take out all of their aggressions and suspicions on someone else...

"Okay, well," Alexa rolled her shoulders, thinking that perhaps Kage had been right. It was time to go to bed and start again the next day. Get on with the interviews just to tie up all the loose ends, and then try to get Marinsburg to join her and Kage on a thorough sweep of the island. Either that or request more forces from HQ. As it was, the CSI team should be arriving the next day, so that would free up the Secret Service agents to help in the search, right?

Thinking of which, Alexa picked up her phone to check any updates from Field Chief Williams. Instead, she found a list of messages not from Williams, but from her dad.

Kiddo. You might want to check the news. Sending love, Pops

"What?" Alexa murmured, moving to open the laptop as she realized she hadn't actually spent even a second on the news so far today. Not that she was a news junky, but she liked to keep informed.

But she had just been so busy, what with one thing after another...

Alexa opened her laptop and fired up the usual sites, to suddenly see what her dad had been trying to tell her about. He hadn't known where she was working, of course, not officially anyway, but she wondered whether Skip Jackson had dropped him an off-the-record, personal message.

All of the news sites and feeds were leading with the same story, told in a variety of different ways.

Murder at Florida Resort!

Three DEAD in possible terror-related incident at Secluded Florida Resort. FBI and Law Enforcement Agencies Narrowly Escaped with their LIVES!!

But none of the above even compared to the most extravagant headlines, which had Alexa blinking at the screen, and suddenly feel very, very small indeed.

Cuba Demands Full Apology and Explanation for the Assassination of Cuban Firebrand Representative, Ramon Martinez, in Florida…

"Oh… crap," Alexa groaned in the dark. It was out. The news was out, and now the entire world would be watching them.

CHAPTER ELEVEN

THE INVESTIGATION DAY 2

XII. 4:10 AM

BRRING!

ALEXA WOKE UP WITH A START FROM SOME NIGHTMARE where she was sitting in an auditorium, watching a stage. On it were people that she had known throughout her life: Kage, her brother, and her father, all of them supposedly giving speeches to a vast crowd of people.

But none of them could see the thin wisps of smoke rising from the sides of the stage. Naturally, of course, Alexa panicked.

There was a fire. Something terrible was about to happen. To explode – but no one, not those on the stage or those watching appeared to be doing anything.

And then on walked her mother, and Alexa felt her heart lurch. She was just as tall, willowy, and blonde as she had remembered, always full of grace, wit, and charm, right up to the very end.

Why aren't they doing anything about the fire!? Why isn't anyone DOING anything!? They don't know what's about to-

BRRING!

"Alexa!"

She woke with a sudden gasp to a dark room and the incessant ringing of her phone – and of Kage, barging in through the door. Alexa felt a momentary shiver of alarm, as she was only wearing a shirt and underwear, but Kage didn't even seem to notice.

"Alexa – it's the main building. There's been an attack. Something's happened-" Kage spoke quickly, already dragging on his shirt as it was clear that he had only just woken a moment before, too.

"What? Crap-" Alexa coughed, rolling out of bed and reaching for her pants at the same time as she snatched up her phone. It hadn't been a phone call but an alert from the secure Secret Service alert system that she and Kage had been added to.

CODE RED. ALL INACTIVE AGENTS. EVENT AT ST. MARTIN'S RESORT. CENTRAL LOBBY. 4:01 AM…

She barely had time to zip up her fly and slide her bare feet into her boots by the time Kage had already left. She ran out of her room, forgoing the jacket as Kage had unlocked their safe box and handed her the service pistol.

Check. Even half asleep, Alexa ran through the mandatory checks, checking that the chamber was clear and then slamming home a new magazine into the service Glock before locking it into her holster at her hip.

"No details, got the alert a moment ago," Kage said as he reached the front door, and the pair were racing out into the night, their boots hammering on the gravel paths as they sprinted toward the main resort building.

It was lit up by the permanent floodlights set on the floor, but Alexa couldn't hear any shouts or screams. A few of the upper bedroom lights were on, but it was eerie to not see the flash of blue and red that Alexa usually associated with emergency services.

That's because we're on an island, doofus, she berated herself, shaking her head to clear the fog of last night's nightmare.

One of the side entrances was already open, and Kage was the first in, skidding to a halt as there was already one of the Service agents in front of them, his gun at the ready. The tall man took a step back as he saw that the sudden arrivals were agents, not attackers.

"What's happened?" Kage said, a little out of breath as the agent motioned for them to follow.

"One of the guests was attacked in the night. I rushed in, she's saying that a suspect matching Figuera's description rushed her, then fled the scene," he explained as he led them back through one of the main corridors and through the main lobby area toward the kitchens, where a woman was seated on a chair, holding a large pack of frozen peas to her head. By her side, a pile of bandages and a bowl of ruddy water sat on one of the stainless-steel countertops.

Eva Montgomery, Alexa recognized her. She was in a long black t-shirt and what looked to be dark yoga pants, while the giant sunglasses had disappeared (unsurprisingly, given the time). Her acres of auburn hair were in disarray, and it looked like there was blood drying on one side of her face. She no longer looked like the floaty, slightly dizzy Californian, but a slim, athletic, scared young woman.

"Eva?" Kage asked, slowing down instantly, his voice dropping a couple of registers as he gave a calming, smoothing gesture toward the woman. "You were attacked," he stated.

"No shit," Eva grumbled, before suddenly blinking, and offering him a small smile.

"I'm sorry. It's been a long night already. I wasn't expecting to get jumped on my way to the kitchens…"

"Did you see the weapon the attacker used? Where they went?" Alexa asked as she hovered by the door. It sounded like the attack had only happened a few moments ago. That meant that the attacker – *Figuera?* – couldn't have gotten very far at all.

"I was too busy falling to the floor and bleeding, actually," Eva said, still apparently tired and not happy at all at the way this night was going.

"But I came down to get some ice water for my room. Didn't see anyone until I came in here, where that guy – one of the staffers, I remember him – was in here. He jumped at me, swung something, and down I went," Eva sighed. "I'm guessing that I'm lucky to be alive, I suppose. But I was starting to wonder how you haven't caught him yet, *or* how he'd managed to wander back in here when there's Secret Service and FBI agents running around…"

Ouch, Alexa thought. *Okay, maybe she has a right to be annoyed.* They were valid points, after all. Alexa turned to the Secret Service agent, whose face was a flat, unimpressed line. He looked at her for a moment, but then, with the smallest sigh, spoke quickly and in a low voice.

"I was the only one on guard at the resort tonight, keeping an eye on… everyone," he said the last word lightly, but Alexa got the gist. He had probably been asked by Marinsburg to keep an eye on the guests, not the staff. And the resort was a big place, with lots of doors and windows. Did Figuera have some sort of access key?

"I got it – Kage?" Alexa said, clearing her throat as Kage looked up from where he was examining Eva's forehead.

"Abrasion. Slight concussion maybe. Nothing bad," Kage commented then stepped back as Eva shot him a dark look.

"Nothing bad!? My forehead looks like I've got a melon growing out of it! I'm lucky to be alive with that madman running around!" she said.

"We're very sorry, ma'am, we're doing what we can," Alexa said, before hissing at Kage to join her.

"The attack was only a few minutes ago. I think we know where he's going, right?" she prompted Kage and the Service agent as a shout came from the lobby as another of the agents left on the island under Marinsburg arrived.

Kage's eyes went large and round in the dim light. "We don't have much time for a full operation."

We don't have the numbers for a full operation! Alexa could have spat. Most of the Secret Service had gone with Skip back to Washington, as their first priority was protection and to ward off any potential future attacks against key government figures. And their backup wouldn't be arriving for a few hours yet.

"You and me, Kage," Alexa nodded, turning to the Secret Service agent as their second arrived. "The abandoned boat shed, northeast, east of here. That's where I think the fugitive will be heading."

It was, after all, where they had found his guns, and there was a working boat there. Figuera couldn't be planning to hide out on the island forever, could he? So he must be planning on getting out of here.

"Figuera was in the kitchens. Maybe he needed food and water for a long boat trip..." Kage said.

"Back to Miami? Or all the way to Cuba?" Alexa frowned. "That would be insane, wouldn't it? After what he had just done?"

Kage shrugged. "Well. Blowing someone up is pretty insane, and Marinsburg was saying that his social media was pretty, well... *intense*."

"Okay. Let's go. Now. Figuera's only ten, fifteen minutes ahead of us. And we can be faster," Alexa said, turning to check with the Service agents.

"I can stay," the original agent said. The second agent, a woman with severely slicked-back blonde hair, gestured that she would go with the FBI agents.

"Hey, wait, what – where are you going!?" Eva called out as they turned to leave.

"Just sit tight. Don't leave the premises!" Alexa shouted out as they all broke into a run, and sprinted for the door, and the hot, sweltering Florida night beyond.

～

The trio ran onto the path that circled away from the resort and ran northwards, away from the moon that hung low over their shoulders. It was still warm, even just before dawn here, and Alexa could see the distant glow of the coastal towns over the dark waters. They jogged, keeping a regular, easy pace as they wanted to get there quickly but didn't want to lose their stamina.

"Why doesn't the resort use like, golf carts, or something!" Kage grumbled, panting for air a little. But despite his grumbling, Alexa knew that they were all in good shape. They had to be, to keep their jobs, and the female Service agent was no exception. She didn't appear to tire or flag once on their twenty-minute jog.

It was the terrain, though, Alexa knew. The path was old, packed gravel mixed with dirt and sand, but the years and years of floods and storms had made even this path boggy and patchy in many places.

There was a guttural croak from somewhere in the shadows, and Alexa wondered if it was alligators or crocodiles. Or both. Or caimans. Or worse. Small creatures hissed and skittered out from the glare of their flashlights as they rounded the bends and kept on, and the night was heavy with the sound of buzzing, twitching, twittering insects.

Everything either trying to eat, bite, or sting you down here, Alexa once again thought, as her mind moved to last night's – no, this night's – dream.

She had been scared for her family and friends. Scared that nothing had happened, or was going to happen to save them.

Scared that she was the only one who'd notice the danger and that she was the only one who could do anything.

"Watch out!"

The Service agent suddenly spat as there was a flash of light from up ahead. Somewhere in the trees, toward the bend.

But there was no one else out here, was there? Or at least, there wasn't supposed to be anyone else on the island.

Crack!

The first bullet that was fired must have been wild, as Alexa threw herself to the floor, her mind quickly snapping into the stop-frame, instant-moment of high adrenaline. She had heard the gun go off, and the whine and buzz of the bullet as it ripped through the undergrowth and the heavy vegetation between them and the beach.

"Down!" the Secret Service agent shouted as Alexa was already skidding across the floor, feeling the painful bite of gravel and really wishing that she had put on her reinforced jacket before sprinting out of the lodge.

Kage was already up. They were turning in the direction of the shot-

CRACK!

Another loud, whining report, and this time Alexa saw the muzzle flash, too. It was in the trees but not far away. Kage and the Service agent were diving to one side as Alexa had taken her gun out and started to raise it, pulling off a couple of hip shots in the direction of the light and the muzzle-fire.

Everything was happening so quickly. Kage was shouting, snarling the words as the flashlight in the forest was suddenly bobbing up and down and flickering as he ran through the trees.

"FBI! ARMED RESPONSE! DROP YOUR WEAPON!" he hollered as Alexa started to take aim, following the light coming from the attacker's hand.

Crack!

Another flash of gunfire as their attacker fired behind him, or over his shoulder. Alexa flinched, but she held her ground. The chance of a running attacker actually managing to shoot them in the dark was almost statistically zero...

There was a sudden puff of gravel nearby as one of the bullets ricocheted, breaking apart not five yards away from her.

"*Crap!*" Alexa jumped to her feet instead, running forward to see that the bend in the path was only a little way ahead. Kage and the Service agent had remained where they were, and they were placing covering fire into the forest after their assailant, but Alexa kept on running.

A darker, solid shadow against the night which was the boat shed from the night before. They were here…

There was a crashing sound from the forest as Alexa spun, just in time to see a shape break cover. A man in a tracksuit and dark clothes leaped up onto the raised embankment of the path, crashing through the mangrove vines.

His flashlight had gone off, but a moment of silvered moonlight revealed the gun that Miguel Figuera was holding in his hand. Alexa saw the wild, glaring whites of his eyes as he saw her, as he shot his hand out toward her.

CRACK.

Her shot was instinctive, barely a twitch of her wrist and a twist in her hip as she landed a bullet to his upper thigh. The bullet sent him spinning around and hurtling to the floor with a pained shout and a thump.

"DROP YOUR WEAPON! DROP IT!" Alexa shouted as Kage and the Service agent started forward. Alexa had her gun trained on Figuera as the man groaned, his hand flailing in the air for a moment as he cried out in agony.

"Drop it, Figuera! I don't want to have to shoot you!" Alexa held her position, sighting down her barrel at him as she pointed this time not at his leg, but his chest. The next shot would be the finisher. If he was stupid enough to try to fire.

"Okay! Okay! I give up!" Figuera cursed, dropping the gun as he held up one hand in the moonlight air, the other clutched to his bleeding thigh.

"Landers!?" It was Kage, arriving hot and fast as he crossed the distance between them, quickly kicking the gun aside and stamping down on Figuera's wrist, eliciting another snap of pain.

You really don't need to do that, Kage… Alexa thought. *I had him covered. He wasn't going anywhere.*

"Any other weapons? Show me your hands!" Kage shouted as the Service agent came to a panting halt, her gun lowering as she saw that the FBI clearly had the situation under control.

"A knife. My pocket… Agh dammit, this hurts!" Figuera was starting to cry as Kage cuffed him and then beckoned the Service agent forward to get some first aid to him.

Was that it? Alexa was left reeling, her blood still pounding with adrenaline as she slowly lowered her own gun, realizing that the threat was now gone.

Was it over? It had to be. They had just caught the killer after all, hadn't they?

CHAPTER TWELVE

XIII. 9:05 AM

"I'M TELLING YOU, IT WASN'T ME!"

Miguel Figuera insisted again, for what must have been the third or twenty-third time since Alexa and Kage had started questioning him.

The trio had set up a small interrogation room in the resort's storage basement. It was a small and crowded room, but it was secure. Probably the most secure site on the entire island, Alexa considered – as the walls were steel girders lined with block and concrete, as it had to be, given the low-lying nature of the island.

Figuera sat opposite them with his hands cuffed behind him on a small chair, with one of the kitchen's steel tables between them. The light was bright under the glare of the strip lights, and Alexa had done her best to oversee that all dangerous or potentially dangerous items had been taken out, but there were still racks and cases stacked with giant, industrial-grade cans of food.

"Mr. Figuera, given the fact that you shot at me, my partner, and members of the Secret Service, and apparently had been stockpiling weapons and maps of the island in your room, you'll understand if I find that just a little bit hard to believe..." Alexa stated in a rather bored way.

The fact was, she was bored of this show. Or rather; she was frustrated by this little, uptight man and his inability to accept the fact that he had been beaten.

"We found your maps. We found the stash of guns."

"They're not mine!" Figuera claimed. Alexa's only response was to clear her throat and lay out the sheets on the table, photocopies of the photos that she had taken in his room, along with print-outs of his hidden 'Cuban Truther' profile that the Secret Service had uncovered.

"Here, you will see this is a map from your room of the island, with a pencil marking the location of the boat shed. Why did you mark it if you had no knowledge of it?"

"I've never seen that before in all my life," Figuera stated, holding his chin up defiantly.

Alexa looked at him. *Seriously? You're going to try and play me for a fool?*

It wasn't her who went hard-cop though, it was Kage, suddenly slapping the metal table with his open palm, making a ringing sound.

"C'mon, man. You fired at us! Why on Earth did you do that? I've got a witness that says you attacked her and ran. And guess what – we headed straight for the place marked here on your map – and there you are, too!" He barked an angry, mocking laugh. "You know this looks bad, man. Do you think any jury in the land would acquit you? *Especially* after you tried to shoot us?"

"All the juries in this land are corrupt. They're in on the conspiracy," Figuera said, a feverish sort of intensity coming into his eyes.

Okay, let's try a different approach, Alexa silently sighed to herself.

"This conspiracy," Alexa interrupted. "Do you think that Representative Martinez was a part of it? That Skip Jackson was?"

Figuera shot her a look as if she were mad for a second, and then said haughtily.

"Martinez was. Jackson probably is in the inner circle, as far as I know…"

"So you tried to kill them both. To rid the world of their evil, right?" Kage said, leaning back in his chair. Alexa could feel the waves of satisfaction rolling out of him. This was it. This was the angle.

"Can you describe the conspiracy to me, Mr. Figuera?" Alexa asked.

The man squinted a little at her, suspiciously. "Why? So you want to know how much I know? How much I have managed to figure out? Get me a reporter from one of the main stations, and I'll reveal everything!"

Damn it. He thinks this is a negotiation.

"Mr. Figuera," Alexa sighed. "We are going to charge you with multiple counts of attempted murder, including intent to kill federal officials. We are also going to charge you with handling illegal items, with terrorist acts, and with the murder of one international politician and the attempted murder of another…"

"What!?" Figuera hissed in annoyance, jerking in his seat as his rage bubbled through him.

"If you are lucky," Alexa carried on loudly, "you will be tried here in the United States. If you are *exceedingly* lucky you will serve the rest of your life behind bars, but given Florida's severe penalties, I am not sure that you will."

"What are you talking about!? Get me a reporter!"

"If you *aren't* so lucky, then the powers that be – those people you think of as part of the conspiracy, I presume – will bow to the international pressure to have you committed to Cuba, where you will serve out *their* justice penalties. And it seems from your writings online that you have quite the issue with Cuban authorities at the moment, don't you?"

"You can't. You wouldn't dare! That would be delivering me into the belly of the beast!" Figuera screamed.

He's desperate. He's on edge. It won't be long until he breaks, Alexa thought. She turned to nod to Kage, who pulled out the next series of paper reports. This time, they were print-outs of some of the top headlines from papers and news websites.

CUBA DEMANDS CHARGES BROUGHT IN DEATH OF RAMON MARTINEZ...

CUBA APPROACHES U.N. FOR INTERNATIONAL INQUIRY...

CUBA VOWS 'REPERCUSSIONS' AS ONE OF ITS TOP POLITICIANS IS ASSASSINATED...

"You can see, they are being quite vociferous at the moment," Alexa said, leaning forward to tap the last one. "I particularly like this one. To be honest, it would be really easy for the United States government to just ship you down there and not have to worry about you at all ..."

"Yeah, you'd love that, wouldn't you? Making some dirty deal with the dirty Soviets in return for a few more years of life? More control?" Figuera shot back.

What the hell is he talking about? Alexa thought, wondering just how crazy Figuera was. At this rate, he might even get out on a mental insanity plea. He had even refused any legal counsel because 'they were all in on it, too.' But not if he was extradited to Cuba. She didn't know much about Cuban laws, but she couldn't imagine they'd be any more sympathetic to his case than the United States.

"I don't 'want' anything, Mr. Figuera, I just want the truth," Alexa said, as Figuera paused, blinked, and looked at her accusingly.

"You really want the truth?" he seethed.

"That is why I am here," Alexa said. "Yes, yes I do. And for the record, there haven't been 'Soviets' since before you or I were born."

Figuera had such a sour face on him that Alexa was sure that he didn't believe her, but he surprised her by continuing to speak anyway.

"The US and Cuba aren't at war. They're people-smuggling. Huge numbers of refugees from South America and Africa, selling them to the highest bidder, flooding larger countries like America with them so that they destabilize western democracy..."

Wow, Alexa had so far specifically not researched too deeply into the 'Truther' movement. Right now, she was glad she hadn't.

"...all the major countries in the world are in on it. Why do you think everything is going to hell all the time? There's all this unrest and street gangs and violence? And they're trying to convince us the world is warming, when actually it's just them, making sure we don't see what they're doing to us!"

The words rushed out of Figuera now that his tongue had been let loose. It was a dizzying, confusing array of ideas that Alexa didn't see how it all fit together. There was anti-environmentalism in there, anti-government, anti-everything. Even some bizarre rant about implanted mind-control microchips. Alexa let him rant on for a while, making shocked faces every now and again, and pretending to take notes.

"So you see, that is why something has to be done! That is why-" Figuera ended on a flourish, and that was when Alexa cut in.

"That is why you planted the bomb that killed Ramon Martinez?"

"What? *No!*" Figuera suddenly blinked, surprised out of his reverie. "I keep telling you, that was nothing to do with me! I never wanted to kill him; I wanted to kidnap him. Get him to talk. To admit it on international television what he and the rest of the ruling cabal are up to!"

Alexa paused, cold ice water running down her back.

He could be lying. He must be lying, right?

"You *didn't* blow up the helipad?" Alexa stated the question very exactly.

"No! No – why would I? That wouldn't achieve anything. I want the truth to get out, and killing him would do absolutely no good at all, right!?" Figuera said in a tone that appeared completely rational and logical. It even made a weird kind of sense, not that Alexa believed him entirely.

"Then why the boat shed? The guns, the map?" Alexa prodded a little deeper.

Figuera hissed in annoyance. "I was going to take him off the island. Record Martinez making a confession! *That* was going to change the world, but – but – I got up early, snuck out just as I had intended to, but then the explosion went off, and I knew that you would be coming for me. So… So I got scared-"

Suddenly, Figuera's lip wobbled, and he broke down in front of them. He started to sob, his shoulders shaking with shame.

"I couldn't do it. I couldn't face going to prison for something I haven't done. I'm telling you that the explosion wasn't me. *It wasn't me!* I wouldn't even know how to do something like that! But I knew you would blame me, and I had worked so hard, so very, very hard… So I hid. In the wilds, and then came back to get water for the trip…"

"Where to?" Kage asked steadily.

Figuera shot him a shielded, wary look. "Away from here. Maybe even Cuba. Maybe I could have got footage of the actual slaver ships smuggling off from Cuba, and then people would have to believe me…" Figuera's eyes flickered to the table, and his tone went darker. "Who knows? Cuba isn't that big. Maybe if I was in the right place, at the right time, I could stop all of this from happening…"

Alexa wasn't sure that people would believe him at all at this rate, she thought, but this new development was troubling her. Figuera's tone, his passionate, suppressed anger seemed to suggest that he *was* capable of killing… but not like this. He wanted to make a martyr of himself. He wanted to be the one who 'found the bad guys.' And put a stop to them.

"I see," she said, clearing her throat as she collected all of the papers once again and motioned to Kage to meet her outside.

They gave him some water, carefully feeding a bottle to his lips for a moment before Alexa led Kage out of the resort basement and halfway up the stairs beyond, where they could speak in quiet.

"What is it? The guy is crazy as a snake, but I think we've got him..." Kage said.

"I'm not sure," Alexa said heavily. "In fact, I'm not sure at all that he's our man."

"What? He just admitted to plotting to kidnap Martinez!" Kage whispered.

"Yes. He did. But where's the evidence of explosives? Where is his laboratory, or design studio, or whatever? He seems quite clear that he sees himself as a martyr, a whistleblower, not an assassin..."

A public figure, Alexa thought back to her criminology classes at Quantico. There were many types of criminals, of course – as many as who committed crimes – but psychological evaluations generally concentrated them into more exact categories. Certain psychological dispositions indicated certain tendencies. And what Figuera was displaying was a 'heroic complex' – a part of him needed to be the one to be the savior. To be seen, perhaps.

Not the work of an assassin, Alexa thought once more, groaning gently as she pressed her finger to her ear, gently massaging it to get rid of the white noise of remembered bombs.

"It's a bunch of lies. He's just trying to lower the sentence against him. Does he *really* expect anyone to believe that, with all of this evidence stacked against him, this proof that he was plotting an attack, that he didn't go through with it?" Kage pointed out.

Alexa paused and nodded. Kage also made sense; no jury would believe Figuera now that he had admitted what he had, and that they had him on audio and video recording saying so.

And plenty of dangerous people have been taken off the streets with less evidence, Alexa considered.

It was just... There was something that irked her.

Figuera was obsessed with 'the truth' – even if it was his own twisted, misguided version of it. Why would he lie now? What if he actually was telling the truth, and Figuera's nefarious plans were completely independent of another plot to kill the Cuban?

What if the bomber wasn't Figuera, and was still on the island? *But Kage is still right,* Alexa thought. At the end of the day, they had a strong suspect. He had opportunity and motive. Now *they* had to rule out everyone else, and prove it, didn't they? Then why did Alexa feel like he was the wrong man?

CHAPTER
THIRTEEN

XIV. 9:40 AM

T HEIR REINFORCEMENTS ARRIVED EARLY THAT MORNING, in the form of a small ferry that was escorted by the Coast Guard. No helicopters, of course, because the helipad was still a series of large, blackened, and slagged craters.

"Cecil," Alexa greeted the Chief Scientific Officer and head CSI guy for the FBI Miami office, and tried to hide her disappointment that Chief Williams hadn't sent Dee Hopkins instead.

It wasn't that Alexa had anything against Cecil Pinkerton, the thin, tall, white-haired Caucasian man with small glasses forever perched on the end of his nose. He greeted her and she shook his hand warmly as they disembarked from the small but luxurious wharf that was attached directly to the main resort grounds. Theirs was the only boat here, but there were spaces for several such vessels on a number of small piers.

No, it wasn't that she disliked Cecil. It was just that she liked the rather erratic, sarcastic, ebullient Digital Officer Dee Hopkins the more, but Alexa guessed that there really wasn't as much of a digital footprint to this case as might warrant it.

Maybe it was partly that she wanted to see another woman around that she already had a connection with, as well, Alexa told herself as she led Cecil through the grounds of the resort, past the main building to where they had requisitioned one of the private lodges for him, and meanwhile relayed to him the findings from Secret Service Team Leader Marinsburg's findings.

"So, we have multiple sites in play, and almost all of them are past the critical window," Cecil said in a dry, considering voice as he dropped off his bags, but gestured that she could lead him straight up to the helipad at the near side of the island. At their back were a half dozen other CSI people, along with four more FBI agents, here to replace some of the Secret Service members that they had lost – and, from the warning of Marinsburg – were imminently going to lose more.

"The critical window?" Alexa asked, and Cecil nodded. He wore a light blue shirt and dark pants, and looked like he had stepped out of his office and boarded the plane and boat without even considering the oppressive heat of the island. Or the sudden rain showers.

"Yes. It varies depending on weather conditions, temperature, and social activity, but the critical window is the general time frame when we can expect the contents of any investigation site to remain mostly intact," Cecil said as they walked toward the rear gates of the main resort.

Alexa tried not to remember the last time she was here, or the clang as the gates shut and she was stuck on one side, with a ball of black smoke, flames, and a possible dead partner on the far side.

ELLE GRAY | JAMES HOLT

"Like a calculation?" Alexa coughed, trying to keep focused as the gates automatically swung open, and they were presented with the long driveway toward the ruined helipad. Just as before, Alexa could see the smaller figures clustered and working it, only this time they were Service agents busily taking photos of the ground and still searching for any clues.

"Yes, a calculation is exactly right," Cecil carried on. "You see, evidence is always degrading, all the time. We cannot stop time, preserve an event in a mold, as it were, and from the moment that a crime is committed, all of the pieces of evidence, the elements, the objects, the minerals, and substances that make up a scene become vulnerable to movement, decay, entropy, change…"

Oh yeah, now I remember why I would have preferred Dee Hopkins here, Alexa thought. She was tired. She hadn't really slept last night after the alert, and she'd had a late night as well. And she'd been shot at in the godforsaken hours of the morning; now she was being given a philosophical lecture about entropy and evidence.

At any other time, Alexa would probably have found it interesting, but right now was not that time.

"I agree, I'm sorry nothing is as fresh as it could be. We've tried to do our best," Alexa began as they started to walk up the long driveway, and now Alexa was sure that she could smell the burn of asphalt and tarmac.

"No apologies. It is remarkable what we can do." Cecil gave her a small smile, and for a moment Alexa saw a flash of something a bit more human underneath the scientific veneer. That was encouraging, at least.

"Please, list all the sites again for me. I have them written down, but I find it better to actually think while talking *with* someone," Cecil said, already raising his head as he examined the site coming toward them.

"Well, this is the main one," Alexa gestured at what was ahead. The helipad was clearly ruined. A wide crater sat in the center, almost occupying the entire hexagonal landing pad with jagged edges where the tarmac had fallen back in on itself. Alexa could see lines of gravel and grit forming a stratum around one

90

edge, but then underneath that a layer of orange-yellow, wet-looking ground. The crater itself wasn't exactly very deep, more of a shallow scoop that had broken through the crust of the helipad topping.

"Marinsburg – he's the Secret Service Team Leader – recovered the footage of the explosion, that shows it occurring before the helicopter touched down."

"A-huh," Cecil made small agreeing noises as they walked.

"There was a lot of wreckage of course, from the helicopter, but Marinsburg has done his best to recover as much of it as possible and has it cataloging in the larger marina shed over there," Alexa gestured. Even as they walked nearer, though, Alexa could see that there were still small fragments everywhere of burnt and slagged metal along with more mysterious, unidentifiable bits of blackened rubber or shining steel.

"He has a clean tent already?" Cecil asked, alarm clear in his voice as well as his face. When the CSO saw the look of confusion cross Alexa's face before she could ask, he broke in quickly.

"Uh, plastic covers, barrier protection, that kind of thing, that's what I mean. I'm sorry, I spend so much time in my lab with other CSI people that I sometimes forget that not everyone I meet are scientists!" He laughed a little self-consciously and suddenly Alexa liked him just a little bit more, still. He was human after all.

"He said something about that being a problem, and the fact that he didn't have the proper staff and equipment..." Alexa explained as Cecil nodded, turning to one of the small crowd of CSI people following them, several of whom were wheeling handheld trucks behind them, stacked with boxes and bundles. Alexa listened in as he advised them to get suited up before entering the building, and move to install barrier controls and a scrub-down location as their first priority. His team assented, moving out ahead of them around the crater as Alexa and Cecil followed.

"Well, I can tell you right now that this was almost certainly a remote trigger," Cecil commented, indicating the site.

Alexa blinked. The smell of burning was strong in her nose and the back of her throat right now, and her ears were starting to ring with the high-pitched whine of tinnitus once again.

"The device was in the center, hence the crater, the blast radius," Cecil pointed out. "But it couldn't have been motion-sensitive; otherwise, it would have only gone off when the helicopter landed, or it would have been tripped when any number of people walked over the helipad earlier that day."

What!? Alexa blinked, feeling lightheaded. *The bomb could have gone off at any time.*

"No, so I think we're looking at a remote trigger, a wireless or a direct, physical wire connecting to a trigger. Like you see in old construction movies, when people use plungers to demolish buildings, and there are wires snaking away," Cecil stated.

"Wires," Alexa said a little confusedly. "Surely the Secret Service sweep would have seen them?"

"One would have thought so. And general wireless frequencies do not, as a rule, do very well going through physical structures – but they can," Cecil frowned. "You would definitely need quite a powerful receiver and transmitter. A small dish, for example." The man fumbled with his phone for a moment, tapping in a few things before coming up with a picture of a man holding something that looked like a megaphone, only it didn't have a smaller cone inside, but a series of small, hardened plastic antennas instead.

"This is a hand-held version. Military grade, directional so it is less easily eavesdropped. A mobile handheld transmitter like this, when hooked up to a sufficient battery pack, would be strong enough to do the job," Cecil explained, sounding pleased with himself, as if he were already finding solutions and ignoring the fact that a terrible, terrible act had happened here.

"Military grade," Alexa winced. That sounded like bad news. "Would that be restricted sale?"

Cecil looked over his glasses at Alexa for a moment, that cold-eyed lecturing teacher coming back.

"Nothing is restricted if you know where to go, Agent Landers," Cecil said seriously. "We are clearly dealing with someone who knows what they are doing and has experience doing it. That sort of person would have access to dark web or black market contacts from Eastern Europe, ex-Russian or Chinese equipment – all relatively easy to get access to if you know where to look."

"Dark web. Black market. Easy-peasy, right," Alexa repeated, trying to follow the man's warning, at the same time as her head rang with the sound of storms.

Professional. Cecil said their suspect had to be a professional.

The thing was, even in her current state of confusion and disorientation, Alexa knew that Figuera wasn't that level of professional. They hadn't found vast technical or engineering experience so far in his rooms or his background. He didn't seem 'professional.' His grand plan had seemed to be to steal canned goods from the kitchen, power a small boat down the coast, across the Florida Bay, and past the Keys, and then somehow personally invade Cuba!

CHAPTER FOURTEEN

XV. 11:40 AM

"HEY, ALEXA, LOOKS LIKE YOU'VE ALREADY MADE THE news," Kage commented as he turned back from St. Martin's small marina and started to walk back toward the main resort.

Alexa waited a moment longer, her thoughts lost in a haze of worry as she watched the large coastal service boat starting to power back to the mainland, spilling white foam in its wake. The skies above were a pristine blue, but there was a warm wind starting to pick up, and she could feel it teasing at her hair as she thought about that boat and what it contained.

Manuel Figuera, that was the main thing it contained that worried Alexa. They had completed the chain of custody handover, and the Cuban Truther was now in the hands of three of Marinsburg's men, heading first to Miami for holding, and then perhaps to one of the nearby security max detention centers as his arrest and charges were processed.

We got our man? Alexa frowned. They had to charge him, of course. He had fired at federal agents and had admitted to an attempted kidnapping, as well as assault. Illegal weapons, theft, his rap sheet was filling up quickly.

But international terrorism? Alexa still wasn't sure. She was also worried about losing more of Marinsburg's Secret Service agents, even though their numbers had been replaced with extra FBI agents from the Miami office.

"Huh?" Alexa said, turning back to see Kage holding up his phone for her to see a headline emblazoned across it.

Suspect Charged in Murder of Top Cuban Official…

"What?" Shock shivered through Alexa in a sudden blast that made her cold, despite the warm air around her.

This shouldn't have happened. How did the media know someone had been charged!?

"Wait, that's not all…" Kage said, taking back his phone to flick to another tab.

PROFILE: Alexandra Landers, The Woman Who Saved US-Cuban Diplomacy?

"What!?" Alexa repeated dumbly, as she felt the marina underfoot suddenly rock as if they had been hit by a seismic wave. They hadn't, it was just her blood spiking and rolling inside her body.

"How do they know me? *Of* me?" she said, snatching the phone out of Kage's hand and quickly scanning through the article.

'FBI Special Agent Alexandra Landers is one of Miami's best-kept secrets. A rising star in the agency, she attained top grades at the FBI Training Academy in Quantico, and it seems is angled for great things ahead…'

"I don't get it," Alexa said in confusion, her angry eyes scanning Kage's in horror. The job of any agent was supposed to be behind-the-scenes, out of the way, semi-secretive. They certainly weren't supposed to be the lead feature in some Floridian lifestyle magazine!

"Don't look at me! I had nothing to do with it. But maybe you deserve it…" Kage suggested, his sharp, handsome face still crooked with a smile; until he saw just how serious Alexa was.

"No, you don't get it. They *shouldn't* know anything about me. Or about anything that's happening here on the island, should they?" Alexa pointed out, her eyes turning back to the column, alongside a picture of her from when she had been a graduate sophomore, looking thin and frowny.

'Landers was one of the key agents to crack the mysterious murder of Russian oligarch, Aleksandr Budrov, last year, resulting in (I am sure readers will remember!) a terrifying shoot-out inside Miami's very own University Hospital!'

There was a grainy CCTV still of Alexa holding out her gun, aimed across a waiting room while other patients cowered under the seats and chairs. The image didn't depict the mercenary that she had been chasing, and who had come to the hospital to kill Kage; or the fact that the killer had been, at the moment, holding a nurse hostage.

"It wasn't exactly a shoot-out. He didn't even get a chance to fire," Alexa muttered, wincing as the article started to make her sound not heroic and responsible, but reckless and brash.

'This impressively young woman has been elevated past her training post straight into frontline duty, which isn't usual for regular FBI rookies, as our expert commentator, Leeroy Styles, attests…'

"And who's Leeroy Styles?" Alexa asked grimly, for Kage to mutter that he had no idea.

But there was never any shortage of self-appointed experts, was there? Especially when the public was considering the actions of the federal government, Alexa considered... But none of that mattered. What mattered was the fact that this article had correctly identified her, and-

"They've reported on the arrest, see here?" Alexa handed Kage's phone back to him, where it stated that one suspect had already been detained and arrested for the murder of Ramon Martinez.

"We detained him only last night. This paper was updated this morning," Alexa pointed out, as she saw Kage catch up with her assumption.

"And because no one on the resort has access to a phone-" he murmured, before blinking. "No one but us and the staff, I guess..."

Alexa was already spinning on her heel, turning back to march toward the resort at a fast clip. Anger reverberated from every movement of her hips and the stamp of her feet.

"We've got a leak. Someone on the island has been breaking the order!"

~

"Well, I assure you, ma'am, that I-" spluttered the large, fleshy lips of the equally larger Bartholomew Price, resort owner and manager.

"Agent. Agent Landers, if you please," Alexa hissed.

They stood in Bartholomew Price's office, where there was indeed a phone sitting in a cradle on his desk, looking as incriminating as if they had stumbled in to find Bartholomew playing with a stick of dynamite.

"Agent Landers, I assure you that I haven't even picked up that phone all day and all night! I wouldn't dream of talking to the press about anything other than how a stay in St. Martin's is the best thing one can do with their money!" Bartholomew said, his face flushing pink with anger.

Probably true, Alexa thought. The profit motive for this fool seemed pretty high, after all.

"What if they contacted you, though?" Alexa countered back at him. "I'm not suggesting you directly decided to screw with my investigation, but if you got a sudden, unexpected call from a friendly reporter? Is that what happened, Mr. Price?" Alexa said, her eyes blazing as she felt like she could slap the table, or him.

To his credit, Kage didn't intervene on Alexa's behalf, but stayed by the door and glowered. This wasn't going to be a good cop and bad cop routine, but a bad cop and even meaner cop.

"No! No, I assure you that no one has called in since the incident happened! I assumed that you had done something to the phones! You can check the call logs, our systems log, everything, you know!" Price spluttered and huffed. "The very idea that I would endanger the privacy of my business by running to tattle to the nearest tabloid is just sensational!"

In fact, the only thing that really made Alexa question Price's guilt was the fact that the paper had written a fluff piece, mostly positive, on *her*. If their recent interactions were anything to go by, Price would not care at all if she fell off the back of a boat, and any subsequent profile article that came out of anyone interviewing *him* would probably have extolled just how evil and stupid she was.

Pfgh! Alexa sneered at the thought. Price was just another one of those 'traditionalists' who viewed her, a woman, as someone not capable of the job. As too weak, or 'crazed with emotions.' Those sorts of guys resented taking orders from a woman, just as much as they resented being told what to do at all.

"Agents Landers, Murphy?" There was a softer tone behind them as the door opened, and standing there was Secret Service Agent Marinsburg, the overhead bulb gleaming off his bald pate as he clutched a sheath of papers in his hands.

Alexa hadn't been aware that he had caught the conversation but must have, since Price had made no attempt to lower his voice.

"Mr. Price is telling the truth. All the calls to and from the resort are logged through their internal system, which, of course, we had to make a few adjustments to," Marinsburg explained, proffering the sheets of paper to Murphy, who handed them to Kage.

You mean the Secret Service tapped them? Alexa wondered but didn't ask. Who knew what the Secret Service was capable of, or what special legal loophole they existed in when it came to protecting the good and important of the nation.

But on the sheet, there was a printout of all the calls made and received, their duration, and their destination and sender numbers. All the calls to the resort came through a main switchboard, and the dates on the page went back for almost a week. Where possible, names sat beside the caller ID, and Alexa saw a large number of calls to suppliers, boat rentals, and ferry taxi companies.

And there had been none since the explosion.

"We turned their main switchboard off," Marinsburg stated. "No calls in or out."

Price shot them all a vindicated, victorious look that Alexa would have been very happy to slap from his face, were it not for the sudden mystery presented to her.

"Then how did the paper know about Figuera? His arrest last night?" Alexa frowned. "How did they know that *I* was here?"

Alexa and Kage had discussed this on their short march over to confront Price. The security leading up to the operation had been tight, necessarily so with the inclusion of the Secret Service and Skip Jackson. That had meant no external communications about where they were going, and especially not about where the presidential advisor would be at any given time.

No one should have known the names of the security agents working the operation, nor of the operation itself. That would only open the opportunity for blackmail, threat, extortion, and compromise.

But once they had my picture, then I guess the media would easily be able to track me down, Alexa figured. The case of the murdered Russian oligarch hadn't exactly been small, and although their names had been kept out of the papers as per traditional FBI policy, there would have been plenty of witnesses, police officers, hospital staff, hotel managers, and more who had seen or met her during that investigation...

But there was still no way for that information to get out in the first place, was there? At least, that is what Alexa would have supposed.

Not unless someone here, on the island, had leaked a photo of her, and was cataloging the events of the last few days!

"Thank you for your confidentiality, Mr. Price," Alexa said abruptly. "I trust that you will continue to follow our guidance on that matter."

"Why!? You've caught him, haven't you? It's over! My guests can go about their business again, can't they?" Bartholomew Price bristled, half-rising from his chair.

There was the smallest of coughs from Kage as he shifted his weight forward. It wasn't exactly a threat, but it was undoubtedly a readiness if Price proved unable to contain his anger.

As it was, the small movement was enough to get across everything that Alexa didn't want to say. She saw Price flush a deep, almost purple crimson once again and heavily sit back down. His hand slapped the top of the hard-wired phone on his desk.

"I guess I should just throw this in the trash, shall I!? You know I have a business to run, don't you!?" he snapped.

"You have made that abundantly clear, Mr. Price," Kage stepped forward to say a little testily. "I am sure all of this will be over very soon – and *then* you will be the only resort manager in all of the United States who has the story of the century, huh?"

Kage offered a little lighter, and Alexa saw Bartholomew blink for a second before he caught the officer's drift.

"Hm. A memorial to that Cuban fella. A resort of international significance and world history…" Bartholomew muttered softly as Alexa gave a disgusted snort, already turning back out of the room, and catching Marinsburg as she did so.

"Is the main switchboard to the resort still off?" she asked.

Marinsburg nodded.

"And we still have everyone's phones?" Alexa pressed.

"Everyone that we know of," Marinsburg pointed out.

That was it, wasn't it? Alexa thought. Someone on site had a phone. Someone was leaking important facts about the investigation.

Of course, the other option was that someone in one of the services is leaking important information, Alexa considered briefly. But that would be huge. A Secret Service or FBI agent willfully breaking several national security laws to talk to the press?

She didn't think it likely, but she also knew that neither Williams nor Marinsburg would be taking this lightly. They would be conducting their own investigations behind the scenes, poring over not just the resort records, but the phone records of every employee they had, including her.

"We need to search the rooms for that phone again," Alexa said abruptly, walking up the hallway, back into the lobby to see some of the assembled people there. The Lucas were in their rooms, as was Mr. Angry Hipster Kendricks apparently, and the attacked Eva Montgomery, leaving just the older man in the shorts and baseball cap, Saul Staniforth.

"I gave them access to their rooms as you suggested last night, and now they are free to move within the resort building, but not outside these walls," Marinsburg stated as they walked forward. But he paused, his hand moving to touch Alexa's elbow just briefly before she could cross in front of the reception area to the rest of the main room.

"But, Agent Landers, there is something I have to tell you…" Marinsburg said.

"Yes?" Alexa looked at him before remembering the man's position. Some sort of senior officer of the Secret Service itself. "Sir?"

"As soon as your suspect is charged with the murder of Representative Martinez, then the state of emergency will be void. As it stands, the statute of emergency powers will be expiring this evening, no later than seventeen hundred hours, unless a further application is made."

"Damnit!" Alexa whispered. Although she didn't want to inconvenience people's lives any more than she had to, she knew what that would mean. That they would have to give back the phones to every citizen here at the resort and allow them free movement to leave.

"But, the case looks strong against Figuera. No extra time may be needed," Marinsburg pointed out, and Alexa pursed her lips in response.

He isn't the guy, her gut was telling her. He was too messy, too chaotic. This murder had been planned for a long time and had been conducted with skill and precision.

But what do I have to prove that? Nothing! she thought in frustration. She felt like she was racing against a clock because the Cubans and the US and the entire world were going to want results on this case, now – and they even had a man in custody.

"Seventeen hundred hours," Alexa nodded. "Can you facilitate the searching of the rooms? I want to finish questioning the guests."

Marinsburg grimaced. "With help. Send me two of your new arrivals, and I'll organize another sweep."

Alexa thanked him and that was it. Done. She turned back to the room where there was only one man waiting for her.

"Mr. Staniforth? I suppose now is as good a time as any to take your witness statement?" Alexa said lightly.

CHAPTER FIFTEEN

XVI. 1:45 PM

"YOU'RE RULING HIM OUT?" KAGE ASKED AS HE STOOD up from the chair in the conference room where they had been interviewing Staniforth. As before, the room was far too large for the job that Alexa and Kage had requisitioned it for, but it was what they had.

The fierce Florida sunlight streamed in past the gauzy white curtains, and the gentle *whub* of the ceiling fans formed a constant backdrop to their conversation, but there was no denying that it was getting hotter.

"I'm not ruling anyone out," Alexa clarified as she caught a glimpse of the skies past a gap in the curtains. The blue porcelain was gone, and now there were deepening drifts of gray, moving fast up there. Was it Alexa's imagination, or could she hear the relentless whipping of wind out there, as well?

"He's a bit... old?" Kage said, casting a similarly furtive look up at the skies beyond the gap in the curtains. There was no denying that the weather was picking up. Alexa was glad that they weren't out there searching through the mangroves and the old boat sheds, as it looked like it would turn into strong gales coming off the Florida-Cuba Bay later that afternoon.

"Old? I suppose so..." Alexa blinked when she checked her actual details, revealing him to be 66 years old. That wasn't technically old in her book, not at all. Staniforth had reminded her of her father, actually. He had that same compact, bullish sort of presence and an assumption of competence that always belied his actual years.

They had a recording of the interview, and Alexa was busy summarizing her notes.

Saul Staniforth was a widower, who had *"spent too long in the garage after my wife died – and a good time before it, too, I'm ashamed to say,"* as he had put it.

He was a man with a scattering of white hair on his head, long enough for him to still grease it back, but clearly racing backward at pace. His skin was weathered and a little pale, but otherwise, he seemed in good health. What impressed Alexa the most had been his general, practical attitude. Alexa read out what they knew about him.

"A widower. Ex-National Guard. Was too young by a couple of years to go to Vietnam-" (*"a fact I thank myself for every day, believe you me! Too many men in my age range and above are still drinking themselves out of a family and job thanks to that stupid war,"* he had said).

"Carpenter and house builder in his later years. One long marriage, his wife died young, and he's only just decided to try and break out of his shell now," Alexa said. She felt a pang of sorrow for the man, and for the years that not only a tragedy can take from you, but also the fear that came with it, or after it.

Just like Dad, Alexa thought, her heart cramping just a little.

"He was up but wasn't out of his room yet at the time of the explosion," Alexa read out with a sigh. "Although he has stated that he thought there was a thing going on between our Eddie Kendricks and Eva Montgomery?" She looked over to Kage, who gave her an amused grin. "But if I seriously believed that was true, then maybe I should be looking for another job!" She thought about the pure, unadulterated disdain that she had seen the younger woman display for Kendricks, even though both of them looked fairly compatible in that symmetrical-faced way.

"I heard that bit," Kage affirmed, shaking his head. "But my money is that it's true."

"What?" Alexa frowned up at him. "Did you see the pound of flesh that Eva tore out of Kendricks the other day – heavens, was it just yesterday?"

"You told me about it, but that's all the more reason why I think they had a thing going on," Kage laughed.

"Think about it. Two young people, full of hormones, get away to a premier resort on the Florida coast. They're not bird watchers. Kendricks claims he's some kind of deep-sea fisher, but that's not what's on his mind, is it? They're here for one thing and one thing only, so on night one they don't care who the other person is … They're rich, they're used to the people around them being out for the party life, or being entirely invisible in the case of the staff…"

Alexa frowned. This sounded all too plausible.

"They're here to have fun, and they are used to taking whatever it is they want, without worrying too much about it. They get it on one night or whatever…"

"Kage, I think you are enjoying this far too much," Alexa said dryly.

"It's funny," Kage laughed. "Then the next day they realize just what an awful decision they made, and that they have to see the other person for the rest of their vacation. Not good. Hence why they hate each other so much," Kage concluded.

"Speaking from experience?" Alexa asked, and Kage's face fell for a moment, and a look of pain crossed his features before he rebuilt himself quite suddenly.

"Nah, no – well, not for a long time. But I remember all the Spring Break stories from college," he explained jovially.

Damn. Gone too far, Alexa thought. Kage was so good at playing the frat boy, even though she knew that wasn't who he was. When he had been shot during the last mission, one of the doctors had confided to Alexa that Kage had been married and lost his wife to an accident. All of this bravado and humor was a sham.

There was a momentary silence between them, and Alexa was about to fill it with something. Anything. A confession that she knew, perhaps – but then Kage was laughing it off.

"Y'see? That is why I am sure that Eva and our Eddie Kendricks got it on. When did Staniforth say he'd seen them?"

Alexa looked back at her notes, the moment lost. Inwardly she cursed her stupid, stupid timing.

"The day before the attack, that day, and that evening. He thought it was one of the night cleaners, but actually, it was Eva and Kendricks, out by the pool in the middle of the night," Alexa said.

Which, okay, might be suspicious, she thought. In any normal situation that would indicate some sort of emotional entanglement, for sure. But she wasn't sure if that qualified in this instance.

After all, all of the guests were trapped on this island, weren't they? If they couldn't sleep or they were still working off their mini-bar jag, then there was nowhere else to go, and nowhere else to see, other than each other.

"So. What's the theory? If you don't like Figuera for the bombing, then which of these mostly middle-aged guests do you prefer?" Kage asked, turning to Alexa. There was a hardening in his stature, and Alexa could tell that he had been hurt, even if it was only by the memory of something that he had lost.

But it was a good question. A very good question.

"The problem is *none* of them really have alibis for the morning of the explosion. Not really. Not any alibi that would stand up," Alexa said.

"But none of them have motive, either. Figuera did. He thought Representative Martinez was a part of some weird evil cult!" Kage pointed out.

"True," Alexa groaned. "But there is no sign that Figuera had the skill to pull something like that off. The technical know-how…"

"Nothing pointing to any of the rest of them had it, either?" Kage said and then rocked his head from side to side.

"Although, didn't Kendricks say that he was in something to do with software? Technology? It's a stretch…"

"And Staniforth was a carpenter. Spent a lot of time in his garage," Alexa said. It hadn't meant to be a joke, but as the pair of agents looked at each other, they slowly started smiling at the sheer uselessness of it all.

"Okay. Maybe we got nothing. Not yet, anyway," Alexa continued as she tried to envisage her room in the private lodge. The bits of paper that she scattered everywhere, helping her make sense of what was in front of her.

Motive.

Expertise.

Opportunity.

Those were the three vectors of investigation, according to FBI training. They were like overlapping circles rather than pillars, and where they intersected, there could usually be found the killer.

"But not always," Alexa breathed to herself, as she mentally tried to slip everyone that she had met so far into one of the above categories.

You always have motive, and you always have opportunity, but expertise is more varied.

The problem was that, traditionally, all of these three things are obscured, and motives and opportunity the most hidden of all three when a crime has been committed. People try to hide their skills, they lie about where they were, or why they were there.

"Let's dig a little at this Kendricks and Eva connection," Alexa said with a groan. Staniforth had agreed to have his room searched, more thoroughly, for a second time, and so far no extra phones, tablets, or communication devices had appeared elsewhere in the resort complex.

"It's not exactly a lot," Kage winced.

"No, but it's something. We still need solid evidence that someone had the opportunity and skills to plant the explosives and the remote detonator. If we can find anything tying anyone to the crime scene, the better," Alexa said.

And after all, Eva had been attacked by Figuera in the middle of the night, hadn't she? What if that wasn't a mistaken brawl with a desperate man? What if something else had been underneath it all?

"And our Mr. Angry Kendricks has sure been committed to getting off the island, hasn't he?" Alexa said, standing up, and moving to the door.

CHAPTER SIXTEEN

XVII. 2:15 PM

"**M**R. KENDRICKS? IT'S SPECIAL AGENTS LANDERS and Murphy – open up!" Alexa said, rapping on the door smartly with her knuckles.

Eddie Kendrick's room was, like all of the others in this chic, prestigious resort, almost a full penthouse suite. It occupied one entire side of one of the floors, as another of the suites – Eva Montgomery's – sat on the far side, beyond the central wall columns, stairs, and various spa rooms.

There was a flicker of movement in the corner of her eye, and Alexa turned to see that Kage had caught it, too. It was one of the last remaining Secret Service men, heading for the stairs to go up to the next level, where Staniforth and the Lucas stayed.

There was a muffled set of thumps from inside the room, and Alexa thought she heard a voice.

"Mr. Kendricks!" she shouted again, this time pulling the managerial key card that Bartholomew Price had given her.

There was a muffled scrape on the inside of the door, another muffled curse.

"It's Special Agents Landers and Murphy. We're coming in!" she called out, flashing the card and then seizing the door handle, as she barged it with her shoulder.

Alexa hadn't pulled her gun, but she instantly wished she had as she barged in. It was stupid to wander around this place without guns out, particularly when there was a killer…

On the far side of the door was a narrow hallway (narrow by resort standards) that led to a wider, conjoined living and bedroom area. Alexa could see the graying, heavy skies beyond, and a small balcony that must have led down to a lower level of the giant, elite resort rooms.

"Ffu-!"

There was another muffled, sudden swear and a scrape from beyond the balcony, and Alexa and Kage broke into a sudden run, racing past the open door to a well-tiled and palatial bathroom, to see Eddie Kendricks in the center of his living space, with one of the long, low sofas half-turned on its side, as he was trying to jam something long and rod-like back into the upholstery underneath…

"FREEZE!" Kage cried out.

Eddie Kendricks didn't freeze but perversely continued to barge and fumble the cylindrical object into the bottom of the lounge seat for a split second. But he did look up, his face frozen in a rictus of shock and fear.

"Kendricks!" Alexa jumped the steps down to the lower part of the penthouse living area, her gun at eye level, sighting directly at him. "Stop it. *Now*."

This time, the rest of Kendricks's body *did* catch up with the alarm that was clear on his face. His hands froze, and he cast a furtive look down.

He was holding some sort of black carbon plastic rod, and at its ends were rotator adjusters.

Explosives? Radio detonators? The thoughts flashed through Alexa's brain, and she wished that she knew just a little bit more about what she was looking for. She didn't know. But whatever it was that Kendricks was holding, he had been trying to hide it from them, the Secret Service, everyone.

"Good. Now I am going to ask you a simple question. Does that item you are holding pose a threat to life?" Alexa asked, easing her steps forward, as internally, her mind raced. She could hear a rising sound of white noise in her ears, a fast-ascending boil that was like the roar of fire, the blast of smoke-

Didn't Kendricks say he was some kind of tech guru? Technical. Mechanical?

What the crap are the procedures for bomb disposal? Keep distance. Evacuate the building. Call in experts.

...experts that are hours away by boat or plane...

"It's safe! It's not dangerous, I swear!" Kendricks was visibly shaking. "It's a camera pole. A camera pole!" he explained, his hands moving to lift it in the air.

"Hey!" Kage was at the railing above Alexa, and every line of his body was taut and tense. Kendricks froze immediately as there was the sound of running feet behind them. It was one of the last remaining Service agents, who must have heard the shouting.

"Look, it's a camera pole, I swear to you. I haven't done anything. Nothing at all!" Kendricks was starting to blather, as Alexa's ears rang and whined.

He's losing it. He's going to fall to his knees any moment, Alexa thought as her eyes scanned the object that Kendricks was holding. She couldn't see any wires, but then again, she couldn't see the far end of it, either.

And if it is volatile, he wouldn't have been jabbing it into the sofa so quickly to hide it, would he?

She could see branding along its length. A set of numbers with 'PRO' written after it, in fancy retro machine-plate writing.

Alexa took a chance, stepping forward as she lowered her gun, placed one hand over Kendrick's own, and firmly pulled on the device.

"Agents? You got this?" whispered the Secret Service agent behind Kage, as he stepped out to go to the other side of the room, so that they had Kendricks in a triangle of fire, if they needed to. The Service agent also had his pistol up, and he had the same one-pointed, complete stillness that Kage was exhibiting. Neither of them would hesitate to fire if Kendricks did anything.

"I think so," Alexa breathed, pulling on the object to see that it was indeed a long cylindrical pole, like a mountain hikers' pole, extendable in the center, and, as it came out of the upholstery, revealed a set of bulky attachment clips at the far end. A tripod of stabilizing struts could be pulled out at the end she was holding, meaning that it could stand without support.

Camera bolts, Alexa recognized, turning to hiss at Kendricks immediately.

"Where is it. The camera?" she said.

Kendricks blinked at her, but he didn't try to hide this time, nodding back to the sofa.

"In there. But I didn't mean to-"

"Get it," Alexa said, her eyes narrowing as she watched Kendricks nod dumbly, then crouch to reach into the sofa, past the heavy canvas underlay.

"Slowly," Kage warned, which made Kendricks flinch, then slow his movements to a crawl as he fumbled around inside the hidden aperture between springs, wooden frame, and straps, finally drawing forth a small black device that was barely bigger than his hand.

"A camera," Kage announced the obvious. "Why were you trying to hide a camera?"

"Maybe because of this?" Alexa had already dismissed the man, turning behind him to the coffee table where there was a laptop already open, its screen dark before she swiped across the touchpad to reveal a video program with a black screen.

A video program, Alexa saw – as in there was a panel of participants, and next to it a box for chat/comments. A message was superimposed over the app saying 'WIRELESS CONNECTION TERMINATED,' but Alexa could still read the last comments in the chat.

MikeBoy73: *You freakin' what!? You're at GroundZero, Dog, could be WW3 if Cuba calls in Russia!*
SensationalMews: *It's one of the feds. I bet ya. Inside job, always is – just like they did to JFK...*
AIOA-^^: *Nah, my money is on the resort owner. It's a trap, isn't it? I bet he was working with the CIA...*

"This is a video stream," Alexa said, turning to look at the two offending items in Kendrick's hand, the camera mount and the camera itself.

"Care to explain what is going on, Mr. Kendricks?" she asked seriously, as Kage and the Secret Service agent slowly lowered their guns. Eddie was dangerous, but not in the way that they had thought when they had first entered the room.

"We asked you to surrender your mobile devices to us just yesterday because of the very serious and highly sensitive nature of the incident. Where privacy was *paramount* to security. But somehow I see that you have been able to construct a streaming platform," Alexa said rather heavily.

And if you have wireless connectivity, then there is also the possibility you have a transmitter/receiver, isn't there, Eddie? Alexa thought as she remembered what Cecil Pinkerton had recently told her. A mobile transmitter. Everything could be bought, if you had the right contacts.

Kendricks looked at the items in his hands, and at the assembled angry people all around him. It was Alexa who spoke next.

"I think that it's about high time we had that interview, don't you, Mr. Kendricks?"

~

Eddie Kendricks was a tech bro. A *definitive* tech bro, in Alexa's opinion.

Born and raised just outside of San Francisco, attended a good school, and obviously shockingly bright. But had a bad time with his chosen romantic preference; women, apparently (or at least, that is what Alexa surmised) in his college years as he got better and better at coding.

But all hard work pays off in the end, as her father would have said, as he made some sort of database coding infrastructure that was brought out and incorporated into Google in the early days, and he'd been living as a sort of 'Tech Influencer' ever since.

From his scared and incoherent stream of conversation, Alexa found it fairly hard to ascertain precisely what Eddie actually did for a living, but it seemed to be consultation.

Telling people opinions on how to make money online, it seemed to amount to as far as she could see, and she found it difficult to hide her scorn – but she managed it well. She tried not to think about her own brother, Jake, who'd made an obscene amount of money when he'd created one of those online multi-player games, and now brought in twice her salary as a federal agent every month.

How the other half live, she sighed, determinedly not looking too closely at how she defined 'other half' in her context…

"It's news!" Kendricks stated emphatically. "An assassination attempt on US soil!"

"A successful assassination, actually," Kage said heavily.

Around them, there was a press and flow of commotion as Eddie's rooms were being turned inside out by the Secret Service and two of the extra FBI agents. Alexa had been very clear about that; she wanted this place taken down to the smallest level, and so far it had already revealed Eddie's tablet and WiFi adapter that he was using to stream the 'Kendricks Report!' – where the exclamation point was actually a part of the name.

"So, with these... videos... of yours," Alexa said pointedly. "You basically talk about what you see happening in society and around you," she stated.

You trash talk, she was thinking. She had to watch through the recorded stream so far, and in there were a lot of unverified opinions of who might have been the killer of Representative Ramon Martinez, with each of the guests given their special introduction and description by Kendricks himself.

Oh, and let's not forget the viewer poll as well, Alexa could have screamed.

So far, the Luca couple were the 'outside bet/not very likely – but would be hilarious' vote.

Next up was Staniforth, which was the 'silver fox opportunity' as far as the viewers had deemed.

But the actual contenders for audience-voted assassins seemed to be tied between Eva Montgomery (*'suspicious. Very, very suspicious. And as all my regular Ken-crew know already; you can't trust a woman!'* was one particularly memorable phrase that had fallen from Eddie's mouth) and the secret services themselves.

With myself ('Alexa Landers, FBI Star-let or Russian Spy?') *coming in as the next best option!* Alexa thought. She would have laughed at the entirely provincial, biased and ridiculous 'fan' theories of who the killer was; that was, if it didn't make her feel sick. And angry.

Kendricks had been streaming since last night, off and on every time a new set of slanderous thoughts popped into his head, it appeared. He had leaked everything that had been happening on the island (as much as he knew) and it was quickly becoming clear how the news media got a hold of the story – and her name.

It was rapidly becoming clear that there were some very clever people out there with very little to do, as the anonymous legion of Eddie's followers had matched her photo to the scant CCTV and news footage of her previous high-profile case, the Russian oligarch in Miami, and from those two things – the victim being

Russian, and Alexa being one of the investigators – had gloriously put together two and two to come up with the idea that she must therefore be an undercover Russian agent, sent here to undermine the United States.

Dear saints preserve us, Alexa groaned.

But it wasn't just the fact that Kendricks broke the emergency security protocol. Indeed, while they had the scant powers to expressly forbid communications during an emergency, there were still the legal arguments over whether or not they could continue doing so. Alexa was aware that there was a legal loophole here, and she didn't want to get tripped up in it. Not yet, anyway.

No, what worried her more was the fact that he clearly knew what he was doing with technology. With wireless technology. The very sort of thing that had triggered that explosion.

"Look, I know my rights. And I have a right to freedom of information. As far as I knew, this could have been the start of World War Three! The next Cold War! Don't you think people need to know that sort of thing!?" Kendricks rationalized heatedly, to be silenced by a stark look from Kage.

"It might *not* have become a Cold War type thing if you managed to keep your mouth shut," Kage muttered, which Alexa thought wasn't entirely professional, but was certainly true. She didn't want to look at the headlines out there in the 'real' world to see what anyone else had made of this underground livestream.

"Did you come here with this intention, Mr. Kendricks? To record what you saw?" Alexa asked, her eyes flickering over the camera, WiFi, and laptop equipment.

Eddie looked confused for a moment. "Er... *yes?*"

Kage suddenly leaned forward, "So you knew there would be an attack?"

Eddie paled. "No! No, of course not! But I run the Kendricks Report every weekend. I was going to stream me fishing from my boat-"

Kendricks suddenly stopped, and Alexa wondered what it was.

There was a gap. A pause. Something that he didn't want to say, or...

Or something he wished he hadn't just said?

"Your boat," Alexa said. "You never mentioned this to us. You have a boat? Here, at the island?"

"Yes. I mean – no," Kendricks shook his head quickly.

A boat. A good way to get on and off the island quickly. Especially if you need to make an escape.

"What do you mean? Is it an *imaginary* boat!? Either it exists or it doesn't; which is it!?" Kage burst out. He was better at doing the bad cop thing than Alexa was. She never puffed up or started to shout during interrogations; she found that play-acting stressful and unnecessary. She always just channeled her inner cool rage.

Eddie continued to blink, swallowing nervously. "It's not here. It's moored back at the mainland, on a private marina. But…" He looked nervous, as if he didn't want to say anything.

"Spill it," Kage said, as Alexa leaned back. She was happy to let him lead the questions. He was better at it, and all the fight appeared to have been sucked out of Mr. Angry Hipster Tech-Bro already.

"It's automated. Low-level systems A.I., one of the first of its kind. I sent it over to the mainland so I could order to have some people to put on some more clothes, expensive wine, that kind of thing, then I was going to order it back here for a surprise. Well, I was, but that was before, you know, everything-"

"Before we closed the waterways," Alexa breathed, as she furiously scribbled down the notes, leafing back through to the page in her notebook where she had written '*Opportunity.*'

"Okay. You have a boat. Moored at the mainland. Who's your pilot, or skipper, or whatever you call them? Where are they right now?" Alexa was noting down.

Was this an extra suspect? Someone they hadn't accounted for who had access to the island via private boat? Her heart leaped. That would solve an awful lot of their problems.

"It doesn't have one," Eddie Kendricks said.

Alexa stopped writing, looking up. "I'm sorry, I don't quite follow. If your boat doesn't have a pilot, and you are here and it is over there, then how were you going to get it back over here? Was it a temporary, hired-worker kind of deal?"

"No, the *Azure Future;* that's what she's called; like I said, she's automated. Fully automated. Like a self-driving car, but a boat ..." Kendricks described.

It was Alexa's turn to blink in disbelief. "You have a robo-boat?" she said as Kage lightly touched her elbow.

"Actually, it's not entirely uncommon. A lot of boats' functions are automated these days anyway. The pilot is now more of a manual, gear and stick sort of driver," he said, as he had grown up all around Miami, and therefore all around the sea.

"Oh," Alexa said, suddenly feeling very stupid.

"But what does make it different is if it can start its engine without human interaction. And tie-off from a dock?" Kage turned to Kendricks, who nodded.

"Magnet locks. One of the companies I consult for designed a way where you just ask the computer to depolarize the magnets. They fall away, and the standby power activates the motor." Mr. Angry Tech-Bro Hipster shrugged like it was no big deal.

Alexa scrunched her eyes and tried to breathe through her nose, one, long breath.

Right. Robo-Boat. A wireless transmitter. Someone professional. She tried to put everything back in order in her head, as it suddenly felt like all the pieces were starting to spiral out of her control. Too many variables. Too many suspects, none of whom appeared to have any viable motive apart from one, Figuera, who had the least amount of skill.

"Mr. Kendricks. Can you tell me precisely what you were doing yesterday morning at nine o'clock and just before then?" Alexa said heavily.

Eddie looked at her, then at Kage, and finding equally stony glances returned to him, looked confused.

"Well, well I told you earlier that I saw that little shifty Cuban guy. Y'know, the bomber ..."

"Allegedly," Alexa pointed out.

Eddie sputtered, continuing anyway. "I saw him that morning. I was up, I already told you, going for water-"

Kage looked down at his phone, where he had been keeping his notes. "I think you said you were going to the resort open bar downstairs, actually. And that was seven-ish in the morning?" Kage cleared his throat and looked expectantly back up at Eddie.

"Yeah, yes, that's right…"

Confirmed by the resort CCTV, Alexa noted, which had caught Kendricks stumbling out of these rooms, bleary-eyed and wandering. He had paused at the stairs and looked down, where apparently he must have seen Miguel Figuera, but then carried on.

Both Kendricks and Figuera were up early, Alexa noted.

"And then?" she said.

"Well, well I got my uh, my drink, and came back. I was probably up for another hour maybe, and then I fell asleep until there was the explosion…" the man explained as Alexa quickly scrolled through her notes to where there were the various reports from the Secret Service.

After they had safely removed Skip Jackson from the island, one of the remaining teams had come back to find pretty much all of the guests downstairs in the lobby area, trying to work out what had happened. The Service agents had held them there, taken their phones and devices (or so they had thought), and waited for Alexa and Kage to arrive shortly after midday; it had taken that long, from the explosion around nine up until 12:15 for Alexa and Kage to work out a plan and for the Secret Service to secure the entire site.

A lot of time for the killer to hide, Alexa mused. But then again, everyone had been waiting in that lobby area. They hadn't gone anywhere, terrified that there was going to be another blast.

"When did you arrive at the resort, Mr. Kendricks?" Alexa asked. She already knew this, having read it on his booking sheet. Two days previous – but she wanted to hear it from the man himself. Ninety percent of investigation was, after all, catching people's lies.

"Just two, or is it three, days ago now? Two before the explosion," Kendricks stated.

Drat, Alexa thought. *But, if he had a private boat then he had plenty of opportunity to come and go before then, didn't he?*

Alexa looked at his hands. They didn't appear to be scarred, burned, or bruised. She wondered how much work it would have taken to crack and re-patch the tarmac on the helipad. Could it be done at night? How large a device did it have to be?

Again, these were all questions that she had no answers to.

"And can you document your whereabouts during those days before the explosion?" she asked calmly, as Kendricks licked his lips nervously.

"Of course, uh, well, you can see my feed mostly. I broadcast from the boat a couple of times each day, it's all there. And the times I wasn't online I was here, at the resort."

Double drat! Alexa thought to herself with a sinking feeling. If what Kendricks was saying was right, then his alibi was as cast-iron as it got for the daylight hours, anyway. He would have had however many hundreds of viewers as witnesses to his location during the 'Kendricks Report!' shows.

But not the nighttime, she concurred, making a mental note to go over the CCTV footage once again.

"And, Mr. Kendricks, you claim that you categorically didn't know anything about the diplomatic meeting due to occur here, just yesterday? A powerful man like you with all of your contacts?" Alexa said.

"No! Of course not!" he protested.

"And yet you seem to have no immediate love for Cuba, given your remarks about the suspect in custody?" Alexa pointed out.

"What? What is that supposed to mean?" Eddie coughed. "I – of course I don't *like* Cuba! Who does – apart from their cigars and rum, that is, I'll give them that; they know how to make cigars and rum! But no, Cuba is a controlled communist state, sitting right on our own borders... but I believe in the free market, and I believe that will be good for Cuba, and America," Kendricks said.

Alexa winced, trying to decipher what he was trying to say. Did he hate Representative Martinez or not?

"And the trade blockade coming down would be a good thing for everyone. So, if that was what that guy was here to do, then it would only be a good thing, right?" Kendricks continued.

"You *support* Representative Martinez?" Kage pointed out, and his voice inferred that he was surprised that Kendricks had even heard of him.

"Well, not directly. I support us. The US. But I support the Cubans if they want to buy our stuff because that makes us stronger," Kendricks said with absolute certainty, and there Alexa saw it. Eddie Kendricks' true soul.

He's greedy. An egotist, she thought. Of course, he would want the diplomatic talks between Cuba and America to go well because that would mean he might be able to get some side profits from any of his various businesses, Alexa thought. Any product that his portfolio was attached to. For all she knew, the world of Cuban computing and internet could even present a very profitable new market for him …

"So, like I said, I didn't even know that the summit was going on, but even if I did, I would support efforts to block the Cuban embargo from *our* side," Eddie said at last. "It just makes sense. Sell them stuff, then they'll put down their guns. I think people the world over just want American democracy."

It might be a little more complicated than that, Alexa thought, but she figured that she had heard enough, anyway. She looked over to the Service agent, who had appeared to hover on the edge of their conversation.

The man shook his head. Nothing. They hadn't found anything else incriminating. No explosive equipment. No long-range wireless transmitters.

But still …

"I'm afraid that we'll have to confiscate these," she said as she stood up, reaching for the camera, mount pole, and laptop.

"What!? Wait – that's my livelihood, you know!" Kendricks retorted.

"I'm sure you won't starve, man," Kage muttered under his breath heavily. It was obvious what Kage thought of the man, too, as they stood up to go.

"But, but when do I get them back!?" Kendricks said, indignant all of a sudden.

After I've handed them over to our CSO, and he tells me that you haven't rigged up some wireless detonator in here somehow... Alexa smiled sweetly.

"When we're done, Mr. Kendricks. Thank you for your co-operation."

They turned and left the room, filing out one at a time and leaving Kendricks behind before Kage caught up with Alexa and raised an eyebrow that said *'whaddya think?'*

Alexa shrugged. "Impossible to tell right now," she murmured, as her heart felt like it was crashing.

"We're back at square one. Still no strong clue to anyone here. Anyone at all," she concluded as she checked the time.

3:45 PM. The interview with Kendricks and the search of his room had gone on for a long time as they had gone through every fact, every detail.

"The emergency statute runs out at seventeen hundred hours," Alexa said. "And that is just a little over an hour away. After that, everyone in this resort is free to go. We have to detain them under suspicion, charge them, or let them all go."

"Well, we've got Figuera-" Kage began as they started down the stairs toward the ground floor of the resort.

"I'm telling you, there's something that doesn't add up about him!" Alexa said. Even though Figuera had the opportunity, and he probably had access to the helipad and the materials to patch it back up once the bomb was in place.

But with no solid evidence linking Figuera to the actual blast, Alexa shook her head. It was worse that she knew that, under this much international pressure and media coverage they could probably even get a conviction on the resort staffer – but *she* didn't like it.

"I need the proof," she hissed. "I need to *know*, deep down, I need to be able to look at the facts and see clearly that this led to that, which are irrefutable. Honest," she went on, looking up finally to find Kage looking at her oddly.

He paused for a moment, and Alexa dreaded that he might say something about her state of mind, of the recent panic attack or the after-effect that the explosion might have had on her.

He didn't do any of these things.

Instead, he stopped on the stairs, and put a hand lightly on her shoulder, in just the same way that her dad would have done. It wasn't authoritative, it was supportive if anything. A silent gesture that said 'you got this.'

For a second, her entire world came to a pause, and Alexa was washed back to all the times that her father had similarly said nothing – or very little – but had been there. Steady. Silent.

"Well, with the way that the weather out there is shaping up, no one will be heading off the island tonight, I don't think," Kage said, and Alexa realized that he was right. There was a distant thrum in the air which she had mistaken for the tinnitus in her ears but was actually the sound of rising winds outside the resort.

"But I'll get started with the interviews next anyway, I guess, before anyone has a chance to leave the island?" he said with a small smile.

"Thanks," Alexa nodded. She had been scared that he would try to pull rank on her or berate her into accepting Figuera as the suspect even when there was no fundamental connection. Not for her, anyway.

"I'll start going through the camera footage again. See if there's anything we missed, any time one of the guests or staff left the resort at odd times…" she listed off, although, to Alexa, even her own words were beginning to sound hollow.

A part of her was starting to doubt herself. Starting to think that maybe everyone else was right, that the simplest solution really was the best. That Figuera was the assassin, and he just hadn't admitted it yet.

But that conclusion felt like a stone in Alexa's throat as they carried on down the stairs to the resort floor.

She needed evidence. She needed proof!

CHAPTER SEVENTEEN

XVIII. 4:58 PM

THE RISING WINDS OUTSIDE WEREN'T JUST PICKING UP. They were turning into a storm. The small office that they had commandeered at the back of the resort, right next to the supply store where Eva Montgomery had been jumped by Figuera the night before had one window, high up in the wall, and it was being lashed by a heavy drub of rain.

"Ugh…"

There was a groan from the door as Kage appeared, holding his phone in one hand and his notebook in the other.

"How many?" Alexa asked, pausing the CCTV footage in front of her. This office at the back was where the resort kept its backup generator, and its small computer system, complete with its own single server that held all the video files for the resort's cameras.

Which would have been a pain in the neck, Alexa thought, if she didn't have Dee Hopkins on the other end of the line.

"Is that Kage? How's he holding up with all those swimming pools and tennis courts and private saunas?" The words of Dee on the other end of the line were full of mischief, but there was an edge to her voice.

She was trying to make light of the fact that Alexa had just been complaining to her for an hour straight about the case.

"Hey, Dee," Kage called out to Alexa's phone. "I still haven't managed to take one steam yet, I am sure you will be disappointed to hear. And the resort looks about as appealing as the Glades in hurricane season."

"Don't joke about that. You're in a Category 1 storm at the moment. It's not expected to go beyond a 2, but you should be careful, all the same!" Dee warned as Alexa thanked her. Dee was like that, helpful, but wouldn't take foolishness from anyone. Alexa liked that about her.

"How many?" Kage continued. "I didn't do full interviews, but I checked off as many statements from the staff that I could," he said, waving the notebook in the air for a moment longer.

"Starting with the lobby staff, I got a whole load of nothing. Everything tallies with the statements that they had already given to either us or the Secret Service," he said, pausing as suddenly there was a large crash of rain and wind against the window.

The window itself was double-paned and laced with metal mesh. Probably for security purposes, but she wondered how bad the storms got out here among the hot mangroves and swamps of the South Florida coast.

"Everything was normal operating procedure, people did their shifts, and the staff that worked with each other corroborated that separately. No one apart from Figuera missed a shift, and that was the day of the explosion," Kage stated.

"Yesterday," Alexa pointed out. "That was yesterday."

Kage nodded as he rubbed his eyes and wearily moved back to his notebook.

"Normally the resort would have been a six on, six off pattern, but for the day of the explosion and the day before it, it was nine on and three off because Bartholomew Price wanted to have the place as tight as possible for the proceedings," Kage explained.

"That was what made Figuera's disappearance stick in everyone's mind, and why they were too busy to go check it out. Figuera was supposed to be on that day, and all the other staff members thought he was slacking."

"Did he have a history of slacking?" Alexa wondered, frowning a little as she moved back to the computer. Thankfully, Dee had guided her around the interface, pointing out all of the ones that she could disregard right away – the wildlife trail cameras that fed back to the resort's server. Alexa had spent her hour fast-forwarding and fast-backwarding through the main resort areas; the lobby, reception, the front doors, and as many of the other entrances and exits as possible. It was boring work, and complicated by the fact that the resort didn't have a full security setup, presumably because Price reckoned any burglar wouldn't bother getting on a boat and coming out this far.

"Figuera? No, apparently not. He was a hard worker but kept to himself."

"Makes sense," Alexa agreed. Martyrs and 'heroic killers' (as they deemed themselves to be, Alexa thought back to her training) often did. They perceived the world as essentially against people like them, and it was this outsider quality that engendered their criminal tendencies in the first place.

She was right about to ask if anyone spotted him taking an interest in the helipad when there was an alarming trill from her phone, from an incoming call.

"Dee? Thanks for the help with the resort computers, but that's Cecil. I'll have to take it," Alexa told her, knowing that Cecil Pinkerton was still ensconced at the marina helipad, having set up a 'clean room' to study all of the various bits of evidence that they had so far collected.

"*Sure thing, Alexa. Just remember to copy everything over to the FBI server address I gave you. I've put in the digital seizure form already, but with that storm you have, we won't be able to get any more operatives out to you at least until tomorrow morning,*" Dee conferred, indicating that they would need to seize the resort's computer assets as well. Alexa thanked her and clicked over to the call where Cecil waited for her.

"*Special Agent Landers, we're closing down the lab for the night, due to the storm,*" he began, making Alexa wince.

"Are you returning to the resort? How bad is it out there?" she inquired, hearing the man clear his throat in a disagreeable manner.

"*It's bad, but not overly hazardous, I believe. We'll make the short journey back to the private lodges and continue what analysis we can do on the computer. There is, after all, plenty of data to get through!*"

Alexa gave an affirmative, as her eyes moved to the window above. The sound of the rain was a constant hammer drill of percussion.

"*Thankfully, we've already processed much of the actual explosion site – but it's still a concern. The rain will effectively destroy any trace evidence we were hoping to gather left.*"

"Darn it!" Kage grumbled.

"*Indeed. But we do have some findings to report, which I think you will be pleased to hear-*"

Cecil's mannered tones led Alexa back to her computer, and the secure FBI online file storage that she had been given access to. It was standard operating procedure that agents in the field upload their data to the secure cloud, so at least there would be a photographic or copied trail of evidence at hand for any other investigator, until such time as physical teams could receive the evidence.

The screen on Alexa's laptop glitched and froze for a moment before refreshing.

"Damn storm. It's playing hell with the local WiFi," Alexa said, echoing what Dee had told her just a little while ago.

However, the disruption was temporary as she navigated to the ST. MARTIN'S folder, and then into LANDERS/MURPHY,

LEAD, and on into the various subfolders that they had created within.

"*CSI,*" Pinkerton guided her, and Alexa started looking inside a folder swiftly populating with photographs and documents; all the result of their hard work over the day. Alexa saw mock-up CAD drawings of the helipad before, during, and after the blast, alongside more photos than Alexa thought that she had so far taken this entire year. Every aspect of the site had been photographed, from close-ups of the crater to multiple overview shots, and different pictures focusing on different aspects; radial cracks, tarmac and asphalt melt, strange and unrecognizable pieces of melted metal...

And then there was a set of illustrations of a tubular device, looking a little like a compacted version of a pair of bicycle handlebars.

"*Images 38 to 42 are our suspected recreations of the actual device. You'll see that it follows a classic IED construction.*"

"IED!" Kage barked out. "You mean like the things they find in Iraq?"

"*Yes and no. Following the Afghanistan War, there was a lot of widespread interest in the devices. You could say they became a favorite, albeit this one is far more sophisticated...*"

Cecil pointed out the small wire that stretched out from one end.

"*We found fragments of the receiver chip. Essentially it would have been planted with the wire packed into the tarmac just near the surface. We believe that it was underneath a section of repainted helipad, so it was missed by the Service when they swept the area.*"

"And me," Kage murmured. "It was missed by me, too..."

Alexa cast a quick glance up to him to see his face distraught and broken. She cursed herself for being a fool for not picking up on it earlier. She hadn't seen how devastated he was at having not been able to prevent the explosion.

How could I miss that!? Alexa thought, instantly blaming herself. She had been so caught up in the investigation, in finding proof – and yes, in her own trauma at seeing three people blown to smithereens – that she had not even thought to ask Kage how he was coping.

"It was a professional job, you couldn't have-" Alexa started to say, but Kage just shook his head and returned his attention to her. The mask had fallen down and there he was, as if nothing had happened. No cracks in the armor.

"*Yes. They were certainly professional, and that is for sure,*" Cecil commented, having completely missed the exchange from his side of the phone. "*The wire that led to the tiny receiver allowed it to catch the wireless transmitter's signal. I have already taken a look at the computer and equipment you sent over from Mr. Kendricks' room and no, there was no way that could have been modified or used. The signal strength was too strong and too narrow. We're looking for a transmitter-dedicated unit, such as I described to you earlier, Agent Landers.*"

"Okay," Alexa murmured, briefly explaining to Kage what Cecil had told her just earlier. That there was such a thing as powerful, ex-military WiFi transmitters, hand-held contraptions that allowed powerful short-range beams to be 'fired' at their target receivers.

"How short range?" Kage asked.

"*Well, depends on the device. Some are more powerful than others, but from the gauge of the wire, and my best estimation on the components, we'd be talking about a narrow beam array capable of seven hundred meters or so.*" Cecil's voice started crackling, occasionally jarring and fragmenting as the storm played havoc with the island's larger receivers and communicators.

"Seven hundred meters? That could take it all the way to the main resort building!" Alexa said, earning a measured noise from the other end of the line.

The perpetrator could have used the transmitter from their room, and no one would know...

Which also meant it was more important to complete that room sweep, as thoroughly as possible!

"*Indeed. But that is not all that I have to report. Unfortunately, the construction of the device matches several others in the National Hazardous Materials database,*" Cecil said.

"What does that mean?" Alexa said quickly.

"I have appended several files at the end of the folder that you will see, but essentially, over many years, the FBI in collaboration with other agencies has realized that there is a way to 'fingerprint' devices such as these. Not by actual fingerprints, but by construction, materials, the logic used, the format and mechanisms..."

"What, you mean every device is unique?" Alexa considered how they used fingerprints, which was still one of the most reliable ways to get a conviction, as far as she was aware.

"Yes and no. Precisely the opposite, in many ways. The way that devices are put together, what materials are used, the design choices taken that put some components over here, and utilize one type of trigger or layout over another that forms a sort of habitual fingerprint, we believe..."

"The way some car companies always front-load their engines?" Kage pointed out.

"Or always include certain types of graphene for their brake pads, yes," Cecil said, the static and interruption on the line not getting in the way of his enthusiasm for his subject. *"Certain designers do things in certain ways."*

"A profile. You're saying that you can profile who made the device?" Alexa asked excitedly.

"Precisely. And as you will see, the device used here at St. Martin's Island matches very closely to a device used two years ago in Texas, and even earlier than that, five and six years ago in Wyoming and Virginia."

"You know who it was? The maker?" Alexa leaned forward. This was the break she was looking for. This was the break that they needed.

"No, no. The whole point is that we haven't caught them yet, but we believe that they were all made by the same person. The same bomb-maker."

Alexa scrolled through to the final files to see that Cecil had indeed appended folders on three other incidents of explosions; one was against a medical clinic in Texas, another was directed at a town hall in Wyoming, and still a third had been sent to (and thankfully defused at) a US Army training camp.

"What's the connection here? Kage, are you seeing this?" Alexa rasped as her partner leaned over her shoulder.

"All government facilities?" Kage asked. "Is that what links this? That the killer has it in for the federal government?"

Alexa shook her head and quickly scanned the documents. "No. The town hall would be local, the clinic was a nonprofit organization that provided healthcare to immigrants. And anyway, why blow up a Cuban – unless the real target was Skip Jackson?"

Kage nodded, but Cecil's voice rang out from the speakerphone on Alexa's mobile.

"I'm afraid that it is more complicated than that. The problem is that the bomb maker is not necessarily the same as the bomb trigger. In this case, I would quite strongly hazard that they are different persons entirely," Cecil said.

"What?" exclaimed Alexa and Kage at the same time.

"Those previous devices were claimed by disparate groups. The far-right Sons of America for the medical clinic device, and then the New Dawn Cult for the town hall, and an individual for the Army training camp. They were three different groups, in different parts of the country, with no apparent overlap aside from the fact their device was constructed by the same designer."

"Cecil, I am not sure that I follow…" Alexa stated.

"I am sorry to inform you that there is a professional class of criminals out there, a very small class, who specialize in the designing and creation of such devices, and then sell those devices to others. In this case, it is the same designer who designed all four devices, selling them to the far-right group, the cult, and the Virginia lone wolf vigilante."

Alexa blinked, stunned for a moment. "People… do this for a living?" she stammered, hardly able to believe her ears.

"And a very profitable living it appears to be, too. From the previous investigations against the other devices, it is believed that they cost somewhere in the region of forty to eighty thousand dollars; and given the size and sophistication of this device, I presume that it is in the upper range," Cecil growled, as the rain lashed down against the windows, and once again his voice fractured into static before coming back again.

"Whomever actually planted and activated the device is usually not the designer at all but the buyer."

Alexa's mind started to race as she tried to trace the implications of such a thing. What did this mean for the investigation?

Forty to ninety thousand dollars. Enough to live off for a year or three, if you were frugal, she calculated.

"Figuera could never afford that on his salary," she muttered, earning a sharp, calculating look of his own from Kage. This was more evidence that Figuera had been telling the truth and that he had nothing to do with the blast at all.

"And we have no idea who the device maker could be?" Alexa breathed. It was a lead, at least. If there was any way to tie any of the staff or guests to a previous investigation...

"There is an open joint FBI and ATF investigation case happening, but from the latest updates, it has been cold for quite some time now. The professional designer is clearly very good at hiding their tracks, and usually nowhere near the actual scene of the crime at all."

Alexa swore. What could have been the breakthrough was only the complication. There was no way to tie any of the guests to anything.

"But there are more questions," she said to herself as Kage considered her.

"What's up? You've got a thought, I can see it," he said.

"Yeah, I do have a thought," Alexa frowned, looking at the laptop screen, and then at the rainy window as her thoughts churned.

"Forty to ninety thousand dollars. We're talking someone with a fair bit of disposable cash. And who really wanted to kill the Cuban representative, and presumably stop the entire talk of dropping the embargo?" Alexa thought it through, looking up at Kage as she did so, her voice hard.

"But the visit itself was a state secret, right? Who knew that this meeting was going to happen? Why and who was involved here? We've suddenly gone from a lone wolf vigilante-type event to a conspiracy. A well-funded conspiracy."

Alexa didn't say it, but from the silence in the small resort office, she didn't have to.

Someone big was behind this. Or an organization. Or a state.

"Are you suggesting..." Kage whispered.

Don't, Alexa held up a warning hand but said nothing. She didn't want to be the one to say that something *political* was involved here. Their last major case had seen them questioning the involvement of the Russian Federation. She didn't want to go down that route again – but she would if she had to.

"We sweep every inch of this hotel for that transmitter. And we finish the interviews. If anyone, *anyone* looks to have a connection to something larger than themselves, a company, a country, anything... then that will be our main target."

"Right on it," Kage responded as the lights flickered overhead.

CHAPTER EIGHTEEN

XIX. 6:01 PM

66 I WILL ABSOLUTELY *NOT* BE TREATED LIKE THIS! WE HAVE trees going down all over the resort, and I've just had a report of a leak in lodge 3 and I really must-"

Bartholomew Price was not the happiest of bunnies, Alexa could see, but then again, neither was she or Kage.

"Quit it, Price," Kage spat in a tone that was like hammered steel. To be honest, it shocked Alexa to hear him like that.

Is he blaming himself for the explosion? I need to keep an eye out to make sure he's keeping it together – for both our sakes.

"We need to question everyone again. And we need to search the resort. Again," Kage continued. "New information has come to light-"

"You have your suspect! I saw you haul him off the island myself! Now you have no right to detain any of us any longer, and I have a damn hurricane to deal with."

"Mr. Price. If you do not lock down this site, right now, I will be forced to arrest you for obstructing the course of justice and interfering with a federal agent in the investigation of a crime!" Kage wasn't backing down for a moment, and the tension in the resort lobby where they had cornered the resort manager was thick.

It was only made worse by the sudden and abrupt ring of alarms from the resort staffers at the lobby desk, as their phones had been returned to them, and they were inundated with warning calls from various other staffers who were trying to battle the storm elsewhere on site.

The winds and the rain outside were only increasing, it appeared, and there was a constant, dull roar in Alexa's ears, and a feeling of pressure building up. It shouldn't have been as dark as it looked through the windows at this time of the year, and Alexa was starting to wonder when they would see their first lightning strike.

But we're here for a reason. Alexa held her stance and glared at Price. Bartholomew, of everyone here (perhaps apart from Kendricks), had the forty to ninety thousand dollars to spare, didn't he? Price also had the advantage of knowing much of the itinerary of events beforehand.

He knew some of what was happening on site. He might not have known who the exact representatives and political figures coming there were, but he had known they were important.

There was nothing in Price's file to indicate extremist views. He was essentially an opportunist, in Alexa's book. An entrepreneur who wanted the money and the political cachet, but that didn't mean that he hadn't been co-opted. Or blackmailed. Or that perhaps he had his own, secret reasons for wanting the blockade to be ended...

It's only the facts that matter. Only the evidence, she thought.

As she opened her mouth to back up Kage's strong demand, there came a piercing scream from upstairs. "Aiiiii!"

Kage shot her a look, but Alexa was already moving. The roar in her ears was temporarily forgotten as she broke into a run, one hand moving to the gun secure at her hip as she made for the central reception area, and the large double stairs that swept upward to the first floor.

"*Help!*"

There was another, closer shout as they got to the first floor (*Kendrick's floor,* Alexa mused). She put in an extra burst of speed, taking the steps two, three, four at a time until she got to the first-floor landing.

There was Kendricks, staggering back from the landing with another person nearby. It was one of the resort staffers, a younger woman, who had been the one screaming, with her hands over her mouth.

There was a sudden, glaring flash of white that strobed through the windows, and everything for Alexa appeared to slow, just as it had when the helicopter had erupted.

Everything before her, just for a moment, was illuminated in black and white. Kendricks and the resort staffer were monochrome versions of themselves as somewhere close outside, lightning struck.

WHUMP!

And then, close after, came the thump and crash of thunder. Her body felt it before her mind registered, as she felt every hair on her arms raise, and her head pound with a dull headache before the booming wall of sound.

"What is it!?" Kage shouted as they got to the top of the landing, hearing the resort cleaner screaming as she pointed past them, across the hallway toward an open door.

The open door leading into Eva Montgomery's room.

No. Alexa and Kage moved as one. Alexa could hardly hear anything over her ringing, traumatized ears, but she saw that the door was open, and beyond it was the wide hallway which was a mirror opposite to Kendrick's rooms. There was the small railing ahead of her as she and Kage ran forward, their hearts hammering.

And there, lying half in and half out of the palatial bathroom, was Eva Montgomery, with blood pooling from the side of her head.

"She – she knew!" Kendricks called out behind them. "She knew who the killer was! She knew who set the bomb!"

CHAPTER NINETEEN

XX. 7:27 PM

"BLUNT FORCE TRAUMA TO THE HEAD," SAID KAGE, taking a few steps back and turning from where Cecil's CSI team had set up as much of a mobile crime scene as they could. Eva Montgomery's body had already been removed from the room and taken to the marina warehouse where Cecil had set up his lab, and the entire room was 'tented' with white polythene sheets covering the windows and doors 'to stop any further contamination' as the CSI had stated with no little frustration.

He looks shattered, Alexa thought. Kage's eyes were deep hollows of despair and rimmed with regret. If anything, Alexa would have said that her partner looked haunted.

How long have we been at this? She knew that they had slept last night. She remembered it being broken at four in the morning and waking up to begin their day. The thought crossed her mind about whether they needed to take shifts.

Because if we don't get a breakthrough soon, Kage – or I – might burn out.

"You got this," she murmured as she crossed over to where Kage stood, looked at him, and made an agreeable but disheartened noise.

"I know. It's just. We should have anticipated it. We should have seen it coming," Kage whispered.

Alexa was suddenly struck by what Kage had said just a little while earlier, that he should have done better. He should have been able to stop the explosion – which was patently ridiculous, but she could see that he was dwelling on it. This latest, newest, terrible death was only making his perceived failures worse.

"How? There is no way we could have seen it coming. Who would have thought Montgomery was a target?" Alexa pointed out.

For a moment, Kage was silent as he stared at the white cloth that covered the area where she had died.

"Everyone is a target," he muttered under his breath before shaking his head, appearing to rally a little of his old self – or his old mask, at least.

"You were right. The killer can't be Figuera because Figuera isn't even on the island."

"He's in custody," Alexa confirmed. "And I am inclined to believe that he was telling the truth in his confession. Figuera was guilty of planning to attack Representative Ramon, but not of this…"

Although Figuera did attack Eva, too, the thought flashed through Alexa's mind. Did that mean something? Was it weird that the same person got attacked twice, one time even fatally?

"What do we know?" she said, narrowing her eyes at the door behind them, to hear the muffled voices of one of the Secret Service agents talking to Eddie Kendricks outside. He had already given his immediate statement, but the Service man was going over it again, and closer this time.

"Scenes of a struggle, but Eva was quickly overpowered," Kage directed around the room, pointing toward various small yellow tags indicating evidence points. "The door wasn't broken open, so whoever did this must have had a key – either that or Eva opened the door to them herself."

"She knew the killer?" Alexa murmured.

"Could be. Enough to let them in. Y'see, the actual event didn't happen until down here, by the living space and bathroom." Kage pointed toward where the white tented sheet obscured the floor.

"Eva walked in, presumably with the killer behind her," he said, next pointing to where there was a small occasional table on its side, where it would have stood at the entrance to the bathroom.

"The resort cleaner – she was the one who found the body – said there should have been a lamp there, but it wasn't. It was the murder weapon," Kage said.

Alexa nodded. That had to be it. "So Eva let the killer in, walked ahead of him…"

"But she must have known something was up, or seen something at the last moment, when it was too late to do anything about it," Kage said. "Because the door to the bathroom was open, and there's obvious signs of disturbance. My guess, and I'm no Pinkerton, but my guess is that she got hit, and then there was a struggle before the attacker overpowered her."

Alexa struggled. *Why didn't she scream? Why did no one hear what was going on?* she thought, but then considered the terrible, awful facts of violent affrays. Some people freeze. Some people are too busy surviving. Some are too shocked.

Once more, Alexa shivered and felt a sick, queasy feeling in her stomach as her ears began to ring. This case had already started with one terrible tragedy and was seeming to just get worse.

Breathe, Alexa, think, she demanded of herself.

Eva was killed for something. Someone came to this room to specifically kill her, and it was someone that Eva didn't think of as a threat, not at first, anyway.

"The cleaner found her. When?" she asked.

Kage looked at his notebook, flipped to the last page, and announced, "She reckons a little after six. Their shift pattern has been messed up thanks to, well, everything going on, so Price asked them to do what rounds they could later in the evening, especially after," he flipped the page, "after the Secret Service are still in the process of searching the rooms, after our chat. They had finished with Kendricks, and the cleaner had finished there to come here..."

"Which explains why Kendricks was around," Alexa connected. *Maybe. Convenient that he was here.* The death was only an hour and a half ago. Two hours, now. The killer couldn't have gotten far. They had to still be in the building, didn't they?

"We need him taken in," Alexa said.

Kage closed his notebook. "Already on it. He has been too often in the middle of a lot of things, too often..." he murmured, turning as the voices outside the room suddenly escalated. One was clearly Eddie Kendricks, loudly protesting, and the other was clearly the Secret Service agent, explaining firmly but clearly that he needed to answer some questions.

"Okay. CCTV," Alexa said immediately, when there was a loud cough from the older Cecil Pinkerton, as he looked up from discussing something with two more of his CSI colleagues.

"Special Agents? I believe you will want to see this, right away," Pinkerton said, standing taller than anyone else in the room and as thin as a pine tree. He had the look of a professor with his small, peaked glasses, Alexa thought. But there was also something like tempered steel in the way that his eyes flashed, his words were exact, and his movements economical as he stepped aside to reveal what his team had just revealed.

A small netbook, and a collection of even smaller devices. To Alexa's eyes, they looked like-

"Is that a tape recorder?" she frowned. She hadn't seen one of them in the wild before but had been introduced to them in the past. They were essentially archaic bits of technology, tiny vinyl tape cassettes that were about the size of your thumb.

"It is. A part of the media landscape perhaps twenty years ago, until digital of course superseded everything," Pinkerton said, pointing to the small collection of tapes, and the larger but not by much black plastic 'stick.'

"Mobile annotator. Utilizes micro cassettes. Used by field recorders, naturalists, and of course, journalists."

"Journalists?" Kage said.

Pinkerton grunted. "The netbook was hidden, as were these items, but seeing how naturalists have employed this technology to record bird sounds and the like, perhaps it was overlooked," Cecil judged, carefully putting on a set of blue plastic gloves as he handled the device, checking it carefully.

"But there was a time when they were also one of the chosen items for reporters, too. Small enough that they could fit into a handbag, discreet so as not to draw attention," Cecil said, opening the small tape deck, and inserting one of the cassettes.

Alexa thought back to the airy, breezy Californian woman that she had met, and who was now dead.

To be honest, Eva Montgomery did not seem that much of a naturalist. Not a die-hard bird-spotter, she thought, considering the other guest's choice of light, all-weather and rugged clothing for being out on the semi-tropical island, or even of Kendricks' avowed love of deep-sea fishing. Eva didn't appear to fit anywhere in that milieu at all. If anything, Alexa would have placed her in some sunny beachside retreat, soaking up the sun and complaining about the cocktails.

But then again, no one was who they appeared to be entirely, were they?

"Are you suggesting that Eva was a reporter?" Kage asked as Cecil pressed play on the tape.

There was a hiss and a moment of silence, but what came next wasn't a barrage of bird calls or the sigh of wind in the trees. It was Eva's voice, whispering and intense—and notably, with her valley-girl accent almost entirely gone.

"...*About 3:30, and everything here is an utter shit show. It's terrifying, but I know I have to continue. It seems that there was a terrorist incident yesterday morning at the resort, where the Cuban Representative, Ramon Martinez, was murdered. Obviously, the case against the CIA only grows stronger. The US Special Advisor, who I have managed to ascertain was none other than Skip Jackson, who already has many known links to the military, was here – but I think that they've now left.*

"This is a classic false flag event. One of the staffers, Miguel Figuera, has been questioned and arrested, but I think that he must be an obvious stool. I mean, from what the other staffers at St. Martin's state, he was Cuban himself – or at least of Cuban origin. Isn't it always the case that they blame a disaffected child of immigrants? This paves the way for the federal government to blame the Cubans, call it an internal power struggle or whatever. Keep it out of the private eye..."

"Ugh," Kage groaned, looking darkly at the assembled people around him for a moment.

Funny, Alexa had never pegged him as much of a patriot. But he seemed eager to defend the honor of America.

"Is she going to be another Truther?" Kage whispered and rolled his eyes.

"I don't think so," Alexa frowned. "It doesn't sound like she knew Figuera at all..."

They listened for a few more minutes, as Eva's voice – without the ditzy and dreamy, drawn-out vowels this time – appeared to be discussing just how this could all be an FBI and/or CIA plot to kill the Cuban, and then disperse blame. The dead woman revealed her logic after another twenty or thirty seconds of assumptions.

"*...and therefore the blockade remains up, and the cocaine trade continues, which, as we know, the CIA profits from, using it as currency to infiltrate the gangs in America, or as payment to the counter-insurgents and mafias everywhere around the world...*"

"I get it," Alexa breathed. "It sounds like Eva Montgomery was some kind of reporter? In her own head, at least. She thinks *we* killed Ramon in order to keep the blockade?"

Immediately, and at once, Alexa felt her heart patter as soon as she said it out loud. It was a ridiculous notion. Everything in her training, her upbringing, her childhood, and her profession told her that this wasn't the case.

And yet.

There was another side of her as well. A side that hankered after the truth. After the facts. There was a side to Alexa Landers which was cold and as clear as the day that she had walked into her final Academy evaluations and had walked out maintaining her graduation-with-distinction merit. All that part of Alexa cared about was the truth and the evidence, and now that the lid had been opened on another line of inquiry, it started to relentlessly turn facts over.

It would have been easy for elements with the US government to have access to the site.

The US government knew that this summit and visit was happening ahead of time.

The US government had chosen the site of the meeting.

The US government had filled this place with their own people in the week leading up to the eventual meet.

And how convenient was it that all US personnel had escaped unharmed while the Cuban delegation all died in the blast?

Wait a minute, Alexa breathed. She tried to check her thinking, lest she herself disappear down one of those conspiracy rabbit holes. Externally, the words of Eva continued, discussing how advantageous it would be for the US if they could blame Cuba for the explosion, further discrediting them and, apparently, further strengthening the illegal cocaine smuggling trade.

"Here, this appears to prove that Eva Montgomery was not who we at first thought her to be," Kage opined as he carefully looked through the rest of Eva's assembled belongings. There was a notebook with a list of numbers in the back, as well as the front half being half full of dates and notes and times.

"Bellingfox. Vice. The Green Report. Carrot News," Kage read out.

"Excuse me? I've never heard of half of those," Cecil said, looking sternly over the tops of his glasses.

But Alexa had. "They're news sites. Indie ones. Some of them are pretty firmly on the right wing. But some are definitely left-leaning as well. About the only thing they have in common is that they're on the outside. Radical independent media, I suppose you could say," she said.

Cecil blinked academically. "I don't believe I have ever seen them in the newsstand. I take it these are... *online* publications?" He said the word with a great amount of distaste, which would have made Alexa laugh out loud were it not for the seriousness of the situation.

"Yes. But even if Eva had their contact details, I don't particularly see why she would keep using a tape recorder."

"Oh, that bit I *am* aware of," Cecil Pinkerton said. "I believe that a tape recording presents far easier methods for confidentiality than a digital one, at the moment, anyway. Computers can be hacked and copied, and digital recordings can be made fairly easily, but an actual piece can be physically hidden and destroyed," Cecil said.

That made sense, at least. If Eva had been fooling them all and wasn't actually some kind of Californian airhead but was in fact an undercover independent reporter, then Alexa had certainly fallen for it. And to be honest, she had stuck out amongst everyone else here for *not* having any great love for nature or the outdoors.

Think, Alexa. The facts, she demanded of herself. As fascinating (and terrifying) as that line of conspiracy questioning was, she was here about four deaths. About whom might have killed Ramon, his staffers, and now Eva.

Whomever it was, they hired a professional explosives maker, she thought, as her thoughts started to sidle once more with Eva's conspiracy theory. Heaven alone knew that the secret intelligence services had that kind of money, and they probably had all the means to be able to keep that transaction secret...

No wait, think! But the killer was here, at the resort. They knew Eva, they...

"Kendricks!" Alexa suddenly said, turning to look at Kage in alarm.

"He said that Eva knew who the killer was. The bomber, didn't he!? How did he know that? How!?"

There was only one explanation, of course, and that was if Kendricks had been talking to Eva before she had died. Maybe *just* before she died.

CHAPTER TWENTY

XXI. 8:14 PM

❝ I'M TELLING YOU, IT'S GONE!"

There was shouting coming from ahead of Alexa and Kage as they crossed the hallway and rushed toward the opposite open door of Eddie Kendrick's studio room.

"Sir, I won't tell you again to calm down and sit down," they heard one of the Service agents saying, as they slowed to a jog and for the second time that day entered Eddie Kendrick's rooms.

They found it still in disarray, but now with a considerably angrier Mr. Angry Hipster standing in the middle of the lowered room, with a suited Secret Service agent pointing a finger at him and almost prodding him in the chest. It was clear that the tension in the room was high, and that at any moment Kendricks was about to get himself arrested.

Which, if he is the killer, would make my life a lot easier, Alexa thought as she pushed herself forward.

"What is gone exactly?" she demanded, as Kendricks looked up at her, a furious glare on his face. The sofa was still upturned to one side, now with its bottom stuffing entirely ripped out. Either Kendricks had been even angrier than usual after their last chat, or he hadn't bothered to clean up.

"Sir, I detained the witness in here for questioning, as right now there didn't seem to be any issue," the Secret Service agent, one of the very few handful that remained, explained, when Kendricks exploded.

"You see! You're admitting it! *Detention!* I am being detained against my will! What for? First, you think I'm a bomber, then you think I'm what? A murderer!? Under what power or act am I being held!?"

"Sir-" the Secret Service agent bristled.

We haven't got time for this, Alexa thought as she moved to the edge of the railing.

"Mr. Kendricks. What are you missing? It's important. Or it might be. Tell us now and maybe this goes away," she snapped.

"My yacht key!" Kendricks barked, turning to point down at the upturned leather sofa. "Look at this! Why would you do this? You could have just searched it – I gave you permission to search my rooms."

"Technically, sir, we only need Mr. Price's permission, not yours," Kage reminded him acidly, as Kendricks huffed and puffed.

Not helping, Alexa thought as she struggled to make sense of what was going on.

"You are being detained because you admitted that you were one of the last people to see Eva Montgomery (*if that was even her real name*) alive. That makes you a suspect. A suspect in a murder case, which means we have the right to hold you for up to twenty-four hours without charge. And that is even *before* we start talking about the recent state of emergency…" Alexa pointed out.

Which doesn't apply anymore, Alexa winced. *That was a temporary legal order, which is over now. We have to allow them to leave if they want… although no one could go anywhere in this storm, could they?*

"Preposterous! You've had it in for me from the beginning! You've completely ignored everything I've told you," Kendricks spat at them. The Secret Service agent standing right beside them started to loom, and Alexa was sure that he was going to force Kendricks down to his knees any moment if he didn't tone it down.

And yeah, maybe there was a part of me that didn't like you from the beginning, Alexa thought. She had reacted to Mr. Angry Hipster because of, well, his anger and his entitlement. But she hadn't been unfair to him, she didn't think.

"Then answer our questions. You claimed that Eva knew who the killer was. How? How do you know this? And no, I don't think we have your yacht key. Do we?" Alexa turned to look at Kage and the Service agent. She hadn't remembered any of them mentioning it in their evidence lists.

"Not that I know of," Kage shook his head.

"No, sir," the Service agent shook his head. "We take the chain of evidence very seriously, and we do not have such a thing in your belongings, Mr. Kendricks."

"Then what about my sofa here! What happened to it!?"

"Mr. Price's sofa," Kage corrected under his breath.

"Mr. Kendricks, we hadn't even begun doing a thorough sweep of your rooms yet," the Service agent replied, looking at him balefully.

"Lies!" Kendricks shouted back.

"*Wait!*" Alexa demanded. There was something here. A mystery.

"You said that your yacht key is gone and what, your rooms have been overturned?" she clarified.

"Well, duh, can you not see it? I thought you were the investigators!?" Kendricks said.

Yeah, charming, Alexa frowned.

"My key was there, in the sofa," Kendricks explained, outraged.

"Are you admitting to attempting to hide from us an important piece of evidence?" the Secret Service agent asked when Alexa cut him off.

"Your yacht key. Is that to this automated robo-yacht or whatever it was?" she said, as Kage nodded his agreement.

"Yes! Of course! There is only one *Azure Future!*" Kendricks fumed. "As soon as I realized that I was going to be allowed to leave, I wanted to recall it, knowing that it would automatically pilot itself over here, dock, and then I could get the hell away from all of this madness and on with the rest of my life!" Kendricks paused, his tone dropping to a sulky whisper.

"Only I can't, can I? Because it's not here. The key, which is the controller and the beacon at the same time, is gone."

"Someone stole it," Kage said.

Alexa felt the roar of hissing tinnitus in her ears once more. It was like a storm. A sea. But it wasn't as violent as what was outside. She had that vague, dizzying sensation that she got as if she had just jumped off of a carousel.

Too many moving parts. Too much stuff going on, and all of it out of my control.

The explosion. Eva's death.

Figuera.

Kendricks and his boat.

Eva being a reporter.

CIA assassinations…

But if someone really had indeed stolen Kendrick's yacht key, then it meant that they intended to use it, didn't they? Presumably to get away.

"You claimed that Eva knew who the killer was. Can you explain any of that right now? Right *now*, please. You may be saving lives if you tell us everything, and I mean *everything*." Alexa remained patient as the windows shuddered once again with a hammer of gale-force rain outside.

"I, uh…" At first, Eddie Kendricks tried to prevaricate; Alexa saw his eyes darting as he tried to come up with a suitable cover story, but Kage saw it, too.

"The facts, please. Just the facts," Kage growled, and Alexa saw Kendricks look between the big Japanese-American and herself, and then nod.

"Eva approached me. On the first night I got here. I thought she recognized me from the Kendricks Report, and that she wanted a bit of fun. It happens, you know…"

Oh god, please spare us the details, Alexa thought.

"Turns out she *did* recognize me, but she didn't want fun. She was a reporter. Freelance. Said that she was here to cover an important meeting, and that she was going to break a story that was bigger than God."

Alexa squinted. Her brain leaped from one clue to the next of what she already knew about Mr. Angry Hipster. He was a video streamer, too, so he likely thought he was providing a public service as well.

"And you thought you could what, team up? Join forces?" Alexa asked.

Eddie grimaced. "She saw that I had a whole lot more reach than she did. A way bigger platform. She thought I might be able to get her message out when she uncovered it."

"Uncovered what?" Kage asked.

"She said she was here to uncover some big meeting. A government conspiracy thing," Kendricks said. "But she wasn't expecting the explosion, and all of you showing up. That really shook her up."

"Go on," Alexa prompted.

Kendricks licked his lips, looked at the upturned sofa, and then back at them. There was a wobble in his voice, and Alexa realized just how scared he was. Petrified, in fact.

"She kept on talking to people. Asking questions, but not in your face. Piecing things together. She snooped. That's why we would meet up, why we met by the pool, and why I was supposed to go over to talk to her this evening when the cleaner had found her, found her…"

He couldn't say it, but Alexa did.

"Killed. Murdered. Eva Montgomery was murdered."

"Yes," Eddie confirmed shakily. "She told me that she had spoken to everyone and that she had worked out who the killer was. The one who set off the explosives. More than that, the one who'd made him. She'd seen the equipment, and she needed me to get the message out. I was coming to tell her that you still had my equipment anyway, but that you should be giving it back. I was going to offer to broadcast her report on my show, we'd both hit the roof in terms of viewings and rankings…"

"Wow," Kage muttered. "Don't you even care that a woman is dead? You only care about your damn internet rankings!?"

"No, uh, I, uh…" Kendricks stuttered. His earlier bluster had vanished, and in its stead, there was just fear and guilt.

"Who was it? Who did she say was behind all of this?" Alexa demanded.

Eddie looked at them both blankly.

"Staniforth. Saul Staniforth."

CHAPTER TWENTY-ONE

XXII. 8:40 PM

Saul Staniforth had rented out the rooms on the next floor up from the suites of rooms that Eva Montgomery and Eddie Kendricks had. Again, the floor above was palatial, with its own interior set not just of rooms but also of sauna blocks and private treatment rooms. Alexa was amazed that anyone even managed to get out of the resort at all, as every luxury appeared to be on hand and available to the high-paying, high-class resort guests.

"Is everyone in place?" Alexa whispered as she waited halfway up the stairs, with Kage right behind her, and then another FBI agent behind him. On the other side of the stairwell was another team of three, with two FBI agents and one Secret Service agent. This was all the agent power they had available at the moment, and they had to completely abandon the intense search and sweep in favor of this quick operation.

"We don't know if Eva had the right guy at all," Kage whispered to Alexa who nodded.

Yeah, I get that, but I have to take precautions, she thought, as she had been the one to call in all of the available officers to do this take as professionally as she could.

Because what if Eva had been right? That she had been able to uncover something that Alexa and Kage and the Secret Service, with all of their years of experience and skills, hadn't?

Right now, Cecil was working through the rest of Eva's tapes – which had been found secreted all around her room, presumably so that she could smuggle them out without them being detected, but Alexa knew that they couldn't wait to hear what they had to say. If Saul Staniforth was indeed behind all of this, then he had to be stopped. Now.

According to Eva, the very equipment needed to set off the bomb had been in Staniforth's room. In her estimation, he wasn't just the bomber – he'd made them, too. And though the only word they had to go on was that of a possibly unreliable, and very dead, reporter, Alexa knew they could no longer take any chances.

"We have to do this, Kage," Alexa breathed, and felt Kage shift behind her.

"Yeah," he said, although he didn't sound happy. They didn't have time to evacuate the resort. They were possibly about to lead a live-fire exercise right there in the resort's main building as outside a storm raged.

But we are skilled. We are trained. We know how to do this. I know how to do this, she told herself.

'*Sometimes you just have to trust your training.*' That was another phrase from her father. Alexa briefly wondered how he was doing, somewhere far away, wheezing and struggling around the house that he had built with his own hands.

Alexa felt the slight buzz and pressure in her ears, followed by the pounding of her heart. But no, she breathed through it. She had to focus. She would not let anyone die this time. She was in control.

Wasn't she?

"Okay, Team One?" she whispered, and the three agents on her right readied themselves, two men and one woman, and suddenly jogged up the last of the stairwell as fast as they could, stopping at the top as one of them peeled off down the wide corridor that led further into the building to head to the Lucas rooms, where they would knock on their door, and keep them inside their rooms for the duration of the proceedings. The other two moved slowly in the opposite direction, their service pistols held up as they aimed at Staniforth's door, crab-walking as they did so until they were just a few feet away, one man on one side, a woman on the other.

"Okay, it's us," she said, as she broke into a forward jog, wishing that she had paid more attention at Quantico, and had half of the equipment that you were supposed to have when it came to possible explosive encounters. Full riot shields. Blast shields, preferably – which were giant, human-sized slabs of metal with reinforced, bulletproof windows that you approached confined, possibly hazardous spaces with.

As it was, their amalgamated teams barely even had full body armor, just vests and a few helmets. The protection afforded to the meeting was supposed to be unobtrusive, and the FBI reinforcements had only brought their standard protective wear with them.

Alexa led the way, breaking into a fast-paced jog that moved them forward until she was in the middle, approaching the door head-on as Kage stood behind her, and the FBI agent behind him joined the agent to the left of the door.

"Alexa," Kage said, his hand lightly on her shoulder. Alexa knew what he was about to say even before he said it.

"I got this," she hissed, walking straight up to the door and raising the keycard that Bartholomew Price had given them...

And paused.

Her ears rang and hammered with the memory of an explosion that never fully went away. Her nose felt suddenly full of that thick, black, greasy smoke…

There was a light touch on her shoulder. It was Kage, gently but firmly reminding her. *You got this. I'm here.*

Alexa nodded. *Yes. I got this.* With her pistol up in one hand, she swiped the door lock at the side of Staniforth's room as the FBI agent to her left grabbed the handle and shoved the door open.

"FBI! On the floor!" Alexa shouted as the door swung open in front of her and, the way clear, she ran forward.

There was the hallway, similar to all the others in the complex, with an entrance to what should be a bathroom on one side, and a sleeping area on the next.

"Go! Go! Go!" Kage shouted as he followed just a step behind Alexa.

Blood pounded in Alexa's ears. Everything was movement and noise. She ignored the doors on either side as she made straight for the largest open area.

"Staniforth! On the ground! FBI!" she shouted as she knew the rest of the team behind her would be gathering at the various door openings. Ahead was the main lounge area. There was the railing that separated the small 'upper' from the recessed 'lower' part of the living room.

No one. He's not here. "Clear!" She was already bounding down the steps, heading toward the recessed area at the back of the room, sweeping her pistol across it as Kage turned to cover the far side of the room. The windows vibrated and hammered with the thunder of the rain outside.

Noise. Thunder. It filled Alexa's ears, threatening to overwhelm her as she spun around, but her eyes and mind were laser focused. Chairs. Sofa. Dining table. No people. No Saul Staniforth.

"Clear!" Kage called from his side of the room.

"Bathroom clear!" shouted one of the FBI agents from the room behind and above them.

"Bedroom-"

The two teams of two had approached the two remaining rooms, with one agent opening the door as the other barged inside, gun out.

The second team, the bedroom team, never got a chance to finish their report; as an explosion lifted them off their feet and slammed them into the opposite wall.

CHAPTER TWENTY-TWO

XXIII. 9:01 PM

"A LEXA."

Fire. Smoke. That same, greasy oil smell in the air. A wave of heat against her body, like a sudden, secondary, burning skin.

"Alexa!"

A terrible ringing in her ears. Too loud, the sound of the rain and the storm outside – no. It wasn't the storm. It was alarm bells, shouting at her, warning her, telling her that she had to get up; now!

"ALEXA!"

"Urgh?" Alexa opened her eyes to see the ceiling awash with black smoke and the sudden flashes of darting, brilliant reds.

She was on her back. Something sharp was cutting her cheek, and there was the shape of a man's head – Kage's – above her, looking down at her with a worried expression. She looked up at him as he opened his eyes and said something else, but she couldn't make it out. She couldn't hear what he was saying as her ears betrayed her like a faulty switch on a stereo, at one time filtering out just the top notes, or then going quiet altogether, to suddenly come rushing back to life.

"Alexa, I'm getting you up. You're okay. You're going to be okay," he continued, which Alexa thought was a little rich coming from him, as half of his face was smeared with black soot and dust.

Even though her ears rang and her heart was pounding, she wasn't confused. She knew where she was, and she knew instantly what had happened.

It was an explosion. It was Staniforth, the middle-aged widower all along. He was the one who had planted the explosives, and he was almost certainly the one who had killed Eva Montgomery when she had deduced what he had done and why he was here.

He's probably the one who stole Eddie Kendrick's yacht key, too, Alexa thought as her brain caught up with her body. She was in pain, and it was everywhere, but it wasn't bad. Her body ached, as she had been thrown halfway across the room.

Wham. Suddenly, everything went into normal time as Alexa's adrenaline kicked in. The room they were in was on fire, and there was black smoke billowing out of the hallway toward them, as well as little gusts of flames. As she looked up, she saw a small river of fire race above her head, lick the molded plaster of the ceiling, and head toward the smashed window that occupied one full side of the suite. The glass had been blown out, and it revealed a scene that was equally as dark and apocalyptic. There were rolls of dirty, sand-colored clouds low overhead, and there were driving winds and rain hitting the resort and the room she was in. She could see the palm trees below waving in the winds, just as there was a swirl of air, and another whoosh of flame tore across the ceiling and out.

"The others!" Alexa said as panic spiked through her. Kage was already helping her to her feet, keeping one strong arm on her shoulders to keep her bent over and protected from the noxious smoke all around.

I didn't see it coming. I didn't see the explosion. I should have known. Kage was leading her back toward the stairs up to the hallway, through the smoke, and through the spurts of flames.

"I think most made it out. I don't know. One got hit," Kage commented as he hunkered, waiting for a moment by the stairs as there was another sudden flash of flames.

"We have to get out. Evacuate the resort!" Kage shouted before suddenly doubling over into a coughing fit.

How could I not prepare!? People could be dead because of me!

"Alexa, keep it together, keep close, right behind me!" Kage yelled out, his large hand holding hers in a vice-like, iron grip.

But before he could lunge forward, there was another sound in the smoke. A strangled cry.

"The bathroom! There's people in the bathroom!" Alexa relayed, tearing her hand from her partner's as she suddenly launched herself forward, leaping the steps to the landing as a wave of hot, heavy smoke hit her...

And she turned left, keeping her head down and one hand out as she slapped the wall, found the doorway, and threw herself into it.

"Alexa!" There was a shout from behind her, but Alexa felt disoriented. The bathroom was also full of smoke. She couldn't see anything for a moment but felt the crunch of debris on the floor.

And then a startled moan as she saw shapes moving. There was a hunkered-over FBI agent, and he was hauling at another shape that was folded against the far wall.

The door. I'm walking on the door. Alexa realized that the explosion must have blown the door and the teams into here, or some of them, at least, as she skidded over to their side, half holding a sleeve over her mouth.

"I got him! Get out. Turn left – turn left!" she shouted, grabbing at the more mobile one of the guards, as she shoved him back toward the bathroom opening.

"Alexa, we have to – *yech!*" There was a sudden hacking cough as Kage caught the man, shoved him toward the opening, and appeared through the smoke.

"Here. One's unconscious. I don't know where the others are." Alexa was coughing as she grabbed the FBI agent under his arms and started to lift him up. He was heavy, and somehow his unconsciousness only made him all the heavier, like a sack of potatoes.

Heat was battering against her skin, and her eyes were streaming from the smoke, as Kage slid to the other side, putting the man's unresponsive arm over his shoulders as he seized the other side of him.

"We can do this!" Alexa hissed, taking a struggling step forward, and then another, and another toward the torn-open bathroom doorway.

Whoosh.

Another wave of red burst out through the hallway, followed by a belch of greasy black smoke.

I should have seen it coming. I didn't do anything. I failed them. Alexa's heart was hammering and her ears ringing so she couldn't even hear the roar of the fire or the storm outside anymore. Was she carrying a dead man, or did she feel some movement from his body?

No matter. No one left behind. No one.

They reached the doorway, rocking in place as more waves of heat and smoke hit them. How bad was it? It was impossible to tell, and Alexa's eyes were stinging so much that she had to feel the door jamb with her shoulder and slide along it, as Kage staggered on the other side of their charge.

"S'not far!" Alexa managed to call out before doubling over into a coughing fit. She took a staggering step forward, and then another, and another. Either time itself was slowing down, or the hallway that led back to the main landing of the resort was far longer than she had thought.

It's just the smoke. Keep on going.

Alexa tried to take small sips of breath, but it wasn't doing any good. Every breath she took burned, and each one didn't feel like oxygen at all, rather it was like breathing syrup. She coughed and hacked as spots appeared before her vision, and her ears rang with thunder.

Take a step. Another.

She could feel shaking beside her. Kage was almost doubled over, hacking; she grabbed onto his wrist behind the back of the unconscious man and squeezed, feeling his hand squeeze hers back. They took another lunging step forward, another…

And suddenly there were hands on her shoulders, dragging her forward and out of the chaos into the bright hallway. The FBI agent that they had been holding was taken from her hands as Alexa collapsed to the floor.

"Keep on moving, keep going, down the stairs, here!" someone was shouting in her ear, and she felt rough hands grabbing her own as she was half pushed, half prodded to stumble down the stairs to the next floor before being half carried to one of the side walls.

Something wet and cold was pressed to her face, and at first, she sputtered, shaking her head away, until her body reacted before her mind did, her arms reaching up to grasp at the wet flannel as she held it over her mouth for a second, and then rubbed her eyes and face and lips of the soot.

"The others. How bad?" she choked out but didn't get far as she broke into a series of hacking, wet-sounding coughs.

"Don't try to talk. Standard smoke inhalation. Just stay still, and try to breathe slowly and regularly," the voice instructed, and to her surprise, she saw that it was one of the guests, Maria Luca, who was crouching by her side and pressing a bottle of water into her hands before unscrewing another to start dribbling it over her exposed arms and neck. There were bodies moving around them, and she recognized Kage come stumbling to the other side of the landing, half in the arms of one of the resort staffers, and Marinsburg running up past them with a fire extinguisher in hand.

"It's not a large fire! Control it! Dampen the corridor!" he shouted as he disappeared into the smoke-filled level above.

"The others," Alexa breathed once more, but Maria shook her head.

"I don't know, I don't know," she repeated, keeping her cool remarkably well as she helped Alexa out of her bulletproof vest and shirt, replacing it with an over-large white tee, but not before she splattered her skin with more bottled water. Alexa felt no embarrassment as her head was still ringing with the recent explosion, and Kage on the other side of them appeared to have other things on his mind, like throwing off his hot and scalded outer vest himself.

There was shouting and running from upstairs, and it seemed like Marinsburg had effectively taken charge of the situation, but there was also a commotion downstairs, as Alexa could hear Bartholomew Price shouting.

"Follow procedure! Everyone to the front of the building!"

Followed by another shout, this time from Eddie Kendricks. "There's a storm out there, man! Are you stupid!?"

"He's trying to evacuate," Alexa coughed, realizing that for once, it seemed that Eddie Kendricks was in fact right. They couldn't evacuate out there, where the resort palm trees were at risk of snapping.

"The staff block and the private lodges," Kage wheezed. "They're separate from the resort building. They'll be fine." He struggled to his feet as Maria made a sudden angered, rasping noise.

"You shouldn't move! You got smoked!"

"Ma'am, I have to," Kage coughed, leaning against the wall as he wobbled a little on his feet and nodded once to Alexa. It was a look that said, *I have to do this.*

"You good?" Alexa wheezed.

Kage nodded once again, and then turned and jog-stumbled down the steps toward the ground floor, where the shouting continued.

"The others, I have to help!" Alexa was similarly trying to raise herself, as another of the resort staffers raced up past them with another fire extinguisher, but Maria shoved her back down to a seat with a surprisingly firm hand.

"Uh-uh! You're not going anywhere! You *have* to rest. You have to clear your lungs of the smoke!" she said firmly, and Alexa realized that she didn't have that much strength to argue.

Her head was spinning, and her ears were once again filled with noise as she alternated between sips of water and sips of air. Her mouth burned, as did her lungs, but it was getting better, she was sure of it.

"There! Don't go in! Fire from the doorway!"

She could hear Marinsburg's voice from above them, as well as more stifled cries and running feet.

How bad was it up there? She had no idea. She had gone in with six, and she knew that four agents at least had made it out. What had happened to the other two?

"One of your agents came to us to hold me and Antonio in our rooms," Maria explained matter-of-factly as she looked pensively above them. "Of course, we were annoyed, but we didn't want to bother. No one was going anywhere with this storm anyway. But then there was this almighty bang. We thought it was the storm, maybe the resort had been hit by lightning... but then we smelled smoke. How are you feeling now?" Maria asked. The woman's eyes were a clear, piercing blue, and she reminded Alexa of a teacher. Professional, perfunctory.

"Okay," Alexa croaked, although it still hurt to speak. The voices above them were becoming more and more muffled, and Alexa figured that they must be making their way into Staniforth's rooms, using the fire extinguishers. She didn't remember seeing a sprinkler system, but there was a definite moisture in the air, and the walls behind her were damp.

"Our Service agent ran at the first smell of smoke, telling us to make our way downstairs, but I've had paramedic training. I only did it to have something to do in retirement, and it was a long time ago, but we agreed – me and Antonio – that I could help here. That was pretty much when you turned up," she concluded, offering Alexa another skeptical look and a small, tight smile.

"You have a little color in you now, although that could be scalding, I guess. Can you stand? We'll head downstairs now to the others. See if that fool Price has come up with a plan."

This is all my fault, the thought hammered into Alexa with all the weight of a juggernaut.

Of course, she knew that wasn't true. She knew that it was shock from the explosion and the fire – *the trap that Staniforth had set.* It was classic post-traumatic stress 101, which she had learned about a hundred times at Quantico.

1. During times of high conflict and threat, the body reacts faster than the mind.

2. *The mind tries to assess and understand the threat, and often comes up short.*

3. *You need to TRAIN so that your BODY knows what to do, and you reduce your THINKING.*

There. It was a fairly straightforward way of looking at the fact that Alexa had been suddenly faced with immediate, imminent death and danger to her and her partner while there was nothing she could have done about it.

But there were things, weren't there? I KNEW Staniforth was an arsonist, at the very least. OF COURSE he had laid a trap!

But as much as Alexa told herself that she didn't know, couldn't know, and that they had been going to apprehend him based on hearsay and opinion (Eddie Kendricks' opinion, at that), it still didn't matter to her critical, adrenaline-filled brain.

I should have taken precautions. I should have radioed the mainland and called for reinforcements. A proper explosives squad…

Of course, that probably wouldn't have stopped the explosion anyway.

"Hang on," Alexa muttered to herself as Maria helped her to her feet, and started to hurry down the wide, carpeted stairs.

"I got you," Maria countered as she held onto Alexa's elbow, and mistakenly thought that Alexa was talking to her. She wasn't.

"Staniforth wasn't in there, was he?" Alexa mumbled as Maria startled a little, probably out of fear at the idea that there could be a dangerous killer in their midst.

"That was a diversion, a tactic," she continued. Staniforth was, if their theory was correct after all, a thorough, consummate professional. He had managed to conceal his first bomb so well, it was no surprise he'd be able to do it again.

"If it was Staniforth, then he came here early, he got the job done. Then stuck around, knowing that all hell would break loose ..." Alexa muttered to herself as her mind battled the fogs of smoke and the roar of tinnitus.

At her side, Maria abruptly stopped. "I, I beg your pardon?"

Damn, Alexa shook her head. The smoke must have affected her more than she had thought. She was talking the case with a civilian!

"It doesn't matter. Please, just make sure you are safe," Alexa said to her as she stood up a little taller, realizing that it was *she* who had a responsibility toward Maria, not the other way around.

"Agent Landers!" There was a call from behind them, and the pair turned to see none other than Cecil Pinkerton, his face smeared with soot and black smoke, and his normally crisp blue shirt equally as rent and torn. His arms were wrapped in the white towels of the resort, both of which looked grubby and smeared with black. For some reason, Alexa was startled to see him so actively involved.

"Pinkerton?" Alexa gulped air as she nodded.

Pinkerton's face was grave, but his news was good.

"We're lucky. Very lucky. The fire is contained within the guest bedroom, but the scene is ruined as far as CSI is concerned. Not without an intensely thorough investigation, which will take weeks to fully process. You will want to know, though, that Ms. Montgomery appeared to be correct. Not only have we recovered the remnants of the trigger device for the helipad bomb, but several documents and chemicals and other items that line up-"

"Hold on, what are you saying? Staniforth built the bomb, too?"

Cecil nodded. "We'll have to do much more testing and investigation, but this appears to be the case. Saul Staniforth had the equipment in that room to make a bomb with that exact signature."

He rattled on some more specifics about the specific chemicals and mechanical components they'd found that could only match up to the specific signature of the bomber that had eluded the FBI and ATF for so long. The man still had a way of going into detail, despite the near-death experience that everyone had just gone through.

"Our men?" Alexa asked immediately, for Pinkerton to make small, calming motions with his hands.

"One is badly injured, burns and a broken arm, but no one is dead. The blast, as far as I can see, was intended to cause flames, not to destroy the resort," Pinkerton explained.

"Where are they? Our people?" Alexa asked as Pinkerton pointed ahead of her down the stairs.

"In one of the ground floor massage rooms, doubling up as a medical space. We'll be able to keep them safe and stable until we get them on a boat to the mainland."

For a moment, Alexa was insanely thankful to Pinkerton for his apparent cool head and clear thinking. She couldn't quite believe how much had happened, and she was aware of this itchy, nervy feeling running through her aching limbs as she was still hyped on adrenaline and still expecting danger.

Which there very well could be, she thought, before coughing and wheezing as Maria firmed up her grip on Alexa's elbow.

Staniforth was still out there. That trap was just a distraction. He had been expecting to wait out the inevitable investigation and then – and then do precisely this. Create a distraction while he…

"Got off the island!" Alexa suddenly said, as she immediately knew what was happening here. "Staniforth stole the yacht key, didn't he? That means he must have a way to recall the boat."

Yes, Alexa's fast, adrenaline thoughts could see it now. Staniforth might even have thought that he could wait out the entire investigation, but she had started to order the room sweeps, and that had forced his hand. And Staniforth must have known that Eva was on to him, which was why he had to act. He had to kill her, which would bring entirely too much scrutiny on the resident guests here. It was only a matter of time before Alexa and Kage would have narrowed down the suspects, so

Staniforth acted now. Using the storm as further cover, knowing that everyone would be everywhere.

She looked at her watch to see that its face was cracked from where she had hit the floor, but the numbers were still legible. It was already nearly ten in the evening.

Eva Montgomery had been killed just past six, and the yacht key could have been stolen at any time.

"How far is it to the mainland? By sea?" Alexa asked as she hurried down the steps as fast as she could, her lungs feeling like they were on fire.

"Really, you *have* to take it easy!" Maria Luca called after her as she followed the steps to the main lobby area to see that it was empty, but there was a sound of voices from the other side of the building.

Kage took them away from the fire. He was trying to evacuate them. Alexa started forward, toward the main reception room, past the dining room, to see that in the conservatory room at the rear of the building, there was a gathered collection of people, almost all of them staffers, apart from Antonio Luca and Eddie Kendricks.

"I'm telling you, this is ridiculous. What if a tree comes in through that glass! I don't want to survive getting burned alive just to get my head chopped off!" the tech bro was demanding. Meanwhile, Bartholomew Price was trying to make small, soothing gestures.

"We can, uh, we can go for the staff block. I'm sure we can accommodate everyone."

"Fire's under control, people," Alexa wheezed as she entered the conservatory to suddenly be hit by a wave of dizziness. She stumbled, but Maria was there to grab her and steady her to the nearest chair.

"It's over? It doesn't sound over!" Kendricks contradicted as the masses of assembled staffers looked nervously between their employer Price and Kage, then Alexa. It was clear to everyone that they were scared. Terrified, but Alexa had to hope that Price at least knew what he was doing. Or would stand up for his own employees.

Who was she kidding?

"Then. Then we stay here! Everything will look much better in the morning, I promise you! This is nothing that we can't sort out, together!" Price blubbered frantically. Alexa wondered if he was still just trying to preserve his resort reviews, as this was very clearly beginning to look like the worst vacation for anyone, ever.

"Mr. Price, I would suggest a full evacuation of the resort in the morning, as soon as the storm has passed and it is safe to travel," Pinkerton commented rather severely.

There was a ragged cheer from at least some of the workers (and Eddie Kendricks, who was the loudest supporter of this idea). But Price was still desperate.

"No! A partial refund for all guests remaining! I'll cover your losses! All staff will get double time if they stay and help clean up," Price blustered, but it was clear to everyone that he had lost it, as angry shouts quickly broke out.

"There's no way in hell that I am staying here a minute longer than I have to!" Kendricks swore. "How many murders have we had!? As soon as the weather clears, I'm ..."

You're probably going nowhere, Alexa thought as she beckoned to Kage to come over before turning to Pinkerton.

"Cecil? I shouldn't be asking you this, it's not your job; but can you do what you can here? Smooth things over?" Alexa asked. "I need to talk to Kage. Time is running out, and I am certain that our suspect has already escaped..."

Cecil Pinkerton blinked. "You are not suggesting that I try to hold them all? We don't have the staff, at least."

"No," Alexa shook her head quickly, coming to a last-minute decision. "We don't have the staff. We need reinforcements, but no one is going to be making it over tonight, I'd imagine. These people, the staff, the guests, they've suffered enough. There's been two explosions and now four deaths. They're free to go at first light if they can," Alexa said, admitting defeat in that regard, at least. "Just ... try to keep them from biting each other's heads off."

"Now that I definitely can't guarantee," he said with a wry chuckle. "But I'll try."

"Thanks. We'll contact FBI headquarters, get as many people here as we can. We'll continue the investigation, evidence gathering even without anyone else on the island. We'll have to follow up the interviews in the later days, but first ..." Alexa turned to Kage, who was looking at her with his deep, harrowed eyes.

"Staniforth," Kage said, and Alexa nodded.

"Yes. Staniforth." Her eyes moved to where Kendricks was still trying to argue with Price.

"We're going to have to know everything we can about that robo-boat. It might be too late already, but the storm outside is harsh. It's wild. If we're lucky, then Staniforth is holed up on the island somewhere, and he's going to make a run for it as soon as the wind drops."

Kage turned to look out of the dark glass at the storm raging outside. The sky was dark, and there was no sign of the stars overhead, as the clouds were so thick.

"If he took a boat out in this, he'd be a fool, don't you think?" he murmured.

Maybe not a fool, Alexa thought in response. *Maybe desperate.*

CHAPTER
TWENTY-THREE

XXIV. 10:55 PM

"Y OU'RE TELLING ME THAT YOU HAVE A WAY TO TRACK your boat?" Kage mentioned as they sat, huddled around the small laptop in Bartholomew's office at the resort. Kage sat at the desk, while Alexa leaned against the window frame, and Eddie Kendricks stood in the middle of the room, looking distracted, exhausted, and panicked.

Some of the fight had gone out of him since his argument with Price earlier. Which was understandable, as some of the fight had gone out of everyone once the fire had actually been put out.

There was clearly an understandable sense of panic throughout the building, however, Alexa noted. Those who had suffered burns – all of them FBI agents – were being treated in one of the massage rooms, which Pinkerton had converted into a haphazard field medical station. Maria Luca had signed up to help with minor wound care and provide endless cups of tea and coffee, but it was still a surreal experience.

The Coast Guard isn't playing tonight, Alexa thought, ticking off the assets they had at their disposal. The storm was so powerful that they had listed an alert for all boats in or near the coast and were only going to respond to life-threatening emergencies. As such, when Alexa had just gotten off the phone with them, they had admitted that they were already busy dealing with a few late-comer fishing trawlers further out in the Florida Bay area, and so would not be able to provide 'policing duties' to the island.

Not even if there is one of the FBI's most wanted criminals trying to escape over the water? Alexa once again seethed quietly. It was frustrating, but she forced herself to calm down. The Coast Guard was doing their job. She just had to do hers.

Which, right now, was trying to work out everything they could about Eddie Kendricks's boat, and how Staniforth might have used it to escape.

"I've already called Chief Williams," Alexa murmured as she returned to the laptop. "I've given him as much information about Saul Staniforth that we know; he says that he'll alert all local law enforcement."

The question was whether Staniforth had already successfully left the island or not. Eva's murder had been the perfect cover, and it had happened hours ago, almost five hours ago now. Considering that the strip of water between St. Martin's and the mainland was so small, then Kendricks could already be three or four hours up the coast and halfway to Atlanta for all Alexa knew.

But Eva was killed right before the storm hit, and it was already hitting hard. Staniforth would have been crazy to travel then, wouldn't he?

"Yeah, of course, there's a way to track my boat!" Kendricks responded half-heartedly, with just a ghost of his earlier curmudgeon. He was tired. Everyone was tired. The entire second and third floors of the resort were now declared 'off limits' by Price, Pinkerton and Marinsburg (the latter two who were apparently forming a de facto emergency response situation).

Pinkerton had *estimated* that no serious structural damage had been done, as the device that Staniforth had set had been more smoke and less heat, but Alexa could still feel the anxiety rippling through the entire resort. Or who was left, which amounted to just four actual guests, about fifteen agents of various agencies (the vast majority being FBI), and about another dozen staffers. All of the various people had been allocated floor space on the other side of the resort building, or in spare rooms in the staffer block and the private lodges. Alexa was frustrated that their secure hold of the situation had crumbled, with people coming and going through the doors back and forth from their rooms – braving the storm to do it – but she had no choice.

They had been lucky. The thunderstorm and the broken windows had effectively dampened Staniforth's ruined rooms, flooding the largest area with moisture, and containing much of the heat.

We just have to get through until morning, Alexa told herself. It was already eleven, and the storm – just in her opinion alone, anyway – didn't sound as harsh as it had earlier.

Which made finding Kendrick's robo-yacht that much more important, clearly.

"I don't have the key, which acts as a transponder as well, but I have an app. You'll have to let me have my phone back," Kendricks explained, which was what Alexa had anticipated. She nodded to Kage, who brought out Kendrick's phone from one of Bartholomew Price's drawers. It was a super-large and super-thin black plastic affair, and when Eddie turned it on it immediately started pinging with alerts.

"Ah, that'll be the Report alerts. I have a lot of people worrying about my safety..." Kendricks muttered as he flipped and swiped through his phone, and Kage got ever more irritated.

"Mr. Kendricks, we thank you for your *urgent* cooperation," Alexa heard him say, as she tried to figure out if the storm had picked up, or if it was just her ears.

"Right, sorry. Look..."

The tech magnate turned his phone to where there was a blue and indigo app screen with *Azure Safe Systems* written across the top.

"Might want to choose a better name for your app," Alexa murmured.

"Huh? What?" Kendricks didn't see it, but Alexa just shook her head. There was no time anyway.

"Never mind. So this thing can track your boat. Where is it?" she asked, as Kendricks opened up the app to where its landing page showed a picture of quite a small but high-tech boat in a mixture of blues and greens and whites. The prow was unnecessarily high, Alexa thought, and she would know, as someone who'd spent her life on boats.

But it was smart, Alexa could see. She saw at once that it was really a souped-up motorboat, not a yacht at all. So typical of Kendricks to boast about things being bigger than they really were. Although this picture did include some sails. She figured that it must be a dual-purpose vessel with the ability to self-power as well as have a sail put up if you switched to manual.

"She's just a thirty-footer, so not big at all, but she's the first of her kind," Kendricks described lovingly.

"Her location please, Mr. Kendricks," Kage said in a tad sharper tone than was strictly necessary.

"Right. Of course. She should be at the marina in Sarasota," Kendricks relayed, swiping out of the picture to suddenly visibly startle.

"No! But. Look – it's not there! That damn rat must have activated the recall on the yacht key," Kendricks said in horror. "I should never have tied it to an Internet of Things network. Ridiculous idea. Should have kept it shortwave, Bluetooth at the most..." Gone were his earlier outbursts of rage and entitlement, as if the act of someone actually besting him at his own game –

technology – had suddenly shown him exactly the nature of the awful threat against them all.

"Does it say when it left? When the key was used?" Alexa asked quickly.

"Not without getting into the actual database. And I can't do that from here; I need my workstation, which is back home, so I could find the log times, but he's got my boat *now!*" Kendricks exclaimed.

"But does he, though?" Kage had left his seat to move around the desk and peer over their shoulders.

"You said this yacht key had a transponder, right?" he asked as Kendricks's mind leaped easily to what Kage was trying to get to.

"The key does, and so does the *Azure*, too. It was designed so I would never lose it, and I never figured that some insane person would steal it…" Kendricks related, swiping through the apps until he came to a page where there looked to be a grayed-out search map with a squiggly, thick red line navigating between the two places.

"The *Azure*'s on the move! It's already left Sarasota and is on its way over here, to the island!" Kendricks exclaimed – a fact that didn't surprise Alexa in the slightest.

"But where is the other end of it? The key!?" Alexa hissed.

"Uh, here…" Kendricks expanded the map on his screen, showing where there was a grayed-out sea, and a slightly different green for a land mass, which Alexa guessed must be the island of St. Martin's itself.

"He's at the other end of the island. The far end," Kage said immediately, already standing a little taller, looking at the windows. The rain was still coming down pretty hard out there, and the wind was still howling, but it wasn't as gale-force as it had been.

"Can we get there in time?" Alexa asked aloud. She was dreading having to run across the entire five or six miles of the island, in the dark, in the middle of a storm, and with such little sleep herself but she would. She would without a shadow of a doubt.

"The *Azure* will get there in about twelve minutes, at the rate it's going," Kendricks said, his face alarmed as he stared at the map in his hands, possibly more terrified that his beloved toy was about to be hijacked.

"Twelve minutes?" Alexa shook her head. "We'll never get there in time."

"The resort has little buggies, carts," Kage suddenly said.

"But how fast do they go, ten miles an hour?" Alexa gritted her teeth and groused in rage. "And that's hoping there's no trees down on the paths…"

"Or flooding," Kage pointed out, as he looked warily at the windows being battered by heavy sheets of water.

"We need to get the Coast Guard. Even if they're not doing 'policing actions' we need them. We notify the PD at the mainland." Alexa tried to think it through. They were close. So close to catching him. How could they be so close and yet so far away!?

"We use the buggies. But I know an even quicker way to get to the other side of the island," Kage cut in, as his face suddenly lit up as he turned to Alexa.

"You said your Pops was a Navy man. Does that mean you know how to use a motorboat? Because Figuera left one sitting in that old boat shed, just waiting to be used."

Alexa gulped.

"It's been a long time since I piloted a boat, Kage," she smiled as she was already reaching for her jacket on the back of a chair – and her pistol.

CHAPTER
TWENTY-FOUR

XXV. 11:45 PM

We'll never make it. We'll never make it in time!

ALEXA'S HEART WAS HAMMERING IN LINE WITH HER thoughts as she jogged along the track that led up to Figuera's boat shed. Around them, the storm raged; the sky was pitch black and the edges of the raised track thrashed with the dark silhouettes of trees. And there was so much rain. A constant hammering blow of rain hit her cheeks and the back of her neck no matter how she tried to turn away from the wind.

I thought the storm was supposed to be stopping? Alexa thought as another gust hit her, pushing her skittering steps across the wet and sodden path. This part of the island hadn't flooded, not yet, but from the glimmers of water through the dark undergrowth all around, Alexa was sure that it would happen soon.

There was a small sound up ahead of her, carried on the flurries of the storm-ridden night, and Alexa saw Kage skidding to one side, and then leaping wildly over a dark shadow in the road, where a heavy branch of one of the trees must have come down.

Only then it moved, and Alexa realized that it wasn't a tree.

The far end of the creature raised and thumped against the ditch to the right of the path, as the near end, the part that Kage had jumped over, suddenly swung upward and around as it looked at what had crossed it.

Its head was a long, spear-like wedge, and the moment that it opened its jaws, Alexa could see the glint of dirty yellow fangs.

Alligator! Only it was a big one. A *real* big one, Alexa thought. Or maybe it was a crocodile. Either way, she had no idea, and it was too late to do anything about it as she was only a couple of yards away herself. The thought flashed through her head to reach for her gun, to scare the creature off that had obviously ventured further inland as it escaped the storm.

"Alexa, jump!" The wind carried Kage's voice clearer back toward her, and she saw the large head of the beast swinging toward her.

How big was it? Seven feet? Eight?

Time seemed to slow as Alexa took a long, lunging step, felt her boot hit the wet, slick gravel and mud path as she kicked out, and her boot started to slip on the treacherous land. Everything was so waterlogged, she was losing her balance.

Alexa kicked outward, performing a ragged but high hurdle vault over the creature to land, skidding on the far side, and quickly continued running, almost toppling over as she skidded and splashed, and Kage grabbed her elbow and tugged her forward. She heard a crash behind her and hissed. Gators could be fast, couldn't they? At least that was what everyone told her. If you see one and it's active, don't go near it. Most of the time they were sleepy or tired, but if it was moving, just back away.

Alexa and Kage ran in wild, flailing steps as they tried not to fall over. At any moment, Alexa expected to feel the clamp of massive jaws on her calves, but none came.

"It's okay – it's okay!" Kage wheezed as he slid to a halt, catching one of the overhanging tree branches to stop himself from falling over as Alexa did the same, turning to see the last section of midnight shadow, the rear few feet of the creature's tail, slinking into the undergrowth. Obviously, the storm was too much for it. It would rather find somewhere out of the wind than have the bother of hunting fresh meat tonight.

Thank goodness, Alexa sighed, turning to look at Kage. He was as soaked as she was, and it was almost getting hard to see, the rain was so constant.

"Was this a good idea!?" She had to shout, but she already knew the answer. Staniforth was out there, and she had demanded that Kendricks keep an eye on his robo-yacht app and update them on where he was. She paused, gasping for breath as she fumbled her phone out of her pocket, its black screen instantly cascading with water as she juggled with the touch screen to find his latest message.

Eddie Kendricks: Azure slowing thanks to storm – BETTER NOT SINK MY BOAT! Arriving North tip of island in 7...

When did he send the message? Alexa checked. "Six minutes!" she shouted at Kage, who nodded but didn't attempt to say anything. In his off-hand, he held one of the thin security flashlights of the FBI and waved it through the heavy rains up ahead.

Turning, Alexa saw it glimmer on something between the trees. The edge of the boat shed, the same one that Figuera had been planning his own getaway from, and with the tatters of FBI warning tape streaming from its locked doors.

"Keys!" she shouted, knowing that Price had given Kage the set of keys for the lock that the FBI had insisted be affixed onto the shed after they had taken their evidence out.

Alexa checked her watch. Midnight was coming soon, and with it, the start of the third day of the investigation.

A river of unease added to her own previous tide of anxieties and frustrations, as Alexa knew that the longer and longer that an investigation continued, the worse their chances for a conviction became. There was a 'hot' period after any initial crime, when all was confusion, and then discovery, and the culprits could very easily make a mistake as the law enforcement agencies closed in. As they entered day three, they were starting to come out of that hot period.

Apart from the fact that, y'know, we have the culprit. We have circumstantial evidence against him from Eva's tape and Eddie's commentary. We just need to catch him.

All of this could soon be over. She tried not to think exactly why Staniforth had committed the crime. That would shake out in the later statements and investigations. Right now, she needed to stop a man who had already killed at least once.

"Damnit! The key!" Kage smacked his forehead.

No, please don't say… Alexa was already turning, but it was clear from the way that Kage was frantically turning out his pockets what had happened.

"The gator. It must have fallen out when I jumped it!" he said sheepishly, already half turning back toward where the road was pitch black, sodden, and wet.

"Don't!" Alexa yelled at him quickly. "We don't have time. And besides, I don't want you getting eaten!"

Kage looked about to say that he had no intention of being eaten, but Alexa was already running toward the old boat shed. Its sides were old, rusted corrugated metal, and she could clearly see gaps where the door and the walls didn't quite fit anyway.

Wisps of FBI security tape fluttered and snapped in the air where the storm had torn and pulled them apart. Alexa could see the lock, and she already had her heavy pistol in hand.

"Back behind me!" Alexa demanded as she took aim and then fired. The gun retort was loud, and it took two shots to buckle and destroy the handle that the lock was affixed to, and a further several hammers with the butt of her pistol to break it free from the door.

Got it.

The door swung open wildly as the winds outside pushed it, and Alexa hurried Kage inside, for their feet to suddenly splash in water.

In the center of the boat shed was supposed to be a gulley of water, with two thin wooden walkways running up the insides of the building, toward the open end of the shed where it led straight out into open water.

But the walkways were covered with a couple inches of water, and the boat moored in the center was rocking and knocking against the walkways with each surge and push of the wild waves beyond.

"It's clogged," Kage stated, his light illuminating where a tangle of mangrove branches and storm blow had gathered at the mouth of the boat shed. He instantly splashed forward on the right-hand scaffolding, grabbed one of the long wooden boat hooks that still hung from the wall, and started to stab and poke at the water to pull things aside, as Alexa jumped into the boat.

This is bad. There's no way anyone should be going out in this. She eyed the black waters and black skies through the shed entrance. There were sudden glimmers of light as the waves crested, rising high before crashing down once again, and everywhere, the rain and the wind.

"You got this?!" Kage shouted, and Alexa wasn't entirely sure if that was meant to be a question or a statement, but she nodded.

I hope.

The boat itself was little more than a four-to-six-person motorboat, no cover, no top, just an outboard motor and a small stand-up area behind a screen with a pilot's wheel. It was the sort of boat that was built for summery days and speedily skipping across flat oceans as you played loud music and partied with

---

friends. It was a toy, or at least that was what her father would have called it.

"Not a proper boat. A toy boat..." Alexa could almost hear his assessment in the back of her mind as she ran through the checks.

They had the key that they had taken from Figuera, so thankfully Alexa wouldn't have to hot wire it (which was also a skill that she had but hadn't done since she was seventeen and sneaking off in one of her father's smaller boats. *That* had earned her a whole lot of trouble and almost an entire summer grounded, she remembered).

The fact was that Alexa was born into a naval family, and she was one of the lucky ones. Her father hadn't just become a Navy man because of the job security and the career progression, but because he had been a sailor first and had loved the sea. Still did, and he had tried in Alexa and Jake's early years to instill into them that same love – or at least familiarity – with the oceans as well.

For the Landers family, it meant that their summers were mostly spent on the Virginia coasts or lakes or rivers, on a variety of small boats that her father and mother had variously rented or owned over the years. Alexa could never claim to be a 'good' sailor, but she knew her way around. She had always taken more of an interest in her physical training than in learning the ways of the sea, but she was no slouch. Better than her brother, who had seen boats mostly as a way to look good and impress others.

"Only a fool goes out in a storm..."

Another sage piece of advice from her dad, but one that was quickly followed up with, *"but sometimes storms blow up out of nowhere and you got no choice but to just get along and go through it. Which is why we're taking the boat out today..."*

She had been fifteen when her father had introduced her to 'storm riding.' He had already known that there was a fairly moderate storm blowing up out of the east and had taken their fifteen-footer out early to catch the early squalls, and he had taken Alexa with him, despite her protest.

"If there's a storm, I just won't go out! Or I'll cut the engine and hunker down!" Alexa remembered arguing as she moved around the boat, checking the oil level to see that it was good (Figuera had

RESORT TO KILL

at least filled up his possible escape boat before using it, which she could not be more thankful for).

"*And if you do that, you'll be sure to capsize and be found a hundred days later, washed up in some fish hole in Maine!*" Her father had laughed cheerily, not even regarding the heavy gray clouds that were gathering on the nearby horizon.

"*A dead boat – one without its engine – is just flotsam on an unsteady sea. Remember that, kiddo. You're just as likely to be killed being tossed about inside as you are springing a leak and sinking that way. No. In wild waters, you have to maintain power, and you have to use the waves as best you can.*"

Alexa remembered the time that followed as harrowing and terrifying to her fifteen-year-old self as she had climbed waves that had to be at least twenty feet high, and then dropped down their far side at angles that saw her looking directly at the sea.

Maybe it wasn't that bad. Alexa was sure that her youthful naivety and her imagination had made the experience far worse than it ever had been, and she was sure that her father would never have risked her life so recklessly; but she remembered her feeling of elation and woozy sickness when they had finally cleared the wild waters, and the heavy rain had turned into mist, and they broke out the calmer side of the squall as the storm passed by behind them.

It had felt like being born again. She had felt lucky, she had felt invincible.

And that's all thanks to you, Pops, she mentally threw her far away, hacking and unwell father a psychic kiss.

She had this. She could do this.

"Life jackets!" she demanded, putting one on herself and throwing the other to Kage as soon as he had jumped into the wobbling, shaking boat. He looked confused and a little overwhelmed by it for a moment, and then nodded, hastily dragging it on over his armor vest as Alexa did the same.

"How much time we got?" Kage said, his voice echoing in the shed as he still had to shout past the pour of rain on the tin roof. Alexa checked and shook her head.

"The *Azure* will already be there by now. We'll be quicker than we could ever be on foot, but our only hope is that it takes Staniforth time setting the boat up and casting off!" she called, turning to the boat and indicating that Kage should hunker down behind her.

"Hold the rail! There's straps there, and emergency buoys over there!" she called out loudly before pointing at the box to one side of the pilot wheel.

"Emergency flares! If we get into trouble, fire them straight up!" she called.

And just hope that the Coast Guard gets there in time, she added internally, as she saw Kage squat down and grab the sides of the boat, as she started the engine.

The entire boat shuddered and sputtered initially, and then suddenly it came alive. Alexa remembered this feeling, of movement and tension in the very hull and decks and planks of a craft. It was something her father always called 'awake.'

Alexa cast off the line holding them to the framework, and instantly they started to bob away, the strong wave ebb clanking them against the opposite scaffolding.

"Kage?" she called as she started to turn the wheel, one hand on the throttle lever by her side.

"Yes?" Her partner looked up at her, his eyes wide and white in the darkness.

"Just. Hold. On!" Alexa called, as she threw them forward, into the night, and into the storm.

CHAPTER TWENTY-FIVE

THE INVESTIGATION DAY 3
XXVI. 12:55 AM

Hold the line. Hold the line!

ALEXA BERATED HERSELF AS SHE FELT FIGUERA'S BOAT once again skip across the chop and pitch of the Gulf, rising for a moment before she slammed back down into the black waters.

"Hyech!" There was a small and sudden call from behind her as Kage was once again jostled and thumped against the side of the boat.

"Sorry!" she shouted back, but she didn't take her eyes off what was ahead of her. The rain had died down, but the wind was still high, and that meant that the waves that hit St. Martin's Island and the small reef of islands and sandbanks between here and the mainland were wild and frothy. The shallow waters (more than enough to cover them a couple times over, she guessed, but not much more than that) meant that the water was unsteady; it had no depth or 'gravity' as her father would have called it.

The rain was easing off as Alexa started to round the coast, and she was sure that the storm had passed over them and they were, in fact, only in the tailwinds as it hit the coast. This was good, as it was better to be behind a storm than in front of it, she thought as she spared a look to one side.

The dark mass of the resort island rose on their left, and the waters were starting to glimmer and speckle with the return of distant moonlight. It was freezing cold outside, despite the heavy and cumbersome life jacket – and Alexa wished that she'd had time to study an oceanographic map of the area before hitting the surf.

That's the problem with Florida, she thought, almost answering herself that many people from her neck of the woods thought that there was a whole variety of problems with Florida, and she might even be inclined to agree with them, but right now she was thinking only aquatically.

Florida was low-lying in many parts, and that lent itself to sandbanks and tidal, swampy mangrove lagoons. Which weren't best fit for larger boats, and there would be sudden channels of deeper, fast-moving, or sluggish water that would cause hell with their speed.

I've got to play it cool, as much as I can, she thought as she kept them at a steady throttle, not increasing the pace no matter how quick she wanted to travel. As it was, they were skipping over the waters every time they met another cross-current in the stormy waters (which was often).

"Alexa!" Kage called a shout, and she looked to see that he was pointing toward the horizon, where there was a brighter radiance coming from one side of the island. A misty haze of light that had to be a boat light against the rain.

"On it!" Alexa shouted, slowing them down just a little so that she could turn effectively. She pulled their boat in closer to the coast just by a little, seeing the dark, reaching, and finger-like shapes of the trees and bushes as they moved and flexed in the wind.

Of course, now Alexa suddenly realized that they had to come up with a plan for how to actually capture Staniforth.

"Shock, speed, and skill, kiddo, that's the key."

Alexa wished that she could have her father's intelligence and naval experience here, right now, with her. While he might have always had a warship to command, Alexa had no such luxury. She had a motorboat, a flare gun, and herself and her partner. Their boat hadn't even come equipped with a flood light or a loud hailer.

While our quarry is a professional murderer, and has some super fantastic robo-boat, she thought, as she pushed them a little faster.

"Alexa! Don't you want to surprise him!?" Kage asked, wobbling to his feet as he rested his hand on the butt of his pistol.

"Don't take it out, not yet!" Alexa hissed. "Too easy to drop it. And no – he'll have already heard us coming, or will any moment now. We just have to hope he scares easily."

And the chances of that happening for a man who set off explosions for a living, both Alexa and Kage were painfully aware, was probably next to zero.

"But there's nowhere he can go! He'll know that as soon as he sees us!" Kage said, earning an agreeing murmur from Alexa.

(She didn't say what she was thinking, that there would be no guarantees at sea. Staniforth might have the weight of the entire FBI after him, but he had a boat. How many contacts and unlicensed marinas did he have access to up and down the Florida coastline, and across, down into the Everglades itself?)

All he has to do is scupper us.

She rounded the last curve of the island to see the *Azure*, sitting at the end of a short pier that stuck out low over the dark waters of the Gulf. It was little more than a wooden walkway reaching out into the sea, but Alexa saw the shadow of another simple tin hut further inland from the coast, which she guessed was the equipment shed for whatever fishermen and anglers used this tiny dock.

Eddie Kendricks' robo-yacht was lit up with its own deck lights and its two massive floodlights at the fore and aft of the vessel. Its prow was taller than Alexa had suspected, and it had a full cabin occupying the front third of the craft rather than just a screen.

But still, it wasn't a large boat, Alexa thought. Maybe double the size of theirs.

Good.

"Kage, the flares! Fire one – light her up!" Alexa said as she added a little power to their boat to make sure that they were charging ahead, crossing in front of it. The *Azure* hadn't started moving yet, and Alexa wanted to make sure that Staniforth was confined on land.

Things will get messy if we get out to sea. Too messy.

Kage threw open the box, found the flare gun, and fitted one of the fattened red cartridges into the end to fire low over the prow of the *Azure* as they crossed in front. Alexa watched as the glittering flare fizzed into a roar of life, spilling a broad tail of scintillating pinks, reds, and white behind it.

"FBI!" Alexa shouted, slowing the engine as she turned, then shut the engine off entirely as they bobbed forward in front of the *Azure*, between it and the open waters beyond.

"Hands up! On deck! Turn off your engines!" Alexa hollered, and then hollered again as Kage took up his pistol and pointed it up at the windows of the *Azure's* boathouse. There was no way to see the inside, and no way of knowing if Staniforth was even behind the wheel.

But he has to see that we've got him fair and square, right?

"Get ready to fire a warning shot if there's no response," Alexa began when suddenly there *was* a response.

Only it didn't come from Saul Staniforth, or, not directly anyway.

It came from the *Azure* itself, as it suddenly started forward, white water churning behind it as he must have thrown the boat into full forward throttle, and the boat slid, then raced straight toward them.

"Move!" Kage called out, but Alexa was already on it. She grabbed the lever for the drive-throttle, throwing it forward at the same time as she hauled at the wheel. Their smaller boat started forward, but it seemed agonizingly slow compared to the much more advanced and better-equipped *Azure*.

We're not gonna make it. Not gonna make it.

Alexa felt her palms wet against the tattered leather of the ship wheel. The prow of the *Azure* was high, pointed, and a heavy slate blue, racing closer. It was ridiculously sharp. It would slam into their side and punch a hole straight through them.

"*Stop!*" Kage shouted, and Alexa heard the heavy report of pistol shots as Kage fired up at their enemy. She heard the splintering crack of glass over the roar of engines, and then-

Whumpf!

Their entire boat was rocked, lifting on the bow wave of the charging *Azure* as they missed getting hit by a matter of feet. But they were still far too close, and the surge of pushed, frothing water spilled into Kage as a spray surged over the side of the boat and Alexa felt her feet slip.

"Ach!"

The wheel spun, and their smaller boat was turning wildly, rocking as they momentarily lost control; and the bulk of the *Azure* powered past them.

"Kage! Kage – where are you?" Alexa cried out, even as she staggered to her feet, grabbing the wheel and wrestling it and the boat, steering them out of the frothing wake of the robo-yacht. She didn't have time to look behind her; she had to pray that he hadn't been knocked overboard by the wave.

"I'm here! I'm good!" Kage responded, spitting out water as he scrabbled, catching the side of the boat and clinging on as Alexa turned them in the direction of Eddie Kendrick's speeding yacht, even as it had passed them by more than twenty yards by now.

"It isn't even at full power yet, we have to close in!" Alexa yelled, turning the wheel to point them after it, and one hand pushing the throttle as their boat leaped hungrily forward.

"Kage – hold the wheel!" she instructed as her partner launched himself around her, grabbing on as Alexa fumbled with the ship's radio.

"International frequency. What's the international alert frequency!?" She was snarling, trying to remember what her father had told her. She couldn't remember, was it channel 15 or 16?

Alexa knew that marine radios had pre-set channels, much like their FBI walkie-talkies, which broadcast on a range of pre-set frequencies, with some frequencies being 'reserved' for special traffic, such as emergency broadcasts.

Think, Alexa, think! She tried to recall the many, many times that her father had called her up to the wheel to show her through the instrumentation. The throttle, the key, the fuel gauge, the radio…

"Fifteen or sixteen!" she hissed once more, picking up the set and turning the volume to maximum as their boat pitched and rocked. Kage was fighting the turbulent and choppy waters, but he was managing to keep them behind the *Azure,* neither advancing nor losing speed.

"Like this?" Kage asked as their boat shook and chopped once more.

"Try to stay out of their wake. To the left-hand side, see!?" Alexa replied, throwing a hand forward to indicate the frothing 'V' line that spread out from behind their quarry's engines. Every time they clipped into it, they started to skip and judder, and Kage started to turn their wheel incrementally, keeping them out of it as the *Azure* started to gain distance ahead of them.

But they're lit up like a Christmas tree. Everyone will see them coming a mile off!

Alexa chose channel fifteen and leaned forward to the speakers to hear the hiss and crackle of static.

Could have been an empty channel. Could just have meant that no one was talking – or that it was a dead channel and no one was monitoring it.

"Mayday. Mayday. Mayday. This is FBI Special Agent Landers on an unknown craft heading north-northwest out of St. Martin's Island. We are in immediate pursuit of the private yacht the *Azure Future*, same course and direction. Shots fired. Repeat, mayday, mayday, mayday. FBI Special Agent Landers on unknown craft heading north by north-west out of St. Martin's Island. We are in pursuit of the *Azure Future*, shots fired. Requesting immediate assistance. Out."

Alexa had no idea whether the Coast Guard heard, or whether they would even answer considering they had told her that they 'would not be available for policing actions.'

But they have to do something. We've got shots fired. A highly dangerous criminal and murderer at large on the sea. Alexa knew that his piloting alone would be cause for immediate intervention, as he was putting lives at risk.

WHAM!

There was movement from the side of the boat, a glitter through the light, and then the water to the left of their boat suddenly turned a pitch white before lifting up from the surface in a blossom of fire and water.

The thunder wasn't loud, and there was no blinding flash of light, but Alexa still felt her heart tremor at the explosion. Their boat had a moment of peace, and then they suddenly shook and spun to one side as the underwater shockwave hit them.

"He's throwing bombs! Staniforth is throwing bombs at us!" Kage exclaimed as Alexa changed the channel to 16 and repeated her message before grabbing the wheel from Kage. He was a steady hand, calm and centered – but they needed an experienced pilot at the wheel if Staniforth was going to be throwing incendiaries at them.

The pair said nothing as they moved, Kage crouching behind her, bracing against the wall as he took aim at the rear of the boat, waiting for his opportunity. Alexa held onto the wheel tightly and increased the throttle.

"Hold on!" she called out and had no idea whether Kage did or not as their boat was suddenly skipping over the surface of the waves at speed, moving faster and faster and suddenly rising over the waters completely and slapping back down again as they started to close the distance between them.

A flicker of movement at the back of the *Azure*.

"Two o'clock!" Alexa shouted, but Staniforth had already ducked back down behind the boat rail. There was a glitter in the air-

Shhhi-!

Alexa turned the wheel a quarter turn in the opposite direction as they suddenly peeled away from their pursuit and the sea behind them erupted with another blast.

How does he have so many explosives? Or did he prepare them out of boat fuel? Alexa turned them back again, this time not heading for the *Azure* itself but ahead of it. She pointed her prow in a dead straight line ahead of the boat and just prayed that they weren't going to suddenly veer off course.

Staniforth isn't at the wheel if he's out there, throwing stuff at us, she reasoned. That meant that he had set the boat on auto-pilot, or had tied the wheel up with a strap and leaned something against the throttle. Alexa wished that Kendricks had found a way to remotely disable his yacht. Why on earth didn't he have a kill switch fitted into that app of his!?

No matter. Either way, she had to end this. And there was only one way to do that.

"Stay sharp!" Alexa hissed as they started to pull alongside the yacht, gaining in speed as they were no longer fighting its wake.

But she knew this was also the most dangerous way to approach it. Each of the boats provided the other with a totally clear route of attack.

"Four o'clock!" Alexa shouted as soon as she saw a flicker of movement. There was a shape on the deck. It had to be Staniforth, running back-

BANG! BANG-BANG!

Kage started shooting, plugging holes into the side of the yacht. He didn't manage to hit their target because he wasn't a sharpshooter, but Alexa saw the man suddenly leap to the floor.

Alexa's eyes flickered ahead of them. She could see a line of brighter lights studding across the horizon. She didn't know the name of the village or town, but she knew that they were close. They had to apprehend him before he got there.

"Alexa!" Kage shouted, snapping her attention back to what was before them as she saw the glint of metal spinning through the air.

She twisted the boat wheel, but it wasn't fast enough. They were too close.

This time there *was* a blinding flash of light as the explosive ignited before it even slammed into the water. Alexa saw the flash before she felt the sudden wave of heat, and strangely enough, the sound came later.

"Aaakh!"

She screamed involuntarily, as her ears went from a crescendo of noise into the sudden high-pitched, ear-splitting whine of tinnitus, as her vision went white for a moment, and then a wave of hot, wet heat washed over her.

And the boat tipped, lifting and suddenly moving as Alexa grabbed the wheel and cut the throttle. She felt a moment of weightlessness as the entire boat skipped across the waters, and then slammed back down onto the waters.

Alexa knew she was shouting, but she couldn't hear her own voice, it was so muffled against the roar of noise in her ears.

Is Kage okay? Am I okay!? She was blinking, looking around and blinking to see that their engine had stopped, but the boat was slowly spinning. There were gobbets of flame sticking to the side of the railing, and a small patch actually on the decking itself. The incendiary device that Staniforth had thrown had been packed, and although it hadn't hit them directly, Alexa figured it must have exploded in mid-air.

That was close. Too close. Had it hit them, right now they would've been sinking... Alexa felt her ears roar with the pound of her blood as her heart hammered and her lungs threatened to hyperventilate.

There was another muffled noise and this time she heard it for what it was. Kage, rolling to his feet as he shook his groggy head, and belatedly started stamping out the flames, and slashing at them with his jacket.

"The boat!" he shouted (although it sounded very small and very distant in Alexa's ears).

Alexa's entire head felt like it was ringing. Was everything happening in slow time, or was she in shock? She nodded dumbly that she understood, turning to look up to see that the *Azure* was ahead of them, but it was turning in a wide half circle.

Like a circling shark, Alexa thought, shaking her head once again, and grabbing the wheel. She turned the key, but just heard a dull roaring, churring sound from their engine as it turned over but did absolutely nothing else at all.

What!? No! She snarled in frustration and turned the key once again. Had they in fact been hit by the explosion? Had some vital component been knocked out?

Another turn of the key resulted in just the same unresponsive, stalling churr of a noise from the engine as she flicked the key back to off.

"I don't want to flood the engine," she said out loud, although her hearing was so shot that her voice sounded far away and like it didn't belong to her at all.

Kage was speaking and pointing, but Alexa couldn't hear him at all. She realized that her cheek was hot, and she wondered how near that ball of flame had come.

Kage was pointing frantically now, and Alexa turned in the direction to see that, unknown to her, thanks to her tinnitus, the *Azure Future* was bearing down on them. Staniforth had turned it around and was now driving straight at them in what was undoubtedly going to be a ramming move.

Idiot! she thought. How strong was the hull? He might even capsize his own boat at this rate...

But not before he had sunk them, too, right?

She twisted the key once again, heard the resistant churr of the engine – and then suddenly she felt the entire boat underneath them 'wake up' as power poured through its engines. She slammed the throttle lever and they pitched forward, sliding out of the way as the *Azure* surged toward them.

"*Hyech!*" Once again, Alexa felt the chop and sudden jolt as their bow lines met, and both yachts shook and jumped over the waves in the near collision. It was close. Too close, and closer still even than the first ramming strike that Staniforth had nearly succeeded in. Suddenly their yacht was starting to turn and slide as it rocked, and Alexa was slowing their throttle as she spun them out of the way, glancing behind her.

Kage wasn't there. He wasn't hanging onto the back of the boat at all.

"*Kage!*" she shouted out, turning frantic one way and then the next to see if she could catch a glimpse of his arms or his pale skin in the waters. He must have been thrown out in the chop and swell of the waters when their two boats had nearly hit each other. But hadn't he taken his life jacket off to quell the flames?

Alexa was turning once again, looking out over the waters and the receding *Azure Future* – to see a small dark shape clinging to the side of the yacht.

It was Kage. He had leaped onto Saul Staniforth's boat, and he was climbing over the rail.

CHAPTER
TWENTY-SIX

XXVII. 1:45 AM

C'mon, push past it, push past.

FBI Special Agent Kage Murphy's mind was a tight focus of determination, rage, and shuddering cold as he clung to the side of the *Azure* by his fingertips.

He hadn't known what he was going to do until he did it. He saw the stolen yacht bearing down on them, his body felt the shift underfoot as their boat started to peel out of the way...

And then it was just like he was back in college, out on the field when the long throw was coming in. He had experienced moments like this only a few times in his life, and they always – later, much later – came as a surprise.

His training and his instincts kicked in, although it didn't feel like that at the time. It felt like the perfect marriage between his body and his gut. He saw his chance. He saw how close they were going to pass by each other, and suddenly he was moving, his body reacting in tune with his emotions before his conscious thought could even get involved. He had lunged forward, kicking out his booted foot, leaping with his arms outstretched as the world suddenly became weightless and his stomach lurched-

Wham!

He had hit the side of the yacht with his elbows, hands, and knees, just like in his assault training courses when he had to leap across the blocks to grab the rope or the brick wall. He felt himself slide, but he gripped onto the railing with his hands and felt the sudden pull and hammer of weight against his shoulders, his back, and his thighs.

And then he was on. He was clinging onto the *Azure* as the wind whipped at him, forcing tears from his eyes, and the frothing, churning water was only a few feet below his foot.

There was a ledge or a seam of blue and green metal that he was barely clinging to, and he hadn't even consciously seen it until he was somehow using it for leverage.

C'mon. Push it! Go!

But Kage demanded more. He demanded more of his body and more of his mind. He had to do this because it was obvious that they were outclassed in firepower, speed, and size. He had to stop it, and he wasn't a good enough shot to take out a running, darting Staniforth on board a moving target.

Kage felt his weight in his arms as he lowered himself just a little, expecting the stern, angered face of Staniforth to appear over the side at any moment.

But then he was pulling himself up, bouncing upward using the strength in his thighs to launch over the side of the railing, twisting as he rolled, and finally hitting the wooden deck of the yacht and tumbling. Everything was slick with spray, and he slid another few feet until he slammed against a metal box-like contraption in the center of the boat deck. He wasn't sure what it was, a sump of some kind? Vents?

Staniforth. Where is he? His thoughts were flashing quickly as he scrabbled over into a crouch, one hand moving to his hip before he remembered that he had lost his pistol in the near crash.

His thinking was too slow. He needed to react on training, not analyze.

I need a weapon! he thought, seeing the cabin ahead of him, occupying a full half of the thirty-foot yacht, with its rear door open and the gleam of light amid a darkened room beyond.

Kage knew that it would be a simple thing to rush in there, grab him from behind, and force him to the floor. Even without a weapon. He was tensing to throw himself to his feet just as there was a shape from the darkened boathouse door.

It was Saul Staniforth, middle-aged and white-haired, but now no longer looking like a robust, retired widower enjoying his twilight years.

Saul Staniforth was dressed in a simple black shirt underneath some sort of waxed jacket with a myriad of pockets across it, and he wore khaki, army-type trousers. It was then, in that brief moment, that Special Agent Kage Murphy saw Saul Staniforth for who he truly was. He no longer looked like a civilian; he looked like a paramilitary operator, an aging one perhaps, but one that had probably seen action, service even, and was very comfortable with doing whatever he needed to do.

His face was a snarl of surprise, but in that split second, Kage also saw the ice-cold blue of his eyes. There was no furious, uncontrollable rage there. It was all prediction. Strategy.

Kage launched himself forward, at the same time as Staniforth did, but the mad bomber had a surprise. One hand flashed forward and in it was a large crowbar.

Kage had no time to slide out of the way and no time to duck. Instead, he threw both of his forearms up to push outward as he felt the powerful *smack*, and the devastating, sudden lance of pain that shot up his arm.

Kage slammed his free elbow forward in a tight curve, but Staniforth was quick, ducking out of the way and suddenly kicking at Kage as he leaped back, out of the way.

"You're done!" Kage barked, feeling the throb in his aching left forearm and sure that it was fractured at the least.

"Watch me, cop!" Staniforth was backing away, swinging the crowbar between them as he edged around the boathouse, heading for the far side.

Kage paced like a hunting tiger. He controlled his breathing, keeping it tight, and tried not to think about the pain spreading up his arm and into his shoulder.

Don't think. Act.

He saw his opportunity; a moment after the backswing when Staniforth's guard was wide and high. And he darted forward, raising his arms as he did so for Staniforth to flinch and flicker his crowbar up to meet the coming attack.

But this was an old trick. One that Kage had mastered back in his wrestling days, and then used at Quantico. He suddenly stamped out with his boot, catching Staniforth against the side of the knee as his enemy's eyes were elsewhere.

"Urk!"

Saul stumbled to one side, but still had the crowbar in hand as he swung it wildly this time, and it would have torn Kage's jaw clean from his skull if he had been there.

But Kage had darted back, feeling the whistle of the bar right in front of his eyes before he stepped forward once again ...

But you can't get away with the same trick twice, not if your opponent is good. And he was good. Staniforth twisted to one side to avoid the kick, and suddenly the crowbar was coming down across Kage's shoulders.

Pain slammed across him, and Kage spluttered, tasting blood in the back of his mouth where he must have bitten his own tongue. It was like a sudden white flash of agony that rippled across his shoulders and down his spine.

"Rargh!" He threw a wild back fist, but it sailed harmlessly in the air as somehow Saul Staniforth – who had to be easily twenty or more years his senior – wasn't there. Kage's enemy had moved

199

fast, angling out of the way and spinning around Kage so that the agent barely had enough time to turn before the next blow from the solid iron bar struck.

This time it wasn't a flat smack, but Staniforth had held it in two hands and driven the end into Kage's side. He was still wearing his jacket, so it thankfully didn't pierce the flesh, but it did knock him sideways to the floor, and felt like getting shot.

(The very fact that he knew what getting shot felt like probably went some way to explaining just what made him leap across a speeding yacht in the first place, the thought flashed through his mind.)

"*Hyurk!*" Kage gasped for air as he stumbled, struggled to one side, and then dropped to his knees as he flailed his hands upward to ward off any more blows.

But they weren't coming. Staniforth was stalking around him, holding the crowbar at the ready for the final swing.

"I've faced plenty of feds like you in my time, *cop*," the middle-aged man spat as the boat skipped and kept its steady roar of a pace. "You think after thirty years in the game that *you're* going to be the one to take me down? Just like that?" Staniforth started to laugh.

"But – but why?" Kage coughed, spitting blood on the floor of the boat, where it was instantly washed in water-like dye.

"Why kill Eva Montgomery? Why take on the Cubans in the first place?" Kage looked up, his eyes sparking with cold determination. "Who are you working for!?"

Staniforth hefted the crowbar, testing its weight in his hands as if making sure that it would get the job done. It would, Kage could see that it would.

"Who said I'm working for *anyone?*" He threw the last word out like it was an insult. "You think the federal government is so hot? It's nothing more than just another bunch of gangsters with blood on their hands," he snapped, pulling back his lips so that his teeth gleamed in the night.

"But that still doesn't explain it. It doesn't explain why you would go to all this trouble to pick a fight between Cuba and the US," Kage countered.

Keep him talking. Every second that Staniforth was talking was a second that he wasn't bashing his brains out. It was a second that Kage was recovering his breath...

"Always a cop. Even to the end, huh? You disgust me," Staniforth said, and swung the crowbar.

WHUMP!

Something hit the *Azure*, and the entire robo-yacht pitched to one side, lurching as Kage and Saul stumbled.

Kage grunted in surprise as he hit the side of the cabin, scrabbling with his feet to brace against the railing as the *Azure* slammed to the water once again. For a second time, Kage was lifted and slammed back into place, as pain rippled through his arm and spine.

"Kage!" There was a shout, and Kage realized what had just happened. It was Alexa. As sound returned to his ears, he could see that Alexa was right next to them in their own borrowed boat.

But Staniforth was gone, Kage realized in the next moment. He had been standing right there over him, ready to deliver the killing blow, but Saul had also been swinging that crowbar for all that he was worth when Alexa rammed the *Azure* to save him.

"Staniforth! I've lost him!" Kage shouted, pushing himself into a crouch, and then to his feet as he looked first back at Alexa and then to the far side of the robo-yacht.

Did he go over the edge?

Panic gripped Kage as he suddenly moved forward, heading for the railing at the same time as he heard a startled cry, and saw in the dark that there was a hand holding onto the edge.

It was Saul Staniforth, hanging one-handed to the side of the robo-yacht as his legs trailed in the frothing water around them.

"*Aaagh!*" Staniforth shouted, looking up to see Kage appear over him.

For one dizzying moment, Kage was certain that Staniforth was going to let go. He was certain that the aging, anti-American, anti-whatever-he-was agitator would prefer to take his chances in the warm, stormy Florida waters than he would allow himself to be saved.

After all, if Cecil Pinkerton was right, then Saul Staniforth was already responsible for *a lot* of murders. He may not have triggered them himself, but he'd sold them to the highest bidder. As far as Kage was concerned, that made him responsible. A lot of bombs had been sold to the very worst dregs of society and caused untold mayhem and suffering over the last twenty years.

And for just one equally terrifying moment, as Kage looked down at the man, he wondered if he was going to let him die, too.

"You've killed so many. So many…" Kage muttered under his breath as Staniforth clung on with just his fingers as the *Azure Future* kept motoring. Kage could see the thick, corded, and bunched muscles of his forearm and shoulder underneath the waxed jacket as he clung for dear life.

No. Not like this. Justice was a better punishment.

"Grab my arm!" Kage snapped as he reached down with his one good arm, grabbing onto Saul's wrist and squatting down.

Staniforth snarled and even flinched in place.

"Grab my arm, damn it!" Kage shouted once more, wondering why he was demanding that this terrible murderer save himself.

Kage leaned backward, bracing his legs against the side of the *Azure's* railing as he felt his muscles across his thighs and his damaged back scream, but it worked – Staniforth came crawling and scraping over the side of the boat to land on the bottom in a wet, exhausted puddle.

And before he could move, Kage had put a knee on his back, his good arm finding the murderer's elbow and twisting it behind him as he held him against the deck of the *Azure.*

It was done. It was over. Kage held Staniforth there until he felt the fight go out of him and his resolve break.

"Saul Staniforth – if that even is your name – I am arresting you for the attempted murder of a federal agent. For interfering with a federal investigation. For the suspected murder of Eva Montgomery. And about a thousand charges of domestic and international terrorism. You have the right to remain silent, you have the right to a lawyer, but so help me if you give me any more trouble I will personally throw your ass in the drink myself!"

There was a thumping and a clutching sound and the boat suddenly rocked to one side, causing Kage to look up to see that Alexa had thrown ropes from her boat to the side of the robo-yacht and was securing them together where they bobbed and stalled in the choppy waves.

A few moments later there was a hand, then a pair of hands, and there was Alexa's washed-out face. Kage saw her eyes widen, then scowl at the form of Staniforth held under his knee.

"You got him. Thank God, you got him," she exhaled, her voice exhausted as she hauled herself over the side of the gunwale.

"*We* got him," Kage said, feeling the tension still thrumming in his body, but now giving way to more pain.

But as much as his body protested; as much as he was aware that he would need to see a doctor, and soon, and that they still had to turn this boat around in the dead of the night and somehow find safe harbor on the coattails of a vicious storm – he felt a wash of relief, too.

They had done it. They had the bomber. It was over.

CHAPTER TWENTY-SEVEN

XXVIII. 10:20 AM

"It's time…"

ALEXA'S THOUGHTS WERE STILL IN AN EXHAUSTED FOG from the night before, as the watery, grayed-out sun bled through the window of Bartholomew Price's office, but she heard the words of her partner loud and clear.

"Okay. Let's get this over with, I guess," she groaned a little as she got up from her seat, once again rubbing her face and taking the last slurp of what was admittedly very strong coffee – at least that was something that these high-class resorts could do well.

She followed Kage out of the office and up the small hallway, her eyes flickering to the bald and compact Marinsburg standing by the small door to the kitchen storeroom, where Staniforth was being kept.

Marinsburg nodded, just the slightest of movements. All was well. Staniforth was still under guard. Everything was safe.

Is it really over? Her tired thoughts found themselves surfacing as she followed Kage up the resort hallway, past the open door to the reception where two of the wide-eyed, weary, and much beat-upon resort staff were hurriedly standing up. Somehow, even despite the fact that they had helped fight a room fire last night and survived a hurricane as well, Price had made them put on crisp and perfectly clean uniforms once again.

And then there they were, walking out into the main lobby area, with the smell of soot and smoke still heavy in the air, and the whistle of the wind coming through the hotel from somewhere they hadn't managed to barricade one of the smashed windows. All of the remaining hotel staff and guests were gathered in the main lobby lounge, which at this point only consisted of some twelve staff, Eddie Kendricks, and the Luca couple.

How many did we start with? Alexa's thought sluggishly. *How many have we lost?* Her gaze slid over those assembled, and all of them – whether staff or guest – had that quiet, wary look of people who had managed to survive, but who also now knew that life could always change direction suddenly and terribly for you.

The look of survivors. The look of the traumatized.

Alexa could well sympathize with that look, as she shared some of the same feelings. she was exhausted, and even though it was coming up to midday already, she had barely had any sleep. It had taken herself and Kage over an hour to get Saul Staniforth back to the main resort with a gun pressed to his back, and then another hour on top of that getting patchy and glitchy messages through to the mainland. The storm had chewed up an awful lot of receivers up and down the coast, it had seemed, but by the time four in the morning had rolled around, FBI Chief Williams had been awakened, alerted, and they had a plan for the morning.

She had wondered if it was even worth it going to sleep at all, but Kage had impressed upon her that at least a few hours would be better than none. The way that she felt right now, Alexa wasn't so sure about that.

But anyway, it's over. Finally.

"People," Alexa cleared her throat and did her best to smile. "Right now there is a large Coast Guard vessel waiting to take you over to the mainland where there will be first responders and police waiting," she said.

"That's it? We're free to go finally?" Eddie Kendricks piped in. His previous anger was defused, and although there was an air of annoyance to his words, it'd been tempered by the ordeal of last night.

It's funny how we find ourselves, Alexa thought as she hesitated for just a second as she looked at him. Mr. Tech Bro Angry Hipster had deep circles under his eyes and looked like he had aged somewhat. She wondered briefly if this meant he would change his online baiting and troll-worship livestream series, but she rather doubted it.

"Yes, Mr. Kendricks," Alexa nodded. "You will be happy to know that you are free to go. All of your remaining devices and belongings will be returned to you, if you would be so good as to sign the release forms, and if we can get some of your staff to help?" Alexa's eyes flickered to the resort owner Bartholomew Price, who was still seated and somehow managed to look deflated despite his impressive girth.

Well, he's probably ruined, Alexa reasoned. The story of what had happened here, from multiple murders, terrorist incidents, and infiltration by hardened criminals would probably be the end of his insurance and patronage by the political elite, at the very least.

Either that or will be the making of him, she considered the other side. Maybe he could turn it around into the story of the century. Who knew? He seemed a pretty enterprising guy, after all.

"Of course, of course. Full refunds will be offered, have no doubt…" Price's voice trailed off into a mumble, and Alexa moved swiftly on. She had no wish to get into the technicalities of blame. That was for the lawyers, and her job was enforcement.

And on that boat is a secure cell and a team of more FBI agents waiting to take Staniforth, too, Alexa thought. He was being held by the last remaining Secret Service agents in the pantry right now, but they'd take him over at the same time a maximum-security van waiting to take him to the nearest security max holding – where the real work would begin. *Her* work. Hers and Kage's.

Like finding out why he did it, and who paid him to do it, as she said something slightly insincere about what a great team everyone had been, how they had been very patient, and how she was impressed by how they had come together to fight the fire last night.

But she didn't apologize for the inconvenience, Alexa was sure of that. The FBI never apologized, as that would mean that they had done something wrong – and she was certain that they hadn't. Not in this case, at least.

"You have been exemplary citizens in very stressful and trying times," Alexa finished.

"I am sure that over the coming days and weeks, you will be approached by news outlets or be tempted to share your stories with the wider world. I have to stress that this is still an ongoing investigation and that we *will* be getting back in touch with everyone assembled here, whether staff or guest, for follow-up interviews."

Especially as we build the case. It was a common misconception held by members of the public that all of the investigation and police work happened in the heart-beating, blood-pumping few days of action. Much of it occurred in the longer, slower, painstaking checking of reports and witness statements, making sure that everything was water-tight for the courts and that no small details had been missed.

What exact time a suspect was seen.

When, and by whom?

What other details were present, or missing? Who could corroborate that?

All of which would lead to a conviction, and all of which had to be checked and rechecked not just by her and Kage, but by Chief Williams and their legal team to make sure it was fit for prosecution.

Not that we have to worry about that too much. Saul Staniforth had attempted to kill them with explosives. Kendrick's stolen robo-yacht had appeared to have his 'mobile ingredients' for making short-fuse bombs. He was the only man on the island who appeared to have the inclination or expertise. It was an open-and-shut case…

But it still irked her, despite that…

Staniforth is a bomb-MAKER. He was never at any of the previous bombings. That means someone paid him to do it. Some individual or group. But who? They were still no closer to finding that out until they questioned him, she thought a little dismally.

"I suggest the first thing we do is talk to our lawyers," Kendricks mumbled a little as he staggered to his feet, already reaching for his few duffel bags and belongings that they had gathered down here in the early hours of the night. There were still camp beds and mattresses strewn on the floor, where they had all assembled and huddled overnight, praying that there would be no more deadly explosions.

He's probably worried about charges, Alexa thought as she shot a glance at Kage, noticing his jaw clenching. They had already discussed the fact that Kendricks had withheld his devices and effectively interfered with a federal investigation.

We're probably not going to pursue charges. As much as she wanted to, considering the scale of the events that had happened last night, that would probably only make the agency look petty. But there was a certain satisfaction in seeing Kendricks sweat all the same.

"So. That's… that's it, I take it?" It was Antonio, the older half of the Luca couple who spoke, his face still smeared with some of the soot from helping clear the gutted upper floor of the resort last night. Like Price, he, too, had seemed to collapse in on himself a little. She wondered if stress had that effect on everyone.

"Yes, Mr. Luca, that's it," Kage smoothly took over, and Alexa sighed a little internally. Kage was so much better than she was at this. He was good with people.

"The governor of Florida, in a joint statement by the President herself, has officially called off the special emergency situation in the state, and so, therefore, you are free to return to your homes. However, I would advise you that there has also been widespread disruption thanks to Hurricane Hildergard last night, so that might take a lot longer than expected. You might not be able to get a flight back right away," Kage announced, as Antonio mumbled agreement and turned to clutch his wife Maria's hands and give them a squeeze.

They're a cute couple, Alexa thought, turning her attention to Kendricks, who was already moving toward the door, where one of the FBI agents was waiting with zip-locked bags of any small belongings they had left, and a clipboard with paper for them to sign indicating ownership.

"Thank you. I know it has just been awful, but thank you for everything you have done." It was Maria Luca who'd spoken, stepping out of the throng to briefly touch Alexa's shoulder.

"Oh, right, thank you – yes, and you, too," Alexa nodded and even managed a slightly warmer smile. Maria was looking at her with concern and gestured toward her head and shoulder, where she still had heavy bruising from the explosion (*or the boat fight. Or the storm*).

"You will take care of yourself, won't you? Remember to drink lots of fluids," Maria advised, once again the ghost of her touch gently patting the back of Alexa's hands.

"Oh, I will, and thank you," Alexa replied. "You stay safe, too. I guess we've put you off vacations from now on?" She managed to laugh.

"Oh, we're not going anywhere after this!" Maria managed to chuckle just a little, throwing a concerned glance at her husband. "We're heading straight back home and then we've promised each other a long fall and winter with nothing but television and home life after all this excitement."

"I can't think of anything better," Alexa smiled wanly, and realized, strangely, that she actually meant it.

Right now, all that Alexa wanted was her bed. And then maybe a long bath. And after that?

Then the case, she considered, knowing that as much as she wanted a rest after being shot at and nearly blown up and not sleeping and all the rest of it; she needed the action. She knew that she needed to keep busy.

After a sleep, anyway.

"Take care," she said to the Lucas as they joined the line of people filing out of the resort. All of the staff were leaving, too, and Price was joining them at the end of the line. Alexa guessed that Price would probably have to look for a whole new set of staff for the next season, if the resort even survived that long.

The resort was in shambles, on many levels. Alexa breathed a deep sigh as she stepped back while Kage was thanking the last of the staff for their effort. Some of the windows had been smashed by the storm, and Alexa knew that the entire upper floor would need to be gutted. Despite the fire being contained just in Staniforth's room, the broken windows and doors had let in the majority of the winds, causing tens if not hundreds of thousands of dollars worth of damage. Even down here, Hurricane Hildegard had managed to force her fists in through unblocked stairwells. Giant potted plants had been knocked over, spilling their earth across floor mats that cost more than Alexa's entire salary for a year. Paintings were askew or had been ripped entirely from the walls, and there was a soggy, damp layer of moisture on everything.

It'll be a complete renovation, Alexa thought, waiting for the last of them to file out of the main resort building before she turned her attention to the next order of business. She wondered whether Price would even bother. Whether he had that sort of cash on hand – a few million, perhaps – or whether he would cut his losses and just sell the development to the next investor.

Who knew? She didn't even care, not really.

"Alexa? You still with us?" Kage said as he appeared in front of her, with the hall and lobby behind him entirely devoid of life.

"Oh, did I fall asleep?" Alexa blinked, realizing that she had missed a few seconds there. *Damnit* – she was tired!

"You ready for this?" Kage asked again, a little more heavily, for Alexa to give herself a shake and then nod.

"Yes. *Yes,*" she said again, and a little more firmly. Four hours of sleep or not, she would be ready. She put her hand on the butt of her holster, unclipping it and drawing it out so that she could inspect the available rounds, and then sliding it back into the holster – but leaving the holster catch off this time.

"Ready," she said, as they both turned toward Marinsburg, then joined by two more FBI agents, their hands hovering over their own holsters, too.

Staniforth.

"The civilians are secure. Let's move the suspect," she said in a growl as Marinsburg unlocked the door behind him.

Smoke. Smoke and lightning and the smell of grease in the air.

Alexa's mind was playing tricks on her for just a moment because there was no such thing in the air as she stepped forward to the small stairs that led down to the warehouse, just the glare of bare light and the nod of the distant agent they had stationed overlooking Staniforth, cable-tied to the same chair where they had held Figuera, and looking up at them under the bald radiance of the light.

Alexa's hand twitched all by itself. She almost drew her gun and trained it on him, even though a Secret Service agent was standing right there, passionless and immobile.

But he's dangerous. He killed Eva Montgomery. He killed Ramon Martinez. He almost killed Skip. He almost killed Kage...

Somehow Alexa resisted the urge to train her pistol on him and instead walked down the small pantry hallway with her head held high and her mouth set in a firm line. She nodded her thanks at the Service agent, and Kage and Marinsburg followed her in a broad circle, filling the room around Staniforth.

"I'm guessing you're not here to dance a jig and sing all's well, are ya?" Staniforth said in an accent that was now broader and thicker than the one he had used before. It was one of those polyglot accents that you pick up if you move around a lot, Alexa thought. There was a bit of a midwestern twang, as well as a slightly thicker east coast accent, she was sure of it.

"Saul Staniforth..." *if that even is your name...*

"You were arrested last night for multiple serious crimes, including murder and attempted murder and terrorism. Today, we will be taking you to one of our secure holding facilities, where you will be questioned. Given the nature of your crimes, you will be held in jail until your appointed date of trial; however, your legal rights to counsel will of course be respected."

"I got a lawyer. A good one, from Texas!" Staniforth said with a broad sneer of a grin.

"I bet you do," Alexa growled back in response. "Just as soon as we get you to where we want you to be, I am sure that you will get your phone call."

"I want my phone call now!" Staniforth spat, his cheeks matching with small, red blushes of rage. He suddenly no longer looked to be a man approaching his sixty-year mark. Even with his almost shaven, thinning blonde-white hair, his neck and arms straining against the wrist and ankle ties were tight and corded, making him look like a being filled with incredible strength and feral hate.

"Simmer down, Saul," Kage cut in acidly, stepping forward so he loomed over the man.

"Let us get you somewhere more comfortable, and I'm sure you can do all the calling you want. The storm chewed up the reception dishes out here, so you're going to have to wait anyway," Kage smiled a broad, shark's grin in return, as Alexa watched Staniforth hold his glare for one long moment, and then turn and shake his head strongly, just the once.

"Pfgh. How's your ribs, big guy? I almost had you, you know. I *did* have you. How does it feel to be bested by a guy twice your age?" Saul taunted, his true, horrible and nasty character finally showing through. Alexa shuddered at how it had been hiding there the whole time.

Kage said nothing for a moment, but his eyes sharpened just a little. Even though Alexa knew that Kage wasn't like that – he was the good one, he was the nice guy – she still wondered just for a moment if her partner was going to slug him.

And maybe that's what Staniforth wants, Alexa realized. *Rile us up enough so that our procedure gets questioned for brutality and mishandling?*

"Take him away," Alexa nodded hurriedly to the Special agent who stepped forward as Marinsburg stepped back to draw his pistol.

There was a tense, taut moment as the agent used a penknife to cut the ties and Kage stepped forward to grab Staniforth's wrists and cuff them rather roughly before holding his hands high against his back, almost a pressure point position, and started to march him up toward the waiting agents in the main lobby, where he would be surrounded and guarded on the walk all the way to the boat, and the secure cell it contained for him.

"Hey!" Suddenly, a thought struck Alexa, as she leaned in so that she could hiss straight into Staniforth's face.

"You might just be thinking you can get some legal weasel to wriggle yourself out of this, but you'd be very wrong. The mistake you made was going for *us,* too. That'll put you in a hole for a very, very long time!" Alexa said. It was all stuff that he must know, of course; but she felt good saying it.

"Hang it, Agent," Staniforth growled back. "You think you got me, but you haven't. You're nowhere even close."

There was something about his attitude that got Alexa's hackles up. Or maybe it was his stupidity. He wasn't infuriating like Kendricks was, he was just...

I hate the fact that he doesn't even care, Alexa realized. At least Figuera had *cared* about something, even if it was some conspiracy craziness. Figuera had thought himself to be a hero. There was a way to understand what he wanted, what he was all about. Kendricks, too, for that matter, was at least passionate about his goals – if that was only himself, and his belief that he was some kind of reporter, too.

But Staniforth? This guy was a mercenary in every sense of the word. He was only here for the job, to get the job done.

"Just tell me *why*, you piece of-" Alexa caught herself before she overstepped the line. "*Why* did you kill Representative Martinez? What was he to you? Was this a job, or was this a personal vendetta? Are you working alone!?" she demanded, feeling her anger starting to bubble to the surface, as once again her ears rang with the sound of whining alarms and tinnitus.

Staniforth's face was only a foot or so away, and she could see his nasty, stupid little grin slowly spreading across it, and she wanted to smack it off of him so badly.

"Alexa."

There was a firming, grounding touch on her shoulder, and she heard the sound of Kage's voice, suddenly bringing her back down to earth, the ringing in her ears dissipating in an instant as she realized that she had grabbed Staniforth with one hand by the shoulder.

"*Hell. Take it easy, kiddo!*" Alexa suddenly blinked, hearing her father's voice in the back of her head as if he were there, and her anger was gone. She was exhausted, and she was tired, and she had spent the last three nights not sleeping, and it felt like these were three separate yet overlapping things all weighing down on her.

She stepped back as Staniforth's eyes only widened in front of her, and Marinsburg was gruffly telling the agents to get him out of there.

"You ain't got *nothing*, Agent! I'll tell you this for free – I wasn't the one who killed the Cuban! You want to catch your man? Well, it isn't me!" Staniforth called out in a loud cackle as he was shoved and pushed up the short passageway to the resort lobby above.

"Yeah? Well, you're still going down, Staniforth! We still got you for more than enough for Florida to convict!" Alexa hissed back.

"But it gets you, don't it?" Staniforth was laughing, even as he was shoved and pushed forward. "You're the kind of person who has to be *right*. And this time, you're not going to get the satisfaction, fed!"

Staniforth laughed, and his laughter rang in Alexa's ears like the sound of sudden, screaming alarm bells.

CHAPTER TWENTY-EIGHT

TAMPA FBI FIELD OFFICE

XXIX. 2:30PM

"I'M TELLING YOU, YOU SHOULD GET SOME MORE SLEEP," Kage said to Alexa as she looked up from the paperwork on the borrowed desk in their sister office that, compared to the underground parking lot which they'd inhabited, had way better light streaming in from high windows on two sides. Tampa had so far been appraised and prepped for their arrival, with Field Chief Williams already commissioning a suite of data analysis and interview rooms ready for their arrival. The Tampa office wasn't as large as Miami, but they did have good coffee, which was a fact that, right now, Alexa was eternally grateful for.

"An hour isn't enough. Not even for you," Kage continued.

"What's that supposed to mean?" Alexa scowled at him, holding up a sheath of papers that composed the witness reports that they had taken at the resort, which she had been busy ticking through, marking off points of connection and corroboration.

"This can wait. We have our man now. Staniforth is in custody downstairs, and we've already arrested him. That means he's going to be in jail for the next week or more before we have to prepare for a court hearing," Kage said, resting his broad hands on the table as even his larger, athletic frame sagged.

"Pfft." Alexa grimaced.

She knew that her partner was right. They had time to build their case now. They had time to build it out, make it water-tight.

Staniforth had been caught red-handed on St. Martin's Resort CCTV going into Eva's room, the last one to do so before she died, then coming out alone.

Staniforth had been caught red-handed hurling explosives around at FBI agents.

All sorts of devices and mechanisms for the bombs were all over his suite at the resort – the bits that weren't burned to hell, and the same suite was booby-trapped.

"And his stash of homemade devices all fit the signature of the bomb that killed the representative and his staff, and the others he'd made over the years..." Alexa's thoughts were racing ahead as Kage just looked at her with concerned eyes.

"Yeah, I know. We got him. He's all over the bomb. We know he made it. What more do we need at this point. Right now – you can get some rest!" Kage insisted.

But it wasn't enough, the thought hammered through Alexa's heart.

"But we need to know *why,*" Alexa pointed out. "For the case. We need to show motive, too, remember. For a jury to convict."

"Motive!?" Kage said, suddenly standing up and wiping his hands over his face in exasperation.

"Of course, yes, we do. But the guy makes bombs for the far right, and the far left, and everyone else. He's clearly anti-fed. Anti-government. Anti *all* governments, maybe. Maybe this was just a chance for him to take out as many politicians at once? Maybe he just really, really hates Cuba – or maybe he was going for Skip Jackson the whole time, and the Cuban just got in the way, huh? *That* would make more sense given his previous crimes, wouldn't you say?"

It was clear that Kage was starting to lose his miraculous patience, even with Alexa. It wasn't just her who had only had a handful of hours of sleep over the last couple of days...

And he has a point. It *would* make sense for an anti-government bomb-maker, someone who was already deeply implicated in attacks against everything from medical clinics to military bases was out to fight 'the system' in whatever guise it presented itself.

Staniforth had a particular set of skills, Alexa reasoned. And he was all too happy to use those skills to take down the highest-profile targets, whether directly or indirectly.

It was never another gang. It was never the mafia, never an individual. Always the government... So with that understanding, it would make a lot of sense for Staniforth to try to take a pop shot at Skip Jackson, one of the President's most trusted senior advisors just for the hell of doing it, right?

It was certainly a motive that they could sell to a jury, and, given all of his previous work, and the evidence right here in this case – the bombs were his, without a shadow of a doubt – and he killed Eva Montgomery when she found out he was the killer... More than enough to pass the threshold of doubt.

But I still don't like it, Alexa frowned to herself, sighing suddenly as she looked down at the papers before her.

Could it be that Staniforth's last message to her had been right? That Alexa herself couldn't abide not knowing? She couldn't stand not being sure of something – and that this mystery would remain, itself, his final revenge against those that had caught him?

"Damn it," Alexa whispered, leaning back in her chair as she slapped the papers on the desk.

Maybe Kage was right, after all. Maybe there were some things they would never know in their job, and they already had what they needed ...

But she still didn't like it. This was one of the very reasons why she had joined the FBI in the first place, and it wasn't just to do something different from her father.

A part of it was wanting to protect people. To stop bad things from happening.

But there was another part of it, a part that she only dared admit, even to herself.

Alexa liked to solve puzzles. She liked to be right. She liked to solve the chaos and the randomness, and have certainty, because ...

Because the alternative was terrifying, wasn't it?

The alternative to having order, to having certainty, to having facts that made sense and that were clear and accurate was a world where anything random might just happen, and at any moment at all. It was a world where people could kill each other for no reason at all. Where people could die for no other reason other than happenstance. Where it didn't matter how hard you worked – you could still feel all the ground beneath your feet shake, and for no reason whatsoever.

For some reason, Alexa suddenly heard the voice of her father in her head.

"Not if you try your hardest, kiddo," he'd said, and she couldn't remember just what they had been talking about.

But I had tried my hardest to love Mom, hadn't I?

Ouch.

There it was, and Alexa's heart swirled away from it just as suddenly as it sensed that pain, like some deep-sea creature suddenly scared off by the glare of a bright light.

But the fact was the same, in some weird and twisted way, wasn't it? That sometimes people died for no reason.

But if you tried hard. If you tried real hard and got things right, then maybe you could stop it from happening ...

(Alexa suddenly felt hot as her cheeks burned, and her ears rang with the roar of tinnitus and crashing alarms, even though she knew that she was safe, and nowhere near that explosion and that greasy, oily smoke. A part of her knew that her thinking was skewed. She knew that a part of her was overcompensating, perhaps...)

But damn it, sometimes overcompensating meant that you achieved more than you could ever hope for, didn't it? There was another favorite phrase of her father's; or had it been her mother's? Right now Alexa couldn't be sure...

"Reach for the stars anyway, kiddo, you might not get there, but you'll get a hell of a lot further than you were if you were looking at the gutter..."

So yeah, Alexa was a proud over-reacher. She was a proud, over-committed, over-determined workaholic.

Even if that did mean that she hardly ever slept and that her wages never really did match up to the amount of effort that she put into a job.

Because it was never about the pay at all for Alexa. It was always about getting it right. About being certain. About *making* certainty. About stopping the chaos of life just that little bit.

The pay.

Alexa shot to her feet, as a feeling of cold electricity ran through her. The ringing in her ears was gone. She felt refreshed, alert, awake, and energized as her whole body thrummed with a connection that she hadn't seen before.

"Alexa?" Kage was looking at her funny, his previous exasperation now given over to full-fledged surprise at the sudden change in her.

"It was always for the pay," Alexa said, blinking rapidly as she let the realization stretch out, settle in.

"What?"

"Staniforth," she said, already turning as she grabbed her jacket and badge.

"Staniforth's previous crimes, everything that we know of, anyway... It has always been about the pay with him. We've been ruling out other suspects. Thinking that *he* was the one who set the bomb, in addition to building it. But that's not his motive."

"Then what is?"

"It's the money. *That* is what his motivating factor is, and *that* is why he is so unfazed about spending the rest of his life in a maximum-security prison. Because he has the best lawyers. He has the money, and probably the contacts if he wants them across every prison in the United States."

She stopped at the door, turning to Kage.

"With Staniforth, *it's always the money.* He does these things for money, and he does them well. His money is his pride. His mark of a job well done."

"What!?" Kage repeated, shaking his head at her that he didn't understand.

Alexa paused, one hand on the door.

"Yes, we can probably make your anti-fed hatred motive stick in court if we want to – but it's not the right one. No, not at all. Remember Pinkerton said that he'd sell his bombs to various extremist groups? Huge hole in our theory. And as good as Staniforth is, if he just wanted to take a pop at a passing politician, he would have done it well before now, and he would have taken out a senator or a governor or a Supreme Court justice, right? No. Staniforth has always worked for the money. He's a craftsperson. And he was there to make sure that the job got done."

Alexa skewered her partner with a sharp glance.

"But I bet you everything I own that he didn't commission the bomb. *That* was someone else. We can make your motive stick – but *I* need to know the truth, and I am going down to the cells to get it. Come along if you want it, too!"

Alexa swung open the door and marched out, and, a few seconds later, Kage hurried after her with more of a harried look on his large and handsome face.

CHAPTER TWENTY-NINE

XXX. 3:00 PM

"I KNOW YOU DIDN'T DO IT, STANIFORTH. I KNOW THAT you're not the one who commissioned the bomb, who wanted Ramon Martinez dead – that's just not your style, is it? So who was the buyer?" Alexa demanded as soon as she had burst into the gray- and white-walled interrogation room where Saul Staniforth was being held.

The room itself was standard across every FBI field office, and probably across every police station and other alphabet agency office the country over. It had functional and simple inner breeze block walls, painted with a stolid paint, half gray on the lower part, and the rest white. The walls were rough and had been repainted many times over as various suspects and people in holding had vented their rage against it, whether physically or artistically.

It wasn't a large room, and it was mostly occupied by a steel table that was bolted to the floor, with another steel handle in the middle of the table, where one of Staniforth's wrists was currently cuffed to. He was leaning his chin on the other, his elbow on the table as his eyes flickered at Alexa.

There was a plate of darkened glass at one end of the room, through which Alexa presumed that Kage had gone to watch the proceedings. But Alexa hadn't brought a tape recorder in with her. She didn't even have her folder.

"Why should I talk to you?" Staniforth cut back, and Alexa stomped up to the table and slapped it with her hand, enough to make the steel ring like a bell.

"Because if you don't then I think that you're going to have a big, big problem on your shoulders," Alexa said.

Staniforth finally leaned back and looked up at the irate special agent standing before him.

"Oh yeah? All I see is a lot of people without a lot of evidence."

"We got you on the boat, and on camera," Alexa laughed. "We got you going into Eva Montgomery's room the same hour she was killed. You came back out; she never did. Now come on. You can do better than that."

"Maybe so," Staniforth shrugged. "But you can't tie me to the Cuban. I was in the resort gym at the time. You can check that blessed resort footage of yours if you want…"

What!? Why didn't I hear of this before!? She took out her phone, trying to look casual as she fired a text at Dee Hopkins, the FBI Cyber Officer.

Alexa Landers:
Dee, the time of the explosion. You got eyes on the guests? Where was Staniforth?

It didn't matter. It doesn't change anything. Alexa smoothly returned the phone to her pocket and lifted her head to smile coldly at Staniforth. The man must have seen her moment of hesitation, as he was leaning back, confident, self-assured.

"You have me walking into a room. Big deal. Anything can happen behind closed doors," he said confidently.

Which was true, Alexa felt a flurry of frustration bubble up through her. It was enraging. It threatened to spill over, pour out of her throat.

They didn't have eyes on the actual murder. And that meant a whole lot of circumstantial evidence. A lot of conjecture. If Staniforth had a top-class lawyer (and a man in his profession had surely made quite a few contacts in his years) then they could mitigate the sentence. Turn a probable murder into a suspected manslaughter. Or even a crime of passion. That whittled a life or a twenty-five-year sentence right down to fifteen, ten, seven…

They'd found the materials right there in his room. But proving he'd actually built them was another task entirely.

Alexa needed to get him cornered. She needed to get him scared.

"You know what your big problem is, Staniforth?" Alexa said, leaning over him.

He grinned back. It was a cold, cold grin.

"The Cubans. You killed one of their own. Not just any one of their own, but one of their darlings. Their golden boy. The guy who was going to end *el bloqueo*. You killed Representative Ramon Martinez, and my god, they are *baying* for your blood. And you know, I'm sure diplomatic tensions can be somewhat eased, depending on just how badly they want satisfaction," she continued, pausing to let that sink in. "Maybe we just cut out the middleman and send you right on down to Guantanamo. Best of both worlds."

Staniforth's eyes blinked.

"You still don't have anything," he insisted, but this time there was the subtlest quaver to his voice.

It was the same line they'd used against Figuera, and it was just as true then as it was now.

"You messed up this time," Alexa said, ignoring his insistence. "You should have stuck to the shadows. Not get directly involved, just like the other bombs you made."

Alexa leaned back, a satisfied smile spreading across her features.

"We got you throwing bombs at federal agents. We got a bomb-making kit with you on the yacht you stole, with your fingerprints all over it. Plus all the stuff in your room. And you want to know something about your profession?" Alexa said.

"Enlighten me..." the man snarled.

"Every device you make has a signature. A way you put things together. A signature that is as personal as your fingerprint. And we have already matched the bomb used to kill Ramon Martinez to the one that blew up the Rio Grande Valley Clinic, as well as an attempted attack on an Army base. Now that we have your kit, who knows how many more cases we'll add to that list? You're not just going down for Eva Montgomery, you're going down for a whole lot more."

Staniforth's eyes flickered once more. He swallowed. She was getting to him, and he knew it.

"When we present all this evidence, tying you to Eva, tying you to the other devices. Do you *really* think they won't convict you for the one that killed Martinez? And do you think the Justice Department would hesitate for even one second before pinning every one of these crimes on you?"

Staniforth was silent.

"I'm guessing it was the bomb commissioner, right?" Alexa continued. "The one who hired you to do it? What was it – this was such a big job that they wanted you here, in person? They pay you extra just to make sure that you got the job done right?"

Alexa shrugged as if it was no consequence, but actually, she was watching him like a hawk.

Staniforth was holding his own. He wasn't saying anything. He was cautious, wary.

"Oh, I'm sure you didn't like it. Maybe you even told them that you don't get involved, that it wasn't your style. But the pay was just too damn high, wasn't it? Or maybe that was the deal breaker.

They said you *had* to be on St. Martin's, on-site; otherwise, you wouldn't get paid at all, would you?"

Staniforth flinched.

Bingo.

"So you're there, against your will, but you do the best that you can do. You try to get the job done because you're that kind of guy, aren't you, Staniforth? The kind of guy who prides himself on his work, who likes to get things done, right?" Alexa said. She was self-assured now. She could see the case. She could see what was needed, what parts made sense, and what didn't.

Staniforth was never the one to actually pull the trigger. Not usually. And he wasn't the one to select the targets. He was all about the job. The technical skill. He was ALWAYS the craftsperson. Not the killer.

"And that is why you even stayed on site after the explosion. You knew that there was someone else who was the real culprit. The one who brought your services. You think that you got lucky when we picked up Figuera, right? You thought that you'd get off without a hitch... But then things got more complicated. We stayed. The storm happened. Eva Montgomery figured out who you were, and *why* you were here..."

Alexa skewered Staniforth with her sharpest glance.

"Just tell us who paid you, Saul. Whose plan was it? Who hired you to plant the bomb?"

Eva thought it was an inside job, Alexa remembered as she watched her suspect, still saying nothing. From all her notes and recordings, Eva had thought that the United States government themselves had ordered the murder of Ramon Martinez.

Alexa's inner certainty rocked. That was something that she instantly rejected. There might be corrupt politicians, even senators – but the idea that they would take out an enemy dignitary, on their own soil?

Nah. The blockade of Cuba might be imposed by the United States, but it coming down – which was what both Martinez and Skip wanted – would only have meant that the United States' free-market capitalism came flooding into Cuba, wouldn't it?

Which would mean the Cubans became consumers. US businesses would immediately seize the market opportunity.

All of which would only be good for the US. It sounded almost like one of the crazy theories they'd been debating all along.

But still, Alexa hardened her heart. If the trail led toward that theory, then she would follow that, too. She would go where the truth was. She would go where the facts were.

Brrring!

Her phone vibrated in her pocket and Alexa casually leaned back, took it out, and looked at it as if she were dotting the i's and crossing the t's.

Dee:

Hey hun. No ball, no play. We got the footage from the resort last night. All cameras went down after the storm, but we have the morning of the explosion. Staniforth was in the resort gym from 8:30-9:30 AM

Alexa tried to control her reaction, but internally she could have screamed.

Dammit! It would have been so easy if Staniforth had been unaccounted for. Or had been out of the resort complex, supposedly 'hiking.' Opportunity and expertise, right then and there.

But no. He was in the gym, under the eye of the resort cameras, which she guessed was a little odd in itself; Alexa gritted her teeth. The explosion happened a little past 9:00 ...

Light. Heat. A wave of brilliance and blistering air as her world shook, and her ears screamed in a high pitch whine.

Alexa felt those first few seconds once again, but she breathed through it. Yes. Staniforth had been at the resort gym. The alarms would have gone off all over the resort at 9:15, 9:20 maybe – *and Staniforth just keeps on jogging or rowing or working on his glutes for the next ten minutes!?*

But either way, it meant that they didn't have a cast-iron case for him as the trigger-man. It meant that Staniforth had a tiny, tiny amount of wiggle room, and that annoyed her.

But they could still get him. Even if he had an alibi at the time of the explosion, they could put him away for a long time on the whole crazy chase alone. Cecil Pinkerton, FBI Miami's Chief Scientific Officer, had said that the device that killed Representative Martinez had been a short-wave, narrow-band WiFi transmission. Surely Staniforth knew of a way to automate that process? Maybe he had set something up the day before, or two days before, and then all he had to do was to get in ten thousand steps while the world burned...

Yeah, Alexa thought. Given Staniforth's experience and previous crimes, they could make it work before a jury, if they had to, she was sure of it. She pressed on.

"The Cubans are angry. They know we've made two arrests, and they already want Figuera to be extradited and tried in a Cuban court, even though we haven't released details of his case yet. They want *you,* too. They won't settle for anything less," Alexa smiled in a sharp, brittle way.

Get him scared. Get him so scared that he wants to talk.

"You'll either have a very short life on American soil, or just a little longer one behind Cuban bars if you don't cooperate. Do you know how many Cuban-influenced gang members there are in American prisons? How many committed radicals there are in Cuban ones? How long before they get to you on the inside? Before one day the guard turns his back?" she said.

A part of her hated herself for saying things like this, for *having* to say things like this, but Alexa's determination came from the fact that she was right. She knew she was right. She was on solid ground, and these were just the facts.

"You wouldn't. I'd be a vulnerable prisoner. I'd be protected," Staniforth said, but Alexa could see that his confidence was shaken. His eyes were darting from one side to the other.

"Would you?" she asked quietly. "We'd try our best, certainly. But you tried to kill federal agents. Law enforcement. You know how it's different if you do that."

That, too, was true, Alexa knew. It was a terrible, terrible fact, but it was still a fact.

Staniforth breathed heavily. He was nervous.

Come on, just make the logical step, it's not far, Alexa was willing him.

"Witness protection," Staniforth said at last.

There you go! That wasn't so hard, was it?

Alexa nodded. "You got a name for me, then we can talk. I want who commissioned the bomb. Who hired you. I want who wanted Representative Martinez dead."

Even if it led all the way up to the US government.

"I don't know that!" Staniforth shook his head violently. "I swear! I promise I don't know! All I know is that I got paid to make them, to turn up at the island and book myself in, in case anything went wrong and they needed help with the detonation. I didn't even know where it was being planted!"

"*They?*" Alexa asked, suddenly confused. Was Staniforth lying to her? Because what he was suggesting...

"Are you telling me that you *didn't* blow the device that killed Representative Ramon Martinez?" Alexa narrowed her eyes and leaned in.

He didn't even plant it. Someone else went out there in the middle of the night and dug up the tarmac and re-patched it.

"No! Of course not! It was blown by a short-wave transmitter/ receiver. That's what I advised they get anyway, and I told them the frequency that would activate the bomb. But I didn't actually have one on me. I never do. All I had was the casings to make flash-bangs. Mini-detonations. Not wireless-tripped ones, just in case..."

In case you had to do exactly what you did do, Alexa thought. *Cause a lot of chaos and distraction while you tried to escape. And. Well. That hadn't worked, had it?*

"And you can check when I got to the island! The day before. No time to run around planting bombs on helipads!" Staniforth explained. His resolve had broken, and it was clear that he was starting to worry about the prospect of prison.

"You are telling me that there was someone else on that island who actually set off the bomb, as well as planted it? You expect me to believe that!?" Alexa frowned at him. This was starting to sound ridiculous. The only people left were the staffers, the elderly bird-watchers, and the haplessly incompetent Eddie Kendricks.

I should have paid more attention to the staff.

"Yes! There was! Look, if you promise me witness protection, I'll get you the messages. They're encrypted, but I'll give you access. But you have to promise first, through a lawyer."

"No promises," Alexa said heavily. "Not until I speak to my team. Then we'll see what we can offer."

"Then you'll lose them," Staniforth said urgently. "You know you will. I got paid a hundred thousand dollars for that device. One hundred thousand for me, and who knows how much for the ones who actually planted the bomb and set it off."

"That kind of money buys you a lot of things. It buys you ways out, and fast ways out, too," the older man said.

That kind of money wouldn't come easily, would it? Alexa thought. One hundred thousand for the bomb maker, and what, another hundred for the planters and detonators?

Nearing two hundred thousand. Almost a quarter million. Who has that kind of money? Alexa felt her heart start to beat faster and faster.

And Staniforth was right, too. If he was telling the truth and there *was* another killer somewhere on the island – who Alexa was now thinking of as 'the detonator' – then they already had several hours to get wherever they wanted. A boat from the island and a flight out of Tampa across the country already, and from there, who knew? Canada to Europe? Mexico?

If Staniforth was telling *any* modicum of truth, then Alexa had to move fast.

"Give us those messages, and we'll cut you a deal. I can't promise full witness protection because you killed people – that sort of thing has consequences. But you can get security for your sentence. A proper secluded wing. One with round-the-clock guards," Alexa nodded. "You get a life."

Staniforth pulled a long face. "A life. What kind of life is that? Behind bars?"

Alexa was resolute. "It's a life, which is more than Eva Montgomery gets now. Maybe you find God. Maybe you write your memoirs. Maybe you even get parole, but I wouldn't count on it. You get a life," she repeated. "Which is all that any of us gets, in the end."

"Now give us those messages," she finished as she took out her phone and started hurriedly typing in messages for Kage.

The other guests. The staff.

Who was there before you swept the helipad?

We need local law enforcement on the others NOW. Who traveled home? Who's still traveling?

CHAPTER THIRTY

XXXI. 4:40 PM

"Landers, you have to wait. The sort of requests you're asking-"

THE VOICE OF CHIEF WILLIAMS WAS BRUSQUE ON ONE END of the phone as Alexa was hurrying through one of the hallways, with Kage a half step behind her. She found the door she wanted and threw it open, cradling the phone against her shoulder as Cecil Pinkerton looked up alarmed from his gray and white plastic desks covered in heavy white, dust-resistant sheeting.

The door slammed shut behind them and she finally put the chief on loudspeaker.

"Sir, I know. But I'm convinced Staniforth is telling the truth. He might have been the one to design and make the device – but I am sure that he wasn't the one to plant it, *or* detonate it, let alone commission it. We're no nearer the actual source of this than we started."

"*Special Agent!*" Even over the phone, the way that Chief Williams said the words was enough to bring a raging bulldog to heel. It was an authoritative bark of command.

"*You are asking for a Florida-wide mobilization of local PD, Highway Patrol, heaven knows who else we can rope in, to immediately get eyes on some seventeen people associated with the resort.*"

"That's right, sir. All the staff, the owner Bartholomew Price, Eddie Kendricks, and the Lucas. If I'm right, one of them is probably on a plane or booking one right now."

"*Alexa. That is a HUGE undertaking. There are clearances. Special jurisdictions. Court Orders. You're even asking for flight lists from private airlines, now!*"

"But, sir, I am sure of it."

"*We have Saul Staniforth in custody. A suspected arsonist and terrorist, with multiple murders already on his hands, by the sounds of it. Why would you question that? We have our man, Landers!*" Chief Williams yelled, sounding stressed. "*I've got the governor of Florida on the phone every goddamn hour. He's pretty pissed at having to call the special emergency, right before he has to deal with Hildegard. I've got the Select Justice Committee expecting a report, and this morning I had the President herself saying that we'd better hurry up as the Cubans are presenting their complaints to the United Nations today!*"

Yeah, so Williams was stressed. But then again, Big Chief Williams from the Miami office always sounded stressed. Alexa remembered her father wearily mentioning something once about how the political was always a hundred percent worse than the operational.

"*You think it's better when you got stripes on your shoulder, kiddo? It's not. It's like walking back into the damn shark tank, only this time all the sharks are wearing suits…*"

But Alexa had a purpose. She didn't care whatever was irking the governor of Florida right now, or what complaints the Cubans took to the UN.

There was the case. And there was the truth.

"Staniforth wasn't the one to set the bomb or to blow it. Of that I am certain," she said once again. "Staniforth isn't a lone wolf figure. He isn't a tormented martyr, either. He's a craftsperson. Someone paid him to do this job, and he is claiming that he has the encrypted messages showing the money trail. We follow the money trail, that leads us back to the real culprit," Alexa said, taking a breath before continuing.

"I can get you the evidence, sir. And Staniforth will be going down anyway. He knows that, we know that. He's not going anywhere." She looked over to Cecil Pinkerton in his white lab coat, who nodded his head, pointing between the large, flatscreen computer screens along the wall where numerous small designs were drafted, and the myriad small components scattered on the desk, under the heavy plastic sheeting.

"The bomb signatures match. Staniforth is the creator of the devices he threw at you, the ones in Texas and a bunch more, *and* the one that killed Representative Martinez," Pinkerton said quickly.

Alexa nodded. Good. That part of the case was solid, at least.

"Staniforth might not be going anywhere – but the *real* killer is going somewhere, and right now. That is why I need those orders and local law enforcement out there, bringing everyone at the resort in…"

"Landers…" There was a weary growl from the other end, but Alexa could tell that she had convinced him. Maybe it was her utter, complete certainty. Maybe it was the fact that she knew she was telling the truth.

Or maybe Big Chief Williams just trusted her.

"Sir – please. This is the right thing, I promise," Alexa said, as she looked up at Kage, who raised his eyebrows and shrugged. It was an expression that definitely said 'whatever – I'm with you if this is your bag.'

And it was.

"*I'll make the calls. But it's past five now, and that means shift change for a lot of agencies. You might not get the information you want back in a hurry,*" Chief Williams commented.

"*But I'll have a fast jet waiting for you at the Tampa airport in case you need to move quickly. Open charter, I can secure that, at least.*"

Better than nothing, Alexa thought. Even if she could read between the lines of what the chief was saying. The other agencies might be too slow. It might be just her and Kage on their own if they came up with something.

It might be up to them to hunt the killer.

CHAPTER
THIRTY-ONE

XXXII. 5:15 PM

"Landers? I've got the messages you want. It was a hell of a runaround. Staniforth was using an encrypted account based out of Liechtenstein, but with his passwords, it was easy enough. I've copied the unencrypted translations onto the group server."

ALEXA WOULD HAVE PREFERRED IT IF DEE HOPKINS, THE FBI Cyber and Digital Security expert, was here with her; she liked Dee's no-nonsense, can-do attitude, but

Dee was better where she was, surrounded by her 'lair' as she called it of near-elite supercomputers and hacking equipment.

"Is there a name?" Alexa said hurriedly, looking at her assembled stuff on the table of the borrowed office. Her plain, black athletic jacket, special issue with reinforced webbing on the inside; it couldn't stop bullets, but it would take a knife.

And no good against bombs.

Her FBI-emblazoned over jacket, more of a poncho that she could pull on for the final take.

Her Glock pistol and holster in its safe box, one full magazine in the handle, and another two spare. *That* had required more paperwork, too – to have a service-ready firearm signed off at short notice, but Chief Williams had expedited that, too.

And, last but not least, her badge and emergency papers. Another gift from Williams:

'This person is an acting Special Agent of the Federal Bureau of Investigation, and is currently in pursuance of serious crimes. Case Number XA30….'

A simple, de facto letter signed by the chief and stamped with an official FBI seal, with the Miami office special authorization number. If any police officer, airline officer, or any other official for that matter stopped her or Kage in pursuance of their duty, they could phone that number and talk to Williams himself.

It wasn't as good as a specific court order, ordering all outbound flights to be landed, or trains halted, or bridge crossings closed – but those things took time, and the letter would go a long way on the ground, or at least, that's what Alexa hoped.

And the chopper, Alexa knew as she logged into the Miami FBI servers, navigating to her personal cache of case folders to see the ones that Dee had uploaded just a little while ago.

There was a chopper waiting for her and Kage at the Tampa airport, ready and fueled with a pilot that would take them anywhere they needed to go.

All we need now is a destination, she thought as she scanned through the messages.

Your payment of $3149.99 has been approved. Full receipt transcript below:

1 X ITEM
Goods and Services $2149.99
Goods and Services $1000.00

Intnl Tax Code applied.
Thank you for doing business with us.
KCV Alliance Holdings

"Dee? What the hell am I looking at?" Alexa asked, completely confused.

There was a momentary pause on the other end of the line, followed by a chuckle of laughter.

"What you are looking at is a paper trail, Special Agent." Dee sounded pleased with herself.

"There's a LOT of those payments from KCV Alliance right there. A lot, and those are the ones that Staniforth said that we had to look at…"

"How much in total?" Alexa asked, scrolling up and down through the list. There were a lot of messages, and every one that she clicked into showed the exact same format, some three thousand dollars paid into Staniforth's Cayman Islands account, with the last few payments being a few hundred dollars short.

"When you total it all up? Fifty thousand dollars. Exactly," Dee said, again sounding pleased with herself.

"Half," Alexa breathed. "Exactly half of what Staniforth said he was paid."

"Half up front, half on delivery," Dee agreed.

There. This was it, Alexa thought. This was the money trail, right here. All she needed was the names behind KCV Alliance Holdings.

"But I am guessing that Staniforth won't ever see the other half of the money, now that he messed up the job," Dee fairly crowed.

He won't see any of it if I have anything to do about it, Alexa thought. She would have to see if there was a way to put an order for illegal earnings on the Cayman Islands account. She didn't know the ins and outs of it, but the thought of Staniforth having any sort of nest egg stashed away out there, built on the slick of blood he'd spilled in his life made her feel sick.

"We need a name. Something tying KCV to someone at the resort," Alexa continued as there was a slight *tssk* on the other end of the line.

"And here, my fearless field agent, is where we get into the mire and grime. KCV is a holding company, based out of London."

"London? London, UK?" Alexa said in disbelief.

Why on earth would anyone from London want to kill a Cuban politician!?

"Indeed. Luckily for everyone concerned, it wasn't housed in Switzerland, or Liechtenstein, where the rules for financial transparency are effectively zero!" Dee explained.

"The United Kingdom very helpfully has something called Companies House Register, which names all the officers and holdings of the registered companies."

"A name!" Alexa's hopes soared.

"Not so fast. I've included the screen grab in the folder. Date marked, plus KCV..."

Alexa navigated to the image, pulling up a webpage.

Companies House
His Majesty's Government

KCV Alliance Holdings

Incorporated: 01/04/2019

Director: Alexander Mitchels

Alexa's heart sank. She was expecting to see a name she recognized, one that tied back to St. Martin's Island.

"Alexander Mitchels? Who is Alexander Mitchels!?"

"He's a stooge, that's what," Dee answered confidently.

"A stooge? What do you mean?" Alexa frowned. She hated this aspect of the cases they sometimes dealt with; the thick web of contacts and financial back and forth that criminals used to try and make their adventures look respectable.

Sharks wearing suits.

"It's an old British term I picked up watching detective shows in the UK. Did I ever tell you that I did a referral program to their GCHQ once upon a time?"

"GCHQ... their intelligence hub?" Alexa said. Sometimes talking to Dee was like listening to ten conversations happening between twenty people in a small room, all at once.

"Kind of. Their spooks and digital agency. Anyway. Ate lots of terrible, terrible food, but they know their surveillance. Got to see a little of how the old world does it, which, let me tell you, is all velvet gloves and smiles right at the same time as they stick the knife into you. Horrifyingly good at it. Anyway, a stooge is someone put up for a job, but not the actual culprit."

"Oh, a fall guy," Alexa said. "You could have just said that, you know."

"I know. But I like to think I am also the cultural representative in this department. Got to at least try to expand the horizons somewhat. Anyway, Alexander Mitchels is listed as the owner of KCV, the people who paid Staniforth for the job..."

"So he's the director, we can legitimately send an international arrest warrant for him to the UK, right?" Alexa said.

"Sure, we could. But we'd only get someone middle-level. You might be more interested in the fact that KCV is technically registered as an investment hedge fund..."

Alexa guffawed. "Okay. Now I have absolutely no idea what you are talking about."

"Think a bank. People make deposits, KCV invests them, or is supposed to, and pays out the interest on accounts."

Alexa started to connect what was happening here. "So, Alexander Mitchels claims that he is just the director of a bank? And that the payments that went to Staniforth were just his interest payments? Does Staniforth have any statement of investments made?"

"None that he shared with us, but I am sure when we ask KCV, they will be able to concoct some. That's the way this scam works. You incorporate a supposed investment bank from some de-regulated financial authority, and then make up your books. Mr. Mitchels just says that he's the director and has no idea what transactions are going through his bank and there you have it, even if it is just him in an office with a fax machine."

"No one has fax machines anymore, Dee."

"I know, I was being ironic, honey. It's money laundering, really. It'll take the finance team months to detangle it…"

"No wonder Staniforth was so cocky to begin with," Alexa muttered. That was, until she had promised they would get a conviction on him anyway on the other bombs.

"But what you might be MORE interested in is this. I did some digging on KCV and Alexander Mitchels, and the interesting thing is that I am not finding anything about him at all. Anywhere. No social media, no Facebook, no Twitter."

"Plenty of people don't have social media," Alexa pointed out. She had never adopted it, for example.

"Yes, and very wise, too. You know that all social media is basically an open-range social surveillance tool used by corporations to target voting or buying habits, don't you?"

That was another fact about Dee that Alexa both loved and hated. She was one of the most knowledgeable people that she had ever spoken to; her leaps of understanding, of putting fact after fact to achieve certainty was simply breathtaking to someone with Alexa's brain – but often what she said was so bone-chilling that Alexa wasn't sure that she even wanted to know some of Dee's conclusions most of the time.

"Dee. Dee, the case," Alexa tried to steer her friend's gunfire intelligence.

"Yes. Mitchels. He isn't listed on any of the company registers either. You know the ones, like catalogs with company information. Nothing. I'm guessing that he doesn't even exist, or that Alexander

Mitchels was someone's dead brother, or a passport on the dark web that someone lifted," Dee relayed.

Alexa felt her stomach lurch. There at her side, folded on the desk, was her equipment ready to go and catch the killer. It felt like the actual culprit was only getting further and further away, not closer.

"But what IS listed is that KCV Alliance Holdings is owned by another company, Licensing Administrations International," Dee added.

"And who owns that?"

"Right question, wrong puzzle piece," Dee said rather cryptically. *"Licensing Administrations hasn't supplied its officers to Companies House UK because it's not a UK company at all. Guess where it's incorporated?"*

Alexa couldn't even begin to guess.

"Right there in Tampa, Florida. 103 Lakeview in Palm Ridge," Dee said.

"Gotcha!" Alexa said, already rising from her seat and reaching for her jacket. It all made sense to her now: the killer had opened a fake company under a fake name in a different country, hoping that none of it would lead back to them.

"Hold your horses, kid. I take it that you haven't looked at the rest of the files I uploaded yet?" Dee asked as Alexa frowned.

"No. But if we know where the company is, then we order a few squad cars, go in-"

"And find a whole heap of nothing. Take a look."

Alexa sat back down, turning to see that the last few files attached were Google Images, supposedly of 103 Lakeview, Palm Ridge, Tampa Florida.

Alexa squinted. She saw a long roadway with a collection of smaller buildings on one side, and then she saw a whole lot of abandoned, weed-covered lots on the other side. Palm Ridge appeared to be so much in the suburbs of Tampa that it had gone even beyond the industrial and development parks. It was almost just brush and wildlife, and heaven alone knew where the lake was that this street had supposedly been named after.

Dee must be talking about the smaller buildings.

"Which one is it, Dee? Which one is 103?"

"It's the large, empty brown patch in the center of the image."

"But. But… there's nothing there!" Alexa said. No buildings. No people. Nothing but an abandoned lot. How could you have the company, Alliance Holdings, registered to a place that doesn't even exist?

"Precisely. That is because Licensing Administrations International, the parent company of KCV Alliance Holdings, is just another shell company. It doesn't exist as anything at all, but just a way for money to be moved around, and for there to be more of a confusing paper trail between any nefarious payment and the payer," Dee said. She sounded happy, as though she had just worked out an incredibly hard puzzle.

For Alexa, though, it felt like the puzzle was only just beginning.

"But. But how do we find our killer then? How do we prove that this company and these payments had anything at all to do with the hit on Ramon Martinez?"

This was precisely what Staniforth was – unironically – banking on, wasn't it? The fact that the paper trail would sputter and peter out, and nothing would indefinitely prove that he had been paid to make the device that had killed people.

Alexa suddenly wondered if this was it. If this was the end of the road for the investigation. They would still be able to convince a jury of Staniforth's guilt thanks to Cecil Pinkerton's 'signature' evidence. But beyond that? The trail went cold.

And Staniforth will probably get swept off with a sweetheart deal, where the trail will rot or die with him. Alexa felt a swell of anger roll through her, as her ears were filled with the rising tinnitus of screeching birds and sudden alarms.

"All hope is not lost, my indomitable Special Agent," Dee remarked.

"Oh yeah?" Alexa wasn't so sure that she agreed with that.

"I still need to do the digging on who sold all these holdings to whom, and from whom. There will be a trail, there always is. Perhaps it was another shell company, but there will be a clue, I promise you… "

"Okay," Alexa muttered, feeling utterly defeated. Perversely, Dee was still sounding like the cat that ate the canary. How could she sound so deliriously happy when the entire case had just collapsed around their ears?

"But I have some good news for you. Or very interesting news, anyway. I did some digging. There is one thing that DOES exist at 103 Lakeview."

"Oh?" Alexa asked.

"A mailbox. One of those secure depot ones. The kind where people drop things off, and then you come along with a key and pick them up. It's a way for whoever knows about Licensing and KCV Holdings to receive messages and mail, without actually receiving them, if you catch my drift."

"Right. A locked mailbox," Alexa replied. When she squinted, she thought she could see a small spike on the blurred Google Image right in front of her. A tiny stand like a steel cabinet, placed against one corner of the lot, beside the gate and the overgrown ivy.

"I also did some off-book digging, you might say, on some of your residents and guests at the resort, and you will never guess what I found out," Dee continued. "One of your guests recently rented a car out of Pine Ridge, Florida. I thought I'd run a registration check on all the licenses and car rentals, cross-referencing them with the names on St. Martin's Island, and one of them pinged up in the exact same shitty borough where Licensing Administrations or whatever has a site. A long-term rental house. One of those hire-for-a-month deals. Where this locked mailbox is located. What an opportunity to go and pick up some mail – or directions, right? Who do you think it was?"

Alexa had no idea. There were some fifteen or more possible names. Fifteen or more people who had come off that island after the storm, and when the emergency order had been lifted. Fifteen or more people who could be anywhere in the western hemisphere by now.

Dee told her a name, and Alexa gasped.

"Oh."

CHAPTER THIRTY-TWO

OUTSKIRTS OF TAMPA, FLORIDA
XXXIII. 9:15 PM

AND YOU ARE *ABSOLUTELY* SURE ABOUT THIS?" KAGE whispered to his partner as they pulled their cheap, airport rental car to park by the side of the small turn-off for Pine Ridge.

The night was gathering in, and they were losing the last of the light fast by the time they arrived at the private access road; when Alexa raised her head, all that she could see in the western distance was a deep purpling-blue glow where the sun had once been.

The city and the bay had given way long ago to undulating miles and miles of road between the dense pines. It was a rural part of Florida. It would even have been a nice part, Alexa thought, in the daytime. A nice place to raise kids, or retire to, if that was your way of thinking.

Right now, however, the main road behind them burred and hummed with the fast rush of commuter traffic, heading fast up and down the highway northeast toward Orlando, or southeast toward their home, Miami. Alexa stepped out, almost wishing she could still see the distant glow of her adopted home in the distance. Even hundreds of miles away, and far from sight, the eternal Vice City cast a sort of radiance on its surroundings. A dreadful, pulsing glow that blocked out the starlight.

How did a girl get to this? Alexa thought, pausing for a moment as she looked around them in the dark, seeing the sudden whizz and flare of neon lights racing back and forth from the cars. Whenever there was a lull in the traffic, the distant hum of insects rose up once again in the night. Miami was a long way away from where they were now, and Florida was still Florida, even up here, where it pretended to be more civilized. More sedate. More human.

Sharks in suits, the thought flickered across Alexa's mind once again.

"How come I didn't see it?" she whispered to herself as she walked to the trunk and popped it to open the secure gun box inside.

"Alexa spoke the automatic statement as soon as she had placed her hands on the hip holster and Glock, taking it out to secure it with her belt and the thigh strap. They were statutory words, the lines you were supposed to say whenever you took arms out of their secure holding; designed so that every agent and service personnel would know when there was a live weapon in the vicinity.

"I have the weapon, armed and at the ready," Kage copied her, his voice little more than a whisper in the night. There was somehow a tinge more seriousness to this than the other times that she had heard him say it.

Maybe it's because both of us are hoping not to have to use them, Alexa thought, and then answered Kage's earlier question.

"In truth, no, I am not sure. But it's a mighty coincidence. They were at the resort, obviously, and a week before they arrived, he rented a car right in Pine Ridge, Tampa, where the company that owns the company that paid Staniforth for the bomb, is located," Alexa said, as she held up a hand and ticked off the evidence.

"Bomb-maker."

"Payment."

"Location."

"Opportunity."

Kage made an agreeing noise, but Alexa could tell that he still wasn't happy about this. Sometimes coincidence was just coincidence, after all.

"Doesn't mean correlation. Could be bad luck. Right person at the wrong time," he murmured, pausing for a moment as his hands hovered over the holster at his hip.

"That's a pretty good description of any criminal, isn't it?" Alexa countered. "Right person at the wrong time? Who knows what drives someone to do it. Maybe extreme racial prejudice. Maybe they were forced into it. That is what we are here to find out. What they were doing here. What they were planning."

And the fact that their history matches, Alexa thought. Or at least, what they had claimed.

It was a slip-up on their part. They probably never expected the FBI to get this far on the paper trail.

But then again, they had no idea that FBI Miami had Dee Hopkins.

And they must have never thought that we would look any further than Figuera. Or Staniforth.

Alexa locked up the car and started toward a small, tucked-away building that was so far behind the abandoned lot they hadn't seen it from the satellite pictures. There were no lights on at this end of the gate, which was good for them anyway. Alexa nodded to Kage as soon as they got to the gate, and both of them hopped over it with smooth, practiced skill, all signs of their previous exhaustion vanishing as they neared their goal.

The driveway ahead of them curved up under heavy bushes and trees on either side. They couldn't see the house at the far end, but Alexa and Kage had studied the site on Google Maps. The house was a stand-alone residential, with a long garage block to the right. The house itself was in the traditional style, with two floors and probably about five or six rooms inside.

Plenty of places to hide. Plenty of places to shoot from, if the killer had a gun.

Please God, don't let them have a rifle, Alexa thought.

Then there was the garage block, too. It was too much to cover just with two people, but Williams had been good to his word, and the chief had already put a request in for local PD enforcement. Unfortunately, that request was slow in the making. The chief had been right about the shift change.

Kage turned to nod silently at Alexa just once before he peeled off toward the undergrowth on the right, where he would make his way ahead to the garage block, securing it if he had to, and then cutting across to the base of the house while Alexa had the job of walking up to the door and ringing the doorbell.

They were only here for questions, after all, weren't they?

Questions, Alexa grumbled as she was suddenly alone in the dark, with the whine of the passing cars behind her, replaced by the high-pitched shrill of the insects in the dark.

There are still an awful lot of questions. That irked her. It felt like grit under her eyelids.

Why do it? Why plant the bomb? What was Ramon Martinez to you?

The questions rang in her head as Alexa walked, step by step, forward up the path.

The thing that this person didn't understand, didn't see – was perhaps too arrogant to see – was that for Alexa the facts weren't just pieces of information. They were the firm ground that she could walk on. The certainty. The path forward.

And the thing was, that for Alexa, unlike her sea-faring father who always had water underneath him, who was at home in the chaos and the randomness of life, the certainty was always there, under the surface, just waiting to be discovered. It didn't matter what she surmised, what she guessed, what she could make stick – like Staniforth as the ultimate fall guy – for Alexa, the facts were underneath it all, waiting to be discovered.

She had found the paper trail that led to an abandoned lot in the outskirts of Tampa.

That was a fact.

She had found out that there was a car rented right there, in that tiny backwater beside the road strip of a borough by this very person.

Fact.

The same place where there was a mail-only dropbox. A place to pick up information. To leave deposits. To make connections, give orders.

Fact.

A place where, perhaps if you were clever enough, you could order one of the United States' best bomb-makers with just a few choice letters to the right people, the right cover companies, the right people who passed those messages onto the other right people...

And that entire web (*sharks in suits, sharks in suits...*) led you to St. Martin's Island, where Ramon Martinez lost his life, as well as his two aides, and Eva Montgomery, a citizen reporter who was on the wrong route but with the right questions.

Maybe that was all it was in the end, Alexa thought as she saw the vegetation start to peel back on either side of her, revealing the silvered gray of a lawn of grass, dotted with tall pine trees before the traditional, peaked wooden building. A family home.

The right questions. The ones that brushed away the murk, to reveal the facts beneath...

There was a flicker of movement on her right, and Alexa heard the slightest creak.

Alexa's hand went to the holster at her side, but then Kage's voice crackled into existence in her ear.

"*We got the car. Same plates. It must be one of them long-term rentals.*"

Oh.

Strangely, Alexa felt a little sad at that tawdry little fact. Maybe she had wanted the killer to have done a better job at hiding their traces. Or maybe she still didn't think that they could actually be the ones behind the murder in the first place.

Anyway. She wasn't here to have feelings. She was here for the truth.

She took another step forward in the dark, suddenly feeling very exposed and vulnerable as her shadow under the moonlight leaped long behind her. The windows of the house above were black, and the house itself looked uninhabited.

But the car is here, Alexa thought. *The rental car.*

She saw Kage's shadow move along the line of the garage, heading to the side of the building and around the side.

The front door was right ahead of her as Alexa took a step up to the porch.

Creak!

There was a mighty, strong creak of wood underfoot.

Alexa swore softly. She settled her hand lightly on the holster of her gun.

Ridiculous to think that she would need this. Every piece of evidence of this person indicated someone she could best in a moment. Someone who had no physical combat training as she had. But it was pretty easy to fire a gun. So easy, in fact, that anyone could do it, and Alexa had to remind herself of just who this person was.

You stood there right in front of me and lied to my face. You planted a bomb that killed three people and didn't bat an eyelid when a fourth was killed. When Figuera – innocent up to a point – was taken in.

That sort of person was cold. Cold as ice. Cold as cool, hard cash.

She unclipped the safety on her holster, leaned forward, and rapped loudly on the door.

"Antonio Luca! This is the FBI! Come out with your hands up!"

CHAPTER THIRTY-THREE

XXXIV. 9:25 PM

"ANTONIO LUCA! THIS IS THE FBI! COME OUT WITH your hands up!"

Alexa's voice rang out into the night, momentarily silencing the shrill whine of the insects all around.

There was a pause. A moment of silence.

That was the thing about these all-wooden houses. There was a lot of warp and weft in them, especially after all these long, hot and humid Florida summers. Especially if you didn't bother to add enough insulation to the walls and windows, maybe because this whole place was a retirement getaway, and you never expected law enforcement to come marching right up to your door...

There was a creak on the other side. A creak of a floorboard.

And a click. To Alexa's ears, it sounded exactly like the click of someone flicking a safety...

Alexa dove to one side along the porch just as there was a deafening boom, and the pebbled glass plate in the top of the door broke and spat outward, along with splinters of wood.

She hit the porch heavily on her side, rolling as she did so, not feeling anything for a moment as adrenaline flooded through her system.

The report of the firearm was a loud one. It had to be a Desert Eagle or a damn rifle at least. Alexa's brain suddenly sped up, tripping into second-by-second action mode as she skidded to a halt under one of the large bay windows beside the front door.

"Luca! This is ridiculous – we've got you cornered!" she shouted just before there was another crack, and this time the window over her head blew out as someone fired.

Hell!

Antonio Luca was clearly not just another retired investment agent, was he?

Alexa moved, skidding forward to pop up by the far side of the front door, dodging a look inside the ruined oval of burst glass that had once held the pebbled window.

There was the shadow of a little man; the little man that Antonio Luca had always seemed to be, only now he was occupied by a predatory, feral grace. He had abandoned the shorts and the short-sleeve, button-up shirt and wide-brimmed hiking hat. Instead, he wore long, dark clothes, like ex-military gear, and a close, thermal top. No hat, but in his hands was a menacing shotgun.

Antonio Luca must have seen her movement from where he stood in the internal hallway, one foot in the front room and the other in the hallway as the rifle snapped upward toward the door once again.

A gun that size would shoot straight through the door, Alexa saw immediately. She ducked and spun to one side, turning to the right of the building this time as there was another deafening burst, and this time the entire door was smacked open, spilling wood from its center.

Okay. Tried asking questions.

He had the advantage. He had a very, very big gun.

She flicked one wrist above the window ledge of the matching window to the other side of the door, and this time pumped the trigger of her Glock once, twice.

The window cracked and smashed inward, and Alexa was rolling once more, not toward the window but this time back toward the door. Antonio would be flinching from the sudden gunfire. He would want to get out of the line of sight.

And a gun that size could only have three or four shells maximum, right?

Alexa slid to the edge of the door, raising her pistol and looking up inside to see that the entire house was dark. Antonio had very wisely left all of the lights off in the building, meaning that no one but him and his wife knew the layout, not really.

If his wife is even still alive, the thought flashed through Alexa's mind as she saw a movement at the end of the hallway, under where the stairs rose up to the second floor.

She fired. Once, twice. Pinning Luca down. Keeping him out of the way until Kage could break into the back and get a clear.

Antonio fired once, twice, and this his gun clicked. But before Alexa could even press her advantage, he seemed to pull another gun out from somewhere and fired quick bursts.

Thud-ud-ud-ud-duhr!

But then there were parallel burst sounds, and flares of light as two weapons lit up the inside of the house. One was from the gap under the stairs, and the other was from the room past the main house hallway.

In stop-time motion, Alexa saw a table, tiles, windows. The hallway led straight into the kitchen back there, and there was someone in there with the repeating sound of an assault rifle, just like the one Antonio had in his hands.

"Kage!" Alexa shouted, ducking back as the door frame and the polished wood of the porch exploded with the rapport of wasp-fast bullets. Because that had to be whom the second shooter was firing at, wasn't it? It had to be Kage trying to make his entrance through the back door.

Suddenly, Alexa had gone from cornering the suspect to being cornered by two suspects, each with much better firepower than they had.

CHAPTER
THIRTY-FOUR

XXXV. 9:45 PM

"KAGE!" ALEXA SHOUTED BEFORE THERE WAS ANOTHER instant hail of bullets heading in her direction, tearing apart the door frame and across the window frame of the bay windows behind her.

I need cover. Too exposed.

Alexa's heart hammered, and she was suddenly moving, rolling across the porch and thumping to the damp grass below as she heard striding footsteps behind her.

"I think I have this one, my love!" Antonio drawled, his voice now thicker with a faint country accent and twang of something that sounded a little more Mediterranean, a little more European.

My love? The fact that he would even say that was shocking to Alexa as she tried to wriggle past the wooden posts that held the porch up, and into the darkness beyond. But as soon as she moved, she hit something solid. There were things under the porch there. Old piles of firewood, pallets. She got no more than a few feet in before her escape was blocked.

My love. They were still a couple, Alexa realized. Antonio and Maria Luca, the two watchers and retired investment bankers were still a couple, even in their real life.

Investment bankers. The sorts of people who knew how to run an investment hedge fund that could take deposits in the name of KCV Alliance Holdings and launder it so that it came out as multi-national payments to international terrorists.

Antonio and Maria, the people who had helped fight the fire in the resort, who had said that they had seen Figuera leaving the resort, who had helped patch Alexa up after the explosion…

"We got no time for this!" a woman's heavily accented voice sounded. Thicker than the soft twang that Maria had used at the resort, but it was Maria nonetheless.

"Plan B. The passports are in the car. We have to go!" Maria called as Alexa heard Antonio's footsteps hit the porch.

Where's Kage!? He should have made his entrance at the back of the building, but, if the layout was anything similar to the front, the back might only mean the kitchen rear door. Alexa tried to think rapidly as she squeezed herself into the little gap, under the very steps of the older couple with automatic rifles.

She needed to check on her partner. She needed to make sure that Kage wasn't bleeding out on the Floridian lawn somewhere behind the building.

But she also needed to catch the Lucas.

Vrrr! Vrurr!

Suddenly, the phone at Alexa's hip buzzed, and even though she had it on silent, the noise of its vibration was still too loud in the tense night.

Crap!

"There! Under the porch!" Maria yelled as Alexa suddenly broke free, lunging into the dark of the lawn as the wooden slats and floorboards blew behind her, exploding as husband-and-wife killers fired down at the place where she had been hiding.

Alexa heard their cries following her, but she was too busy scrambling and running for the side of the porch and the end of the building. She felt the hot buzz of the automatic bullets hit the wood and thump into the ground at her heels as she saw the edge, grabbed one of the wooden house posts, and used it to swing herself in a wild flinging leap down the far side of the building. There was more cover here. An outside oil tank. A coal or wood chute, maybe, a close, thick palm tree.

Move! Keep on moving!

Alexa hit the floor and skidded, leaping to her feet as she grabbed at the trellis surrounding the oil tank, and dragged herself around it to the far side.

They wouldn't be so stupid as to shoot their own fuel tank, would they? No one could be that stupid, surely.

Alexa's heart was hammering in her chest so loud that she was sure that they would be able to hear it, even from some eight or ten yards away as she cowered behind the tank, with the boards of the house and the black plastic shirt at her back.

Kage. Where was Kage? She needed to find her partner.

But there was suddenly silence. No pursuit. The Lucas must have seen her attempting to flee.

In the distance was the rising sound of sirens, and Alexa guessed what that message to her phone was. It had been the local police department, finally delivering on their promise of reinforcements.

Crap!

Checking her phone, her hand shaking with adrenaline, Alexa saw that she was right.

Missed Call from Detective Lavoy (TLH PD)

New Message from Det. Lavoy (TLH PD):

Inbound. 3 X Squad cars. 8 troopers. What's your situation?

Alexa silently cursed their timing. If they had been here an hour earlier, if the damn paperwork had gone through an hour ago then none of this would be happening.

Alexa fired off a fast return message and prayed that the detective would actually pick this one up on time, as opposed to waiting an hour for the right 'paperwork.'

Alexa Landers:
2 x shooters. Professional. Armed very dangerous. Shotguns. Automatic/AR-15s?? 1 Agent unaccounted. Proceed with caution.

"They're coming! Be ready!"

Alexa could clearly hear the words of Antonio Luca, and the creak of the floorboards as he moved across the front of the porch.

I could do this. I could take one of them out, at least, Alexa mused from where she hid. She thumbed her Glock, ejecting the magazine even though it was still half full, and instead swapped it out for a fresh one. Sixteen shells. It would be more than enough, wouldn't it?

It only takes one, she thought she could remember Kage saying at some point.

Yes, but then again she was up against weapons that could burst fire almost that many in a matter of seconds. If she needed the numbers, then she wanted to be sure that she had some, at least…

But taking out just one of the two shooters wouldn't help her. That would just mean that Maria could shoot her in the back.

And Alexa needed to find her partner. She hissed a dull curse under her breath and turned to thumb another quick message to Detective Lavoy.

Alexa Landers:
I want them alive! We can surround and contain.

She had no idea whether or not the Tampa Police Department were trigger-happy, and no idea if the troopers assembling down there had experience with siege situations or if they were the sort to blunder in quickly. She hoped they wouldn't do that, for all their sakes.

All they had to do was hold them.

And all Alexa had to do right now was find her partner.

CHAPTER THIRTY-FIVE

XXXVI. 10:16 PM

K AGE OPENED HIS EYES AND HISSED OUT A PAINED BREATH. It was dark, very dark, but there were small slivers of a silvered light showing through the cracks in the boards by his face.

How did I get down here? he thought, momentarily completely confused at what could have happened.

For a moment, Kage remembered another time and another place. There was that smell in the air. The smell of burning, of acrid, burnt air. It wasn't the same smell as before, but it was close enough.

Lying on his back and looking up to find his view shadowed and shaded, and for a wild moment not knowing where he was, or why he had ever come to be there...

But the shade back then had been the thick green leaves of St. Martin's vegetation, and he had been looking up from where the blast wave of the explosion had carried him. For just a moment, it had even been a sort of peaceful experience – until his hearing slammed back into use, and he heard the roar of fire, the sirens, the screams.

The air smelled of burning, too.

But right now, he was somewhere very, very different. For one, he wasn't lying under warm and humid sunlight. There was a chill in the air, and it was dark.

Night time. A typically humid Florida night, and he was lying on his back and looking up at where the boards of the back porch were half covering him.

He suddenly gasped in pain as his chest throbbed. The bullet that the older woman, Maria Luca, had fired at him had hit above the place where Staniforth had almost run him through with the iron pole; he supposed he was thankful for that miss – but it still hurt like hell.

Thank heavens he had worn his armor vest under his jacket.

Kage remembered his training, his body locking into the practices that came with being shot several times in the course of doing his duty. He sucked in air, felt the terrible ache and pain in his chest as he did so, and hoped that he hadn't cracked a rib. Maybe. It would mean his arm would have less movement...

But at least I'm not dead, the special agent thought as he took another breath, letting it out slowly, and another.

His breathing was good. Painful because even when wearing an armor vest, taking a bullet to the chest felt like being back-kicked by a horse (he supposed, anyway).

Shooter. Officer down. *Alexa!*

His brain, sluggish at first, now kicked in with everything that he needed to know. There was still a shooter up there; two in fact. And there was Alexa. She was still facing the Lucas alone. A shotgun and an assault rifle against just her, which was bad, bad math in anyone's book. Not to mention whatever other stockpiles of weapons they might have been hiding.

Kage raised his head and saw the back kitchen door to the Lucas' house that he had been attempting to sneak into, now hanging on its hinges. There was the sound of sirens in the distance.

Tampa PD. So they decided to arrive at last.

Although, as Kage started to turn, pulling himself back up into a painful crouch, he knew that the police would present another problem if they weren't careful. The possibilities of friendly fire in an active situation were bad, real bad if you didn't have trackers on all of your agents and officers – which they clearly didn't.

Surround and overpower. Hold, his training told him. That was precisely what they had to do. Get guns on the Lucas from all sides, and demand they throw theirs down. After all, there was nowhere they could-

"Go, my love, go!"

Kage ducked close to the back stairs as soon as he heard the shout of Antonio Luca from inside the house. The sound carried; the rest of the house was as quiet as a mouse, so it was hard for Kage to tell if the couple were in the kitchen or in the front hallway.

"What? The deal was both of us! Tampa to Mexico City. Mexico to Brazil," Maria's voice was tight and annoyed, the sort of voice that Kage would imagine from a strict schoolteacher.

"At least one of us will get away. Both is asking too much, my heart. We always knew it would one day come to this. I will hold them while you run," Antonio instructed, and Kage realized something.

He realized that the murdering retirees of Tampa, Florida were an actual real couple. Probably a real married couple, too. They loved each other. (Or at least, Antonio loved Maria, that much was for sure.) It was just that instead of taking up golf and cribbage, it looked like this power couple had taken up international assassinations as their golden years' hobby instead...

"We always said it would be both of us. Together and always!" Maria's voice was sharp, a passionate rebuke that was angry with all the fierce, terrible affection it contained.

"That was the deal, Antonio. Both. The beach house in Brazil, and enough money for the rest of our lives!" Maria said, her voice suddenly hot and angry.

Kage was entranced and surprised by this display of emotion, but he also knew that he had no time to sit and listen to the drama of other people's lives. Whomever they were up there, whatever loves and loyalties bound them together, they were murderers, and he could use this moment...

He moved into a crouch, easing toward the stairs, and raised his pistol...

The back door was half hanging from its hinges, and he could see a sliver of the kitchen beyond. Suddenly a shape moved across it. A body, but he couldn't see who it was, Maria or Antonio.

Two shots. Leg shots, if I can make it quick enough, Kage told himself as he started to rise, putting one hand on the stair railing.

"Go, my love, damn it, just *go!* I'll not throw our lives away for nothing. Is that what you want? Us both dead, or the rest of our years in separate prisons? Or the death penalty!? Go, damn it – Go!" Antonio spat angrily, turning, and suddenly there was the short, savage bark of a spray of repeater fire from deeper in the house.

Near the front. Front hallway.

"I love you-" he heard someone – Maria – speak aloud, and then suddenly there was the banging of doors from inside, and the wheel of sirens as the squad cars came roaring up the driveway.

She's getting away! Kage thought, and adrenaline surged through his body.

Alexa. But where's Alexa!?

The agent was caught in a moment of awful indecision. There was gunfire rattling off in burst shots from the front of the building, as Antonio was providing cover for his fleeing wife. But where could she go? There were only these two doors, unless they had another way out...

No. But Kage couldn't do this without his partner. He froze, pulled back from racing up the stairs. The Lucas would still be criminals after he found his partner. They would still be catchable, even if it meant horribly long extradition processes from wherever they fled to.

But he only had one partner, and she might be hurt.

He turned back, staying low as he heard the bang of something on the far side of the building, a shutter of a window maybe, and guessed that must be Maria, finding another way out.

"Kage!" There was a victorious hiss from behind him and he turned, feeling his heart thump in joyful relief.

It was Alexa. She was there, crouching by the side of the building.

"Thank god you're okay," she blurted out.

He nodded. He felt the same.

"Maria is making for the garages. She's just gone," Kage said at once, seeing his partner's face harden into grim determination.

"Then let's go bring her in, shall we?" she said at once.

CHAPTER THIRTY-SIX

XXXVII. 10:42 PM

BOTH SPECIAL AGENTS MOVED AROUND THE BACK OF THE Luca residence, as automatic gunfire spat and barked behind them. It was matched by the flashes of muzzle fire as Antonio Luca took warning shots at the approaching police, and the flashing glare of the neon lights as the three squad cars swung to either side of the driveway, forming a defensive block.

"TAMPA PD! DROP YOUR WEAPONS!"

The sound of Detective Lavoy – a man neither of the special agents had met –shouting was almost mechanical on the megaphone he was using. Alexa didn't think that Antonio would listen to them. Not a chance.

But Alexa's mind, as well as Kage's, was sharpened and focused. Alexa felt herself screening out all the other noise, it becoming little more than a background hum of activity as she sprinted low and fast, forward over the cut grass by the side of the building.

Maria Luca.

They were focused on one thing. Their target. They moved like shadows, with Kage just a few steps in front as he slid to a halt at the side of the gunfire house, popping his head out once to check.

"Clear!" he hissed, and Alexa sprinted around the corner to see the long shadow of the garage ahead of her. There was an open window to her right, its curtains still fluttering in the breeze which she guessed was where Maria Luca must have escaped through.

But where was she going? Where is there to go?

Ahead was the garage. It had the rental car, but there was no sound of banging or movement from in there.

"She won't make it past the squad cars," Alexa relayed. Unless they had somehow managed to hide a helicopter in there, then there was no chance that Maria could get away, unless...

"Kage!" Alexa yelled as she caught a flicker of movement from the edge of her vision, right by the tree line at the edge of the lawn around the Luca property.

It was Maria, dressed in the same dark chinos and thermal top that her husband had been wearing (*matching combat suits; partners to the end,* the thought flashed through Alexa's mind), and running fast as she disappeared into the trees that edged the Luca property.

The Lucas had retired well, Alexa suddenly realized. Maybe it was the money from the investment banking, maybe it was the money from the international killing. Either way, they had sited their house on a little rise of ground that afforded them a vantage point and a defensible position on three sides, with a lawn and then a surround of trees before you got to the highway.

And the access roads! Alexa suddenly cursed as she turned on her heel, and peeled toward the place where Maria had disappeared, with Kage quickly gaining to her left.

"The access roads!" she relayed in between breaths, and cursed herself why she hadn't thought about that before. She had seen them on the maps but had also seen the dense vegetation between them and the house. They didn't have the bodies between them, just herself and Kage, to check the two smaller roads that bounded the Luca property, heading north.

But it would be easy to leave a getaway car by the side of the road out there, wouldn't it? Maybe even leave two, a cache of weapons, explosives – anything!

"THROW YOUR WEAPONS OUT AND DROP TO YOUR KNEES!" Lavoy shouted behind them as they crossed the lawn, and Alexa heard Antonio's response come in the form of three quick-fire bursts, matched with the prang of metal as he must have hit the squad cars.

He won't come out alive, Alexa gritted her teeth in frustration. No matter what she had advised Lavoy, the older, seventy-odd Luca would force them to kill him, wouldn't he?

Which means we have to take Maria alive, she considered, looking at the patch of trees where Maria had disappeared into.

Brrap!

There was a glitter of muzzle fire from between the trees, and suddenly Alexa and Kage were both leaping to one side, rolling, with Alexa skidding to the side of one of the ornamental pines, while Kage did the same a good few yards away.

Maria kept shooting at them from the tree line. Kage was already on one knee, aiming back.

"Wait!" Alexa hissed, knowing that there was no way that he could target a shot to wound at this range. She might be able to, with her A1 marksmanship scores, but even she didn't trust her odds, not in these conditions, not in this darkness.

Kage fired, but she saw him flicker his wrist upward just a little at the last moment. He was firing high and wide on purpose, his bullets hitting the leaves and vines and trunks of the trees above where the muzzle flare came.

Alexa waited, her heart in her throat, but she heard nothing. No sound of return fire. No shout or scream.

It was just a distraction. She turned, pushing herself off the pine as she heard Kage seething in shock behind her, but she knew what was happening. She had guessed what the ploy was. Disrupt and interfere with the chase, but just enough to buy herself time.

Time to get to the pre-planned getaway car, which would already be waiting.

Alexa tore forward, as behind her she heard the startled grunt of Kage's annoyance as he followed.

Her stride lengthened. She flashed into the trees, her boots hitting sludgy leaf litter and almost slipping as she heard the sounds of crashing up ahead. Instantly, their progress was slowed by the wet ground and the mulch of the leaves, the tangle and reach of the vines and branches – but there was a winding path of sorts; little more than a track that the Lucas must have used more than once. The leaves were silvered with moonlight, but the dark was all around them on either side. Alexa adjusted her pace accordingly, staggering her breathing as she breathed in tight, fast puffs, always pushing herself near to her limit but not at it.

Save some energy. Keep it back for the confrontation, she reminded herself as she turned the corner.

BRAP-BRRAP!

The dark of the forest ahead once again burst with muzzle fire, and not too far away as Alexa slid to one side, throwing one of the heavier tree trunks between them as bark was torn, chewed up by bullets, and the leaves on the path exploded upward with small puffs of deadly wind.

"You're cornered! We got your husband, Maria! But you can still stop this. You can come out!" Alexa shouted out as soon as the gun report had finished, dropping to her knees as Maria responded.

Brrrr-ap-AP!

Another burst, and this time a furious snarl. *That* was what Alexa had been wanting to hear. She hadn't seriously expected Maria to suddenly give up, but she wanted to hear her voice. To hear where she was.

And she wasn't far away at all.

Alexa was staying low, looking back the way she had come to see that Kage was flat on the ground. He looked up, gave her the thumbs up, and then rolled to the far side of the path, disappearing into the darkness in an instant.

Flanking. He'll go the other side, I'll flush her out, Alexa could almost read his thoughts. It was, after all, the only logical thing to do…

An instant later, there was the sound of crashing once again as Maria must have turned to tear through the woods once more. With a muttered curse, Alexa swallowed a breath and turned, racing up the path, being careful to duck under the heavy outstretched branch that was in the way, and then jumping, leaf-sliding between the downed logs.

BRRAP!

This time the gunfire was much closer, much, much louder. Alexa saw the path widening right ahead of her as she attempted to swivel on her hip, out of the way of the barking fire.

But even Alexa wasn't that good. She felt the sharp slap of air pass her face and her shoulder as bullets thudded into the trees and tore the leaves as she leaped spinning to the ground. She was tripping, hitting the floor and rolling across the small clearing there and skidding across the leaves.

But she still had her pistol in her hand. She flipped over, raising her gun and grabbing her firing wrist with her free hand.

"Drop it." Maria's voice was cold and calculated where she stood over her, just a few yards away, with the automatic rifle leveled directly at her.

CHAPTER
THIRTY-SEVEN

XXXVIII. 11:01 PM

THERE WAS A PAUSE. A MOMENT OF FROZEN TIME BETWEEN the pair as Alexa Landers looked at Maria Luca in the moonlight and saw the cold glint of her eyes. She would fire. She would if she wanted to.

"Fine!" Alexa snapped open her grip, throwing her pistol to the floor just a few feet away as Maria gestured with her rifle.

"You don't have to do this, Maria. Neither of you have to do this. You can both come in. You can be together for a little while, before-"

"Before we never see each other again!" Maria spat, and suddenly Alexa saw the trauma on the woman's face. She did a very good job of masking and holding her emotion, but it seemed her partner was her weak spot. The person she would do anything for, and clearly already had.

"You know what will happen if either of us are captured. The President will personally order our execution. Or the rest of our lives in some rat-infested dungeon."

"It doesn't have to be that way," Alexa replied, although she thought that woman had probably called it. This was political now. It had always been political, and Maria and Antonio must have known the risks from the moment that they had hired Staniforth to build and send them the device.

But what Alexa didn't understand was *why*.

"Why, Maria? You clearly love Antonio so much, and he loves you. Why risk all that just to kill some foreign dignitary?" Alexa breathed, holding both hands in the air as she saw Maria's eyes darting from her back to the edge of the woods. There was more distant, muffled shouting. Antonio hadn't been taken yet, clearly.

Maria's eyes snapped back to Alexa, as did the muzzle of the gun.

"You know nothing. You're in way over your head, little girl," Maria said, her voice cold and thick.

Alexa felt a twinge of anger roll through her. Who did this woman think she was?

"Not even my Pops calls me little girl," she said.

"Good for him. Now, hands behind your head, and stand up real, real slowly..." Maria instructed, once again gesturing with the rifle. "I know there's another of you out there. Your partner. I saw him. Big guy, handsome, but in a dumb-looking kind of way. This way when he comes in, all knight in shining armor, he'll think twice about doing anything rash," she commented as she directed Alexa to slowly turn around.

She's going to walk me back out there into that gunfight, isn't she? Alexa could see the play. *Demand an amnesty. Demand her husband be released.*

But why? Why go to all this trouble?

"I can tell you're professionals, you and your husband. You've done this sort of thing before," Alexa said.

A moment's pause, but then a slow hiss of breath from behind her. "At least we don't come across as amateurs. No more questions, now walk," she said, and Alexa felt the hard nudge of the rifle in the small of her back as she was pushed a few steps back toward the path she had just come from…

"Were you hired?" Alexa ignored her insistence as she stepped forward, this time to feel a sudden harder jab of the rifle in her back.

"You think I would tell you!?" Maria retorted.

Ahead of them, there was the pop of gunfire and the returning powerful shots of the police.

I told them to take him alive! Alexa could have snarled. Two alive meant more chances for a confession. *One might just as easily decide to be a martyr... surely the Tampa PD knows this!*

"If you were, then you have names. Contacts. You know we cut a deal with Staniforth, and he gave us you two. We can do the same for you-*Akh!*"

There was a sudden hardened thump against the back of her head where Maria must have hit her with the rifle. Alexa staggered forward, reaching out just in time to catch herself on one of the nearby trees.

"This is too much effort. You're clearly not who I need," Maria opined, shifting in her place.

"Hey!" There was a shout, a man's shout, as Alexa spun around, back toward Maria, and Kage stepped out of the undergrowth, his pistol pointed straight at Maria. Maria whirled around toward him, her rifle already swinging into place.

Alexa reacted on instinct. She stepped forward, the base of one palm smacking Maria in the side of the jaw as the other slapped the rifle down, and then she started stomp-kicking the woman's stomach, sending her flying to the floor as the rifle went off, a sudden, prolonged burst of fire.

KAGE!

Maria hit the ground as Kage dove to one side, and Alexa lunged down, grabbing one of Maria's wrists as she kneeled on her legs, one fist raised as she looked up.

Is he hurt? Was he shot!?

There was silence for a moment, and then a deep, rasping cough from the dark between the trees.

"I'm good. I think. Thank God for armored vests," her partner wheezed.

Thank God. Thank God, thank God, thank-

Maria's off-hand battered uselessly against Alexa's side until she caught it in her other hand.

"You can't take him! You can't have him! Not my Antonio! Not my husband – take anything but him! *Don't kill him!*" Maria cried out as Alexa grabbed the woman's wrists and held them down.

"No one else is going to die," Alexa countered, gasping for air. "Kage – tell the detective to cease fire. Tell him we got the other suspect, and have him tell Antonio, too."

Kage got on his phone, and a few moments later all firing had ceased, and silence returned to the forest. Under her hands, Maria Luca had stopped struggling, and in the dappled moonlight, she suddenly looked a lot older, all her late sixty or early seventy years came rushing into her in a moment.

"Just let me see my Antonio before you take him away. Let me be with him one last time, and I'll tell you everything," Maria Luca sobbed. "I'll tell you why we did it. I'll tell you who hired us."

EPILOGUE

DAY 4, MIAMI

"*STURMSYSTEME*," FIELD CHIEF WILLIAMS RAISED AN eyebrow as he looked down at the sheath of report papers that Special Agents Alexa Landers and Kage Murphy had just placed on his desk, next to the piles of other reports and papers that made the normal, everyday, emergency ecology of the Miami FBI chief's office.

It was another sunny day in Vice City – not that Alexa, Kage, or Chief Williams could see any of it, ferreted below ground as they were in the secretive Miami field office, which looked like some sort of investment building itself on the outside, with supposedly extensive underground parking underneath.

"Swiss Arms Manufacturers, sir," Alexa informed her chief, as Williams grunted.

"I've heard of them. I've seen their stalls at the Defense and Security Fairs, too," he said darkly.

Huh, Alexa blinked. For some reason, she hadn't thought that Chief Williams would have been the type to go to those. Somehow they seemed the purview of the politicians, or the two-star generals and admirals maybe – but she guessed that even the Bureau had to get its tactical gear from somewhere…

It was the next day following the events of 103 Lakeview, Pine Ridge, Tampa, and the Lucas were currently sitting in two maximum security prisons some twelve hours between them.

As soon as Antonio received word that his Maria had been captured, it had broken the will of the older man. He had crumbled, knowing that she would be extradited to Cuba if he didn't comply. If he didn't give himself up and start supplying names and contacts of what had really happened on St. Martin's Island.

It was a long shot, Alexa thought, but that was why she was standing here, after all, in her chief's office. She figured that the Lucas might be more valuable as assets than as dead scapegoats. It was a gamble, as Alexa knew that she had to argue her case against a whole lot of hysterical newspaper inches.

But that was why the other person was here, on screen, wasn't it?

"A *leading* Swiss arms company, I might say," Skip Jackson said. He sat at a desk somewhere in the White House, with the flag of the United States behind him on one shoulder. He didn't look anything like the kindly old sea dog who used to visit her father and mother, Alexa thought. He wore a powder gray and blue suit, his hair was cropped short, and even this early in the morning his eyes were sharp and he looked precisely like the sort of guy you'd believe if he started talking to you.

The President picks her men for a reason, Alexa supposed.

"I've already done some digging, and *Sturmsysteme* accounts for about twelve percent of our nation's security equipment. That's not a whole can of beans, but it's a sizeable number," Skip explained. "Mostly tactical equipment. Bullets, small arms, that kind of thing. Nothing we can't tender to another, American-made company…"

Williams looked at the special representative, his voice grave. "There will be fallout, sir…"

"There always is, Chief." Skip did that thing that Alexa always admired him for, shooting the chief a devilish, 'who's gonna stop me?' grin. "But I think that the sudden opening in the defense budget will cause a mini-boom for American manufacturers when we announce it, just quietly, at some point in the next few months… keep this business out of the papers, you understand."

It's not the papers you have to worry about these days, sir, Alexa thought as Eva Montgomery and Eddie Kendrick's 'Report' sprung to mind.

But whatever. There was a reason that people like Chief Williams and Skip Jackson were paid their salaries. Let *them* sort that out, Alexa thought, as she concentrated on the case at hand.

She was all about the facts. The truth. And *Sturmsysteme* deserved to be punished, didn't they?

"They hired the Lucas *and* Saul Staniforth for a cool sum of some quarter million dollars between them. All expenses paid, cover stories, equipment, and of course spending money rerouted through the Cayman Islands," Alexa explained, silently thanking Dee for finding that out.

"Maria and Antonio are professionals. They are known as 'quiet hitmen' in the business, and they worked as investment bankers for none other than KCV Alliance Holdings when they lived in Spain, Portugal, and yes, Switzerland," Kage continued.

"It appeared that they had a rather interesting job – and even more interesting contacts that Interpol and the United Nations are *very* interested in hearing more about," Kage added in and nodded at Alexa to continue.

"They were bankers for arms traders, smugglers, and crooks." Alexa cleared her throat and continued. "Bankers and, well, operatives, too. As such, they know a *lot* of the illegal arms movements across the Atlantic," she said gravely, as Skip nodded he understood.

"And, well, some of those arms have been coming from and going to Cuba for the last five years, bought from *Sturmsysteme,* and making them a very tidy profit as well. They get to play all sides, pit them against each other, and drive up the costs of their weapons. And that's not even getting into the black market." Alexa gestured for the next page in the report, showing a small, shoulder-mounted rocket launcher. "This very same device would cost tens of thousands on its own, in the open market. When sold on the black market – which is the only way that Cuba buys weapons internationally, thanks to our blockade – it can cost the Cubans five times that amount…"

Skip nodded. "This is precisely what our team has been afraid of. That trade makes the smugglers and illegal traders a lot of money indeed. It filters into international criminal networks up and down the Gulf…"

"Yes, sir," Alexa confirmed. "And the higher prices make *Sturmsysteme*, or the various shell companies they deal with the Cuban gangs through, a very tidy profit still. That is why *Sturmsysteme* couldn't have the blockade lifted against Cuba, and tensions finally eased. That is why they hired the Lucas and Saul Staniforth to kill Representative Ramon Martinez – and perhaps even yourself," Alexa said the last bit quietly.

For a moment, her father's friend was silent as he looked down at his papers, and then looked back up at the room.

"Very sobering news, Alexa. And I thank you and Special Agent Murphy for your tireless devotion to the pursuit of justice. It would have been so easy to settle for Figuera, or for Staniforth, but this uncovers a web of lies and threats that is truly breathtaking…" Skip paused and then winced.

"Usually, when you save the life of a political figure there is some kind of medal, a star, or award for bravery. But in this case, given that the eyes of Cuba and the rest of the world are on us, and that we have to be tactful in how we next move against *Sturmsysteme*…"

"Understood, sir," Alexa nodded. She hadn't done any of this for the medals or the stars or awards. If she had wanted those, then she would have joined the military.

No, Alexa Landers had done all this because of one simple thing. Because she was her father's daughter. Because her father had taught her how to ride the wild risk of the high seas, yes – but he had also taught her how to value standing on firm ground. Of finding her feet, her courage. Of finding her own certainty when all else around her was ringing with alarm.

Alexa looked around the room to see that all eyes were on her.

"We just wanted the truth, sir. That's all we ever need," she said, and she didn't hear any ringing in her ears, or smell any smoke.

AUTHOR'S NOTE

First and foremost, thank you for choosing to embark on this thrilling journey with us in the pages of *Resort to Kill!*

My co-author, James Holt, and I are immensely grateful for your decision to continue this adventure alongside Alexa and Kage. We are delighted to inform you that the third book in this series is already well underway. The upcoming adventure promises to be a darker and grittier tale, with the Florida Everglades as a crucial backdrop. We hope you eagerly anticipate this next chapter, and we can't wait for you to join us again!

If you are looking for another book series to captivate your heart and to thrill you, I highly encourage you to explore my *Sweetwater Falls Mystery* series. At the time of writing this note, the Sweetwater Falls series consists of three books, with the fourth installment just around the corner. The series has truly found its footing, and you will be charmed by its unique cast of characters and the picturesque small town that harbors hidden secrets and mysteries.

As independent writers, we rely on your support to continue writing and bringing you more exciting novels. So, if you enjoyed the book, please take a moment to leave a review and recommend it to others who love mystery thrillers. With your help, we can keep writing and delivering pulse-pounding and entertaining reading experiences like this one.

Once again, thank you for joining us on this wild ride through the treacherous swamps and sun-soaked streets of Florida. You are our motivation to keep going and to keep delivering the stories that you love.

By the way, if you find any typos or want to reach out to us, feel free to email us at egray@ellegraybooks.com

Your truly,
Elle Gray & James Holt

CONNECT WITH ELLE GRAY

Loved the book? Don't miss out on future reads! Join my newsletter and receive updates on my latest releases, insider content, and exclusive promos. Plus, as a thank you for joining, you'll get a FREE copy of my book Deadly Pursuit!

Deadly Pursuit follows the story of Paxton Arrington, a police officer in Seattle who uncovers corruption within his own precinct. With his career and reputation on the line, he enlists the help of his FBI friend Blake Wilder to bring down the corrupt Strike Team. But the stakes are high, and Paxton must decide whether he's willing to risk everything to do the right thing.

Claiming your freebie is easy! Visit
https://dl.bookfunnel.com/513mluk159
and sign up with your email!

Want more ways to stay connected? Follow me on Facebook and Instagram or sign up for text notifications by texting "blake" to 844-552-1368. Thanks for your support and happy reading!

ALSO BY
ELLE GRAY

Blake Wilder FBI Mystery Thrillers

ALSO BY
ELLE GRAY | K.S. GRAY

ALSO BY
ELLE GRAY | JAMES HOLT

The Florida Girl FBI Mystery Thrillers
Book One - The Florida Girl
Book Two - Resort to Kill